D0354000

A VOICE FROM THE SHADOWS

"Here lies Alesandro de Avallone. Born the seventh day of June in the year of our Lord 1435. Left this world the twenty-second day of January, 1469.

Below that were the words: "I am not an answer to a prayer—nor a whisper—nor a dare—I am but a thought—across time."

She ran her hand over the cold stone, wondering if the Alesandro who had so generously given her the hospitality of his house had been named for the man buried here.

"Alesandro." She murmured the name aloud, liking the sound of it.

"Analisa."

It had been no voice within her head this time, and she whirled around, her heart leaping into her throat when she saw a man standing in the shadows. A man she had seen before. A man she would never forget.

Midnight Embrace

Amanda Ashley

LOVE SPELL   NEW YORK CITY

A LOVE SPELL BOOK®

February 2002

Published by

Dorchester Publishing Co., Inc.
276 Fifth Avenue
New York, NY 10001

ISBN 0-505-52468-6

Printed in the United States of America.

Visit us on the web at www.dorchesterpub.com.

This book is dedicated to Beverly Clemence.
She was the first person to read one of my books.
She was the one who suggested I find a publisher.

Thanks, Beverly. If not for you, I'd probably still
be writing stories and hiding them under the bed.

Midnight Embrace

Midnight Embrace

In the darkness of the night
my angel comes to me
an angel, a nightmare
a love not meant to be

His kisses are edged
with a dark deadly fire
his eyes, like blue flame
blaze with desire

He speaks of forever
as his arms hold me tight
eternity he promises
if I'll surrender the light

I whisper my fears
he kisses them away
my doubts he doth vanquish
like night swallows day

He woos me so tenderly
how can I resist
all I desire can be mine
with one dark kiss

—A. Ashley

Prologue

He prowled the moonlit streets and shadowed by-ways, driven by a relentless hunger and an over-powering need to help, to heal. It was who he was, what he had been born for, until Tzianne swept into his life and literally turned his days to night.

He thrust her memory away. He emptied his mind of all thought and listened to the heartbeat of the city, homing in on the one soul who had what he needed. Who needed what he had.

Gathering his cloak around him, he became one with the dark shadows of the night.

Chapter One

She was dying. She had always feared death, certain it would be accompanied by terrible unending pain and horror. But now, lying on a narrow bed in a darkened hospital room, with long fingers of silver moonlight making ever-changing patterns on the wall, she felt nothing but an overpowering weariness and a vague sense of curiosity about what came next. Was there truly life after death, a place of peace and rest without pain, as the priest had promised her? Or was there nothing beyond this life save an endless black void?

She felt herself slipping away, teetering on the brink of sleep, or perhaps the eternal abyss of death, when she felt it, a sudden coolness in the room, more a feeling than an actual physical chill, and with it the certain knowledge that she was no longer alone.

Fear came quickly, manifesting itself in the nervous shivers that wracked her body, in the sudden dampness of her palms.

"Who's there?" Filled with apprehension, she glanced nervously around the room. "Dr. Martinson? Is that you?"

He appeared out of the shadows, black against black, almost as if he were a part of the darkness itself.

"How are you feeling?" His voice was low, filled with a dark sensuality that sent a shiver of awareness down her spine.

"Who are you?" She huddled deeper into the blankets. "Where's my doctor? Where's Dr. Martinson?"

"The good doctor asked me to look in on you."

She stared up at the hooded stranger, her heart pounding as he moved closer to her bedside. He was tall and broad-shouldered beneath the fine black wool cloak that fell from his shoulders in graceful folds to the floor. She couldn't make out his features, only that his hair was long and dark, blending into the shadows around him.

"Are you a doctor?" she asked tremulously.

"Yes. I am not going to hurt you." His hand on her brow was cool, gentle. "Are you in pain?"

She shook her head, mesmerized by his eyes. They were blue, a deep, dark blue that seemed to be lit from within. Strange, she could see the color of his eyes when she could see little else.

He leaned toward her. She tried to look away, but

it was impossible to take her gaze from his. She felt as though she were being drawn into the very depths of his eyes, until all she could see, all she was aware of, were his eyes. Blue, so very blue, like a fathomless indigo sea beneath a moonless night.

She felt his hand at her neck as he brushed her hair aside and then leaned over her. She felt a brief, sharp pain, as though something had bitten her. Moments later, his gaze captured hers once again.

"Drink, Lisa." She tried to look down, to see what it was he was offering her, but she could not draw her gaze from his face. Something thick and warm dripped into her mouth. "Drink."

Helpless to refuse, she did as he asked and was immediately filled with a sense of euphoria. Gone was the weakness that had plagued her, the weariness that had weighed her down, the coldness so deep inside her. Warmth flowed through her veins, strengthening her, making her feel as though she could leap from the bed, as if she could run. As if she could fly.

"Sleep now."

She didn't want to sleep, not now when she seemed filled with new life, but his voice wrapped around her, low and soothing and seductive. And completely irresistible.

She stared up at him, trying to see his face, trying to fight the sudden lethargy stealing over her limbs. She wanted to ask who he was, what he was, but a blackness as deep as eternity swept her away before she could form the words.

* * *

She woke to the singing of birds and the rattle of the milk wagon on the cobblestones below, woke feeling better than she had in weeks. Almost, she felt as if she could jump out of bed, walk, run. But it was only an illusion, she thought. She had heard too many tales of people lying at death's door who experienced a last, sudden burst of false energy.

Dr. Martinson frowned as he examined her later that morning. "I don't understand it," he murmured as he looked into her eyes, listened to her heartbeat. "How can this be?"

"What is it?" she asked, fearing that death was closer than she thought.

He shook his head. "Nothing." He smiled his fatherly smile at her and patted her hand. "Nothing for you to worry about, my dear. Get some rest."

But she didn't feel like resting. She grabbed hold of his sleeve as he turned away from the bed. "A strange doctor came to visit me last night," she said, still clutching his sleeve. "Who was he?"

Dr. Martinson's brow wrinkled. "A doctor, you say? I'm sure I don't know."

"But he said you sent him."

"I sent no one. Rest now. I have rounds to make."

"But—"

"I'm sure it was just a dream." He tugged his sleeve free of her grasp. "I'll see you later this evening."

She stared after him. Had it been a dream? But it had seemed so real. Overcome by a sense of disappointment, though she couldn't say why, she drew the covers up over her head and drifted off to sleep to dream of a tall, dark man in a hooded cloak the color of midnight.

The chill in the room awakened her, the same eerie coolness she had felt the night before. Clutching the blankets to her chin, she stared into the darkness. "Where are you? I know you're here."

A dark shape detached itself from the deep shadows of the room. Last night, she had fancied that he was a part of the darkness. On this night, she knew he was the darkness.

"Who are you?" she demanded, her voice thin and shaky. "What are you doing here? What do you want from me?"

A soft chuckle floated through the blackness toward her. "Only what I gave you last night. Only what you gave me in return."

"I gave you nothing." She took a deep breath, opened her mouth to scream for help, but he was suddenly at her side, his hand on her mouth stifling her cry.

"You don't want to do that." His voice was as low, as mesmerizing, as she remembered. "Did I hurt you last night, sweet Analisa?"

She stared up at him. How did he know her name? Who was he, this dark stranger with the compelling voice and mesmerizing eyes?

"Did I?" he persisted.

She shook her head, her heart pounding loudly, erratically. He hadn't hurt her, but there was something

17

about him that frightened her. Something dark and intangible.

"I will not hurt you tonight."

She felt a wave of sweet relief wash over her as someone opened the door. Welcome light from the hallway spilled into her room. Thank goodness. Help was here. "Dr. Martinson! I'm so glad to see you!"

"Good evening, Analisa. How are you feeling?"

She stared at her doctor, waiting for him to question the stranger's presence in the room, but Dr. Martinson walked by the stranger as if there were no one there, though she could see him plainly. He was standing in the shadows, as still and silent as death.

"Who's that man?" Lifting her hand, she pointed a trembling finger toward the stranger.

The doctor glanced around the room, his brow furrowed. "What man?"

"You don't see him?" She looked at the stranger, then back at Dr. Martinson. "He's standing right there, by the window."

Dr. Martinson smiled indulgently. "You must have been dreaming again, my dear. There's no one else here."

She stared at the stranger while the doctor examined her, wondering if she was going insane. She saw the cloaked figure so clearly, but if the doctor could not see him, then surely there was no one there. Perhaps she was having delusions of some kind. She had been ill for so long, perhaps in her weakened state she could no longer discern fact from fantasy. But she didn't feel weak and sick today. She felt stronger this

18

evening than she had in weeks. Perhaps the hooded man was Death come for her. Perhaps that was why only she could see him. Her grandmother had told her that Death rode a dark horse. She giggled softly. Of course, he couldn't ride his horse into her room.

Dr. Martinson was smiling when he finished his examination. "I am pleased with your progress, Analisa, though I confess I do not understand it. It is quite beyond anything I have ever seen before."

She nodded, her gaze still on the hooded man.

"If your condition continues to improve through the night, I think you will be ready to go home tomorrow afternoon."

"Thank you, Doctor."

He patted her hand. "Rest well, my dear."

She watched him leave the room, the stranger momentarily forgotten. Home. She had no home, no place to go when she left here.

"Analisa."

The sound of her name on his lips sent a shiver down her spine. "What do you want? Why couldn't Dr. Martinson see you?"

He moved toward her, bringing the darkness with him. "Because I did not wish to be seen. As for what I want with you, only what I desired last night."

She was trembling now. "What did you do to me last night?" She lifted her hand to her throat. "Did you give me an injection of some kind?"

He hesitated. "An elixir of my own making. It made you feel better, did it not?"

"Yes. Yes, it did. But how—"

"Then close your eyes, Analisa."

"Why?"

"Close your eyes, my sweet Analisa. Listen to the sound of my voice, only my voice."

His voice. It moved over her, soft as a mother's caress, soothing her, comforting her, mesmerizing her so completely that she offered no protest when he sat down on the edge of the bed and drew her gently into his embrace. She was aware of the strength of his arms even as her eyelids grew heavy, heavier. Drifting between the awareness of consciousness and the forgetfulness of sleep, she felt again a quick needle-like pain at her throat, and then she was overcome with a familiar feeling of lethargy, of euphoria, that carried her gently down, down, into the velvet darkness of oblivion. . . .

Her blood. It was sweet, so very, very sweet, and he drank and drank, despising himself, despising his inability to control the need that burned through him, yet reveling in the warmth that flowed through his limbs, chasing away the cold that was ever a part of him, giving him an illusion of life, of mortality.

He drew back to gaze at her face, imprinting her image in his mind. She was a beautiful child, her oval face framed by a wealth of ebony curls. Beneath closed lids, her eyes were the color of sun-warmed earth, large, luminous eyes, innocent and without guile. Her brows were delicately arched. Her nose was perfectly formed, her lips as pink as the petals of a wild rose, her skin smooth and unblemished. And warm. So warm, so alive.

How many times in the last four hundred years had he stolen the elixir of life from a child as pure and innocent as the one lying helpless and vulnerable in his arms? It mattered not that he drew them back from the brink of death and gave them life in return. Who was he to interfere with Fate? What right did he have to play with the lives of those whose blood he took?

This would be the last time. When he left here, he would wander the streets in the company of innocent mortals one last time. He would drink until he was replete, and then he would seek oblivion.

Chapter Two

Analisa forced a smile as Dr. Martinson took her
hand in his and wished her well. The smile lasted until
she left the hospital and stepped out onto the street.
What now? she thought. The epidemic that had almost taken her life had succeeded in taking the lives
of her parents and her two brothers, as well as the
lives of most of the other people in their small village.
The cottages of the diseased had been burned to halt
the spread of the disease leaving those who survived
homeless. She had nowhere to go, no place to stay,
no family to take her in. Alone, she thought. For the
first time in her life, she was totally alone.

The thought frightened her almost more than the
thought of dying. Never in her entire life had she been

without friends or family. It was her worst nightmare come true.

"Analisa!"

She turned to see Dr. Martinson hurrying down the street toward her. He was a tall, austere man in his late sixties, but he seemed much younger. It was his eyes, she thought, always so kind and compassionate, and the briskness of his step.

"I almost forgot," he said, pulling an envelope out of the pocket of his coat. "This was left for you."

"For me?" She took the envelope, turning it over in her hands. It was sealed with a dollop of dark red wax that reminded her of blood. She recognized her name, written in bold script. "Who's it from?"

"I'm sure I don't know."

"Would you . . . would you read it to me?"

"Of course." Dr. Martinson broke the seal and opened the envelope. Withdrawing a letter written in a bold hand on fine ivory-colored parchment, he began to read:

My dear Analisa, I am going on an extended holiday and it is my wish that you occupy my family home at Blackbriar Hall. It is an old residence, but I am confident you will be comfortable there. If you find it lacking, feel free to purchase whatsoever you may need, and to stay as long as you wish; I have made arrangements with my creditors to cover your expenses, my servants will obey your commands as though they were my

own. I have included a small amount of cash to cover your transportation and meals until you arrive.
Your servant,
Lord Alesandro de Avallone
Master of Blackbriar Hall.

Dr. Martinson withdrew a handful of currency and a few coins from the envelope and dropped them into her hands, then folded the letter and put it back in the envelope.

"It seems you've found a benefactor," he remarked, handing her the envelope.

She looked at the money in her hands, then up at the doctor. "How much do I owe you?"

"Not a thing, Analisa. Your bill has been paid for. Please take care of yourself."

"Paid for? But how? Who—"

"Lord Avallone has settled your account, and made a most generous donation to our hospital.

"But who is this Lord Avallone? Why should he wish to provide for me?"

"Though I have never met the man, it's said that he is descended from a highborn Italian nobleman. His title is one of respect." He patted her shoulder. "Please, don't hesitate to send for me if you should ever have need of me."

Analisa slipped the money into her skirt pocket. "Thank you, Doctor."

"Go with God, my dear."

He was a kind man, she thought. He had cared for her day and night, knowing when she arrived that she had no money with which to pay him. She was grateful that the mysterious Alesandro had paid her debt. Grateful and extremely curious. Why would a stranger do such a thing?

She watched Dr. Martinson walk back toward the hospital, her hands nervously worrying the envelope in her hands. She watched him until he was out of sight, then turned and walked down the street, avoiding the shallow puddles left by an early morning rain. Winter was coming. There was a decided chill in the air. Yesterday she'd had nothing, no place to stay, nowhere to go. Last night, steeped in despair over her future, she had tossed and turned, wondering what she would do when she left the hospital. She had never been employed, never lived anywhere but at home with her family.

Her family. They had been happy together in spite of their poverty. Even when food was scarce, when the future looked bleak, Mama and Papa had somehow managed to find something to look forward to, some tiny ray of hope. And now they were gone, Mama, Papa, Thomas and Arthur. Why had she been spared and they had not?

Who was Alesandro Avallone, and why had he offered a penniless stranger the hospitality of his home?

Turning onto a path that led through a small park, she sank down on a wrought-iron bench, the envelope still clutched in her hand. If she had the nerve to accept Lord Avallone's offer—if he truly meant what his letter said—all her troubles would be over, at least for the time being.

She couldn't believe it, didn't dare believe it. Why would this man, this stranger, offer her shelter? Blackbriar Hall. The very name sent a shiver of foreboding down her spine. Even in her small village, they had heard of Blackbriar Hall. A dark, sinister place made of gray stone atop a windswept hill. A place wreathed in mystery and superstition. Some said it was cursed, others that it was haunted.

Taking the money from her pocket, she counted it. The letter had said there was enough to cover transportation and meals, but there was enough for her to live on for many months, if she was frugal.

She sat there a moment, overwhelmed by the generosity of a stranger, and then beset by doubts. Why would Lord Avallone offer her his home? Was it some kind of ploy? But if it was, what could he possibly hope to gain? She had nothing of value, nothing save the shabby clothing she wore and the money he himself had given her.

She looked up as a few fat drops of rain landed on her cheek. There was a crack of lightning, a crash of thunder, and the heavens opened, unleashing a torrent of rain.

Jumping up, she ran toward the carriage stand on the corner and flagged down a passing coach for hire. The driver pulled over, took one look at her ragged apparel and well-worn shoes, and shook his head.

"Not working for charity today." Tugging his cap down, he clucked to the horse.

"Wait!" she called, running after him. "I can pay."

The coachman drew back on the reins. He squinted down at her, his expression skeptical. "Show me."

She withdrew a coin from her pocket and held it up.

With a nod, the driver swung down from his seat and opened the door for her. "Where to, miss?"

"Blackbriar Hall."

He looked at her, his close-set blue eyes widening beneath heavy brown brows. "Are ye daft, girl?"

"Maybe so," she muttered, and climbed into the coach.

It wasn't long before they had left the city far behind. The neat, well-tended roads turned into narrow, winding paths lined by tall trees bent by the storm. The houses grew smaller and further apart until they disappeared altogether and there was nothing to see but rolling countryside and an occasional herd of sheep clustered together against the storm.

Analisa huddled in a corner of the carriage, the lap robe pulled up to her chin, the letter clutched, like a talisman, in her hand. She grew more and more nervous with each mile that passed until, too tired to fight it, fatigue overtook her and she drifted to sleep, her dreams filled with a tall, dark, hooded figure and eyes that glowed like indigo fire.

She awoke with a start as a bright flash of lightning lit the interior of the coach. Thunder raged across the heavens, shaking the ground. She shivered, not so much from the cold, but from a sense of unease. The storm was like none she had ever seen before.

A short time later, the coach came to a halt. She heard a rap on the top of the coach and then the voice of the driver. "There's an inn ahead," he shouted, his voice muffled by the wind. "Will ye be wantin' to stop for the night?"

The thought of staying at an inn, surrounded by strangers, sleeping in an unfamiliar bed, filled her with apprehension. "How much farther is it to Blackbriar Hall?"

"About an hour."

"Let's go on then."

"Very well, miss."

She drew the curtains over the windows, then huddled deeper into the lap robe, shivering now as the wind picked up, sneaking through whatever cracks it could find. Belatedly, it occurred to her that she would be among strangers and sleeping in an unfamiliar bed at Blackbriar Hall, too.

She felt a change in the pace of the coach, knew they had begun the long upward climb to Blackbriar Hall. She drew back the curtain and peered out, though there was nothing to see but darkness, nothing to hear but the pounding of the rain on the roof of the coach. She felt a moment of regret for the driver and his horse, comforted herself with the thought that she had the means to pay them well.

A flash of movement caught her eye. Leaning forward, she peered into the darkness, her eyes widening in surprise. Was that a wolf running alongside the coach? A black wolf? A flash of lightning lit the sky, and for a moment, her gaze met the blue eyes of the wolf. She blinked and looked again, but the creature was gone, if indeed it had ever been there. With a shake of her head, she let the curtain fall back into place.

As they neared the top of the hill, a gray mist rose from the ground, floating around the coach like smoke. The road leveled out, widened, ran between a forest of ancient oaks and elms twisted into strange shapes by the wind.

And then, in a burst of lightning, she saw the house, standing dark and sinister in the midst of the storm. Gargoyles leered down at her; tall, arched windows, black in the night, stared at her like sightless eyes.

The coach came to a halt. A moment later, the driver jumped down and opened the door. "We're here, miss," he said, a shiver in his voice that had nothing to do with the chill of the night. "Blackbriar Hall."

She paid him his fare plus a generous tip, then climbed out of the coach and ran up the thirteen stone steps to the front door. Thirteen, she thought. Unlucky. She stood there a moment, shaking the rain from her hair and wondering if she shouldn't climb back into the coach and return to the city, but when she looked over her shoulder, she saw that the coach was already on its way back down the path.

Taking a deep breath, she prayed for courage as she turned back toward the door. It was an impressive entrance. The door was at least ten feet high. The head of a snarling wolf was carved into the heavy dark wood. Taking a deep breath, she knocked on the door, and then knocked again. Was no one home? She shivered as the wind picked up, its icy fingers creeping up her legs.

A moment later, the massive front door swung open, revealing a tall, regal-looking woman clad in a severe high-necked black dress. Her hair, once brown but now mostly gray, was pulled into a loose chignon at her nape.

Raising her lamp higher, the woman regarded Analisa through narrowed gray eyes. "Miss Matthews?"

"Yes."

"Come in," the woman said. The keys at her waist made a tinkling sound as she took a step back to allow Analisa entrance to the house. "We have been expecting you."

Analisa followed the woman down a marble hallway into a large parlor.

The woman set her lamp on a polished hardwood table, gestured toward a curved sofa covered in rich dark green damask.

"Sit, please. Cook is preparing tea to warm you. Sally is preparing your room. I am the housekeeper, Mrs. Thornfield."

Analisa sat down, shivering in spite of the heat radiating from the fire that crackled in the large stone hearth. Preparing her room? How had the woman known she was coming when she hadn't known herself? Or that she would be arriving tonight, and at such a late hour?

"Would you care for something to eat?"

"Yes," Analisa said gratefully. "Thank you."

"Cook made a pot of lamb stew this evening, but if you would prefer something else, you need but ask."

"No, that will be fine, thank you."

"If you will excuse me, I will tell Cook you have arrived."

Analisa nodded, folding her hands to still their trembling as she gazed at her surroundings. The room was larger than the house she had once lived in. The furnishings were all dark wood and forest hues, somber yet elegant. A tapestry depicting a wolf chasing a stag through a field of black briars hung on one wall. A pair of overstuffed chairs covered in muted shades of brown and gold were arranged to one side of the fireplace, a heavy square table between them. Several large rugs were spread over the black and white marble floor. The mantel over the hearth was made of the same black and white marble. A single vase, looking very old and very fragile, sat empty on the mantel. Heavy green and gold velvet drapes covered the windows. A glass-fronted cabinet was against the wall across from the hearth.

Rising, she crossed the floor to look inside the cabinet. One shelf held a collection of animals carved from what she thought might be jade: a large dragon spewing fire, a bat with wings spread wide, a wolf with teeth bared, a mountain lion sleeping on a tree branch, a tiger hunched over a kill.

31

The second shelf held a series of small, thick books bound in rich dark brown leather.

The third shelf held an assortment of objects that might be collected by a child: a bird's nest, a sprig of what looked like dried heather, a white sea shell, a shiny black stone.

The sound of the housekeeper's keys warned of her approach. Analisa whirled around, feeling guilty without knowing why.

"I did not mean to startle you, Miss Matthews," the housekeeper said. "Would you prefer to eat in the dining room or in here, before the fire?"

"I'd like to eat in here, if it isn't too much trouble. And please, call me Analisa."

"You may do as you wish, Miss Analisa. The house is yours, and I, like the other servants, are yours to command."

Analisa blinked at the dour-faced housekeeper. Hers to command? She had never been in command of anything, or anyone, in her whole life. "How many servants are there?"

"Myself. Sally Kent, who is our housemaid. She will also be your personal maid, if she pleases you. Farleigh is coachman at Blackbriar. Dewhurst is the groom. Elton looks after the grounds. Annie Cullen is the scullery maid. And there's Cook, of course. Lord Avallone has not seen fit to replace Hal, who served as footman until a few months ago. We are a small household. We have no butler, so Sally and I fill in as needed." She gestured at the sofa. "Please, be seated, miss," the housekeeper said, and left the room.

Analisa sat down, thinking seven people hardly seemed sufficient to look after such a large estate.

The housekeeper reappeared a short time later and placed a pewter tray on the table beside the sofa. The savory aroma emanating from the soup tureen caused Analisa's stomach to growl loudly. She felt a flush heat her cheeks at the housekeeper's knowing glance, but the woman said nothing except that she would return later to collect the dishes.

Analisa stared at the bounty laid out on the tray. The fine china tureen held enough stew to feed a family for a week. There was a loaf of brown bread still warm from the oven, a pot of tea, as well as a small pitcher of milk, a dainty sugar bowl, a pat of butter, a pot of honey.

She spread the white linen napkin on her lap, filled a soup bowl with savory stew, poured tea into a pretty flowered china cup, added milk and sugar, spread a thick layer of butter and honey on the bread. The stew was delicious; the bread tasted warm and yeasty; the tea chased the last of the chill from her bones. It was, she thought, the best meal she had ever eaten.

She had no sooner finished the last bite than the housekeeper reappeared, followed by a slender young woman wearing a long gray dress and a blindingly white apron. Her curly brown hair was bundled beneath a frilly white lace cap, her brown eyes wide and friendly.

"I have taken the liberty of drawing you a hot bath," Mrs. Thornfield said, taking up the tray. "Sally will show you to your room. Will you be wanting to see the rest of the house after you bathe, or would you prefer to wait until the morrow?"

"Tomorrow, I think." Analisa smothered a yawn behind her hand. "I find I'm rather tired."

"As you wish. I shall bid you good night, then," the housekeeper said, and left the room.

"This way, miss," Sally said, and led the way down a short hall and up a winding staircase that led to a long corridor.

Analisa followed Sally, passing room after room until they came to a carved mahogany door at the end of the hall. Sally opened the door and Analisa followed her inside, her breath catching in her throat as she took in her surroundings.

It was a large square room. A cheery fire blazed in a white marble fireplace. Thick carpets covered the hardwood floor. There was a large wardrobe made of cherrywood, the double doors carved with flowering vines, a matching vanity, and a dainty stool covered in burgundy velvet. Drapes of the same rich color were drawn back from the tall leaded windows, giving her a view of the storm.

A canopied bed was situated across from the hearth; there were dainty cherrywood tables on either side.

"Oh, my," Analisa breathed. "It's lovely. And so . . . so big."

"The bathtub is in there," Sally said, pointing to a

34

door in the corner. "I've laid out clean towels, and a robe and gown. And slippers."

"Thank you."

"The privy is the last door down the hall to your left," Sally said. "If you don't want to go that far, there's a chamber pot under the bed."

Analisa nodded.

Bobbing a curtsey, Sally left the room.

Later, after a long soak in deliciously warm scented water, Analisa sat in a chair in front of the window. Wrapped in a long blue velvet robe, she stared out at the storm. The rain fell steadily, punctuated by bright flashes of lightning and long drumrolls of thunder. She wondered, fleetingly, who had picked out her night rail and slippers and how they had known her size, or that her favorite color was blue.

Mrs. Thornfield had come in a few minutes earlier, asking if there was anything she required before the staff retired for the night. Somewhat shyly, Analisa had asked for a cup of hot cocoa.

She sipped it now, unable to believe she was here, warm and safe. She had lingered in the tub until the water grew old. Clean hot water, scented soap, toweling that was soft against her skin. Never in all her life had she known such luxury, such comfort. A cheery fire burned in the hearth, casting dancing shadows on the high ceiling and the pale blue walls.

Why had Lord Avallone invited her to stay here? She did not even know the man; certainly he did not know her, yet he had opened his home to her. Why?

Blackbriar Hall. It was a house shrouded in mystery and legend. Though some claimed it was haunted, Analisa had never been one to believe in ghosts or goblins. Her fears had been of hunger and disease, but here, in this place, it was easy to imagine the spirits of the dead walking the long, dark corridors. There were numerous alcoves and shadowed corners where any number of otherworldly creatures could hide.

She drank the last of her cocoa and set the cup on the floor.

Feeling warm and sleepy, she crawled into bed and pulled the covers up to her chin. Turning on her side, she closed her eyes. The storm had calmed and she drifted to sleep, serenaded by the music of the rain.

She woke abruptly, overcome by a feeling of being smothered, of being trapped in darkness, unable to breathe. The high-pitched wail of a wolf sent a shiver down her spine.

Bolting upright, the covers clutched to her chest, she glanced around the room, her heart pounding wildly.

She didn't know what she expected to find lurking in the dim light of the dying fire, but there was nothing visible. She had never been afraid of the dark, but now she lit the lamp beside the bed, peering into the corners, flouncing down on her stomach to look under the bed.

It was a long time before sleep came again.

*　　*　　*

In the morning, with sunlight streaming through the windows, her fears of the night past seemed foolish. Sally came in to light the fire, and then, while Analisa snuggled under the covers waiting for the heat of the fire to chase away the chill of the night, Sally brought her a cup of hot cocoa and a sweet roll still warm from the oven.

Analisa thanked the girl. Except for the weeks she had spent in the hospital, no one had ever waited on her, nor had she ever stayed abed so late. At home, she had risen at dawn to milk their old black and white cow and fight the chickens for their eggs.

"Now," Sally said, going to the wardrobe, "what shall you wear today?"

Analisa was about to say she had nothing but the much-mended dress she had worn the day before when Sally opened the wardrobe doors, revealing at least two dozen gowns in a variety of colors. Velvets and satins, silk and challis, gabardine and serge, cotton and muslin and dimity.

"Oh, my," Analisa murmured. She had never seen so many gowns in one place, at one time, never owned more than two dresses in her whole life.

Sally glanced over her shoulder. "So, miss, which shall it be?" She pulled out a soft gray dress of fine-spun wool, and a rich gold and brown striped taffeta with a high collar, both of which looked far too fine for the likes of her. "Or perhaps something more cheery," Sally suggested, and pulled out a flowered muslin with short puffy sleeves and a froth of delicate lace at the throat.

Analisa shook her head in wonder. At home, she'd had two choices: black or gray. "Whose gowns are these?"

"Why, yours of course." Head cocked to one side, Sally regarded her a moment. "This one, I think, miss," she decided, laying the gold and brown taffeta on the foot of the bed.

An hour later, clad in the striped taffeta, her feet encased in soft black kid boots, her hair coiled in a loose knot at her nape, Analisa went downstairs to breakfast.

The dining room was large, as were all the rooms she had seen thus far. An elegant mahogany table surrounded by a dozen high-backed chairs stood in the center of the room. A matching sideboard took up most of one wall. The carpet, drapes, and chair upholstery were all done in shades of forest green and burgundy. There was a large painting of a ship sailing turbulent waters on one wall; a chandelier, as delicate as a spider's web, hung from the ceiling on a thick silver chain.

Sally bade Analisa to sit down, then hurried into the kitchen.

Mrs. Thornfield appeared to wish her good morning and asked if she had slept well. The housekeeper wore black again, relieved this morning by a crisp white apron. A large ring of keys hung from her belt. A white cap covered her hair.

A moment later, Sally returned bearing a covered tray, which she placed on the table in front of Analisa. The maid lifted the lid, revealing two thick slices of ham, three slices of bacon, fried tomatoes, toast, scrambled eggs, potatoes, kippers, and a pot of tea. There was also a bowl of jelly and two pats of butter.

Analisa looked up at Mrs. Thornfield. Was she expected to eat all this? At home, breakfast had been little more than a slice of brown bread and a cup of weak tea. Dinner and supper were bread, potatoes and pork or mutton. If meat was scarce, Analisa and her mother went without, leaving it for her father and brothers, who had to work the fields.

Mrs. Thornfield shrugged. "Cook wasn't sure what you liked. Perhaps later today you can write a list of your likes and dislikes, and any particular favorites."

Analisa bit down on her lower lip. "I . . . I . . . that is, I . . ."

Mrs. Thornfield regarded her a moment, and then nodded. "You can tell me," she said, "and I will relay your wishes to Cook."

Heat flooded Analisa's cheeks. "Thank you."

"Sally, go tidy up Miss Analisa's room."

Sally glanced from Analisa to Mrs. Thornfield, her expression saying all too clearly that she knew her presence was no longer welcome. She bobbed a curtsey and left the room.

"Do you not know how to read and write, child?" Mrs. Thornfield asked when they were alone. "I can teach you, if you wish."

Analisa's eyes widened. To learn to read and write had long been a dream of hers, one as out of reach as the sun and the stars.

A faint smile softened Mrs. Thornfield's usually

stern countenance. "From the expression on your face, I will assume this is something that would please you. We can begin this afternoon, if you would like."

Analisa nodded. "Oh, I would! Thank you so much."

"Enjoy your breakfast before it grows cold," Mrs. Thornfield said. "I shall see you in the library at two."

Analisa smiled, too overcome by her good fortune and her surroundings to speak.

What had she ever done, she wondered, to deserve such a reward?

Chapter Three

Analisa met with the housekeeper at the appointed time, and for the next two hours she concentrated on learning her letters. Her parents had seen no reason for her to know how to read or write anything except her name. She was a girl, after all, and a poor one at that. And likely to be poor all her life. Knowing how to read and write wouldn't help to put food on the table, or find her a good husband.

For all her stern bearing and sharp tongue, Mrs. Thornfield was infinitely patient with her pupil, and pleased with Analisa's eagerness to learn. They agreed to continue Analisa's lessons each afternoon at two o'clock.

"I shall send to the city for some lesson books, some easy ones to begin with," the housekeeper said briskly. "But now I have other duties to attend to."

"Of course," Analisa said, and then asked, somewhat timidly, "What shall I do?"

"Why, whatever you wish, child," Mrs. Thornfield replied. "Cook serves tea at four. Dinner is at eight. If that schedule is not to your liking, you must let me know, and I shall advise Cook."

"No, no, that's fine," Analisa said, horrified at the thought of disrupting the household.

"Very well." Mrs. Thornfield offered one of her rare smiles. "As I've told you, child, the house is yours for as long as you wish to stay. You may do whatever pleases you while you are here. You need not ask anyone's permission. If you wish to go into town, you have only to let me know, and I will have Farleigh bring the carriage around. Accounts have been opened for you at all the shops. You may buy whatever you wish."

Analisa could only stare, overwhelmed by a stranger's generosity, and by the house itself. Hers, for as long as she wished to stay? Why would anyone ever want to leave? Again, she wondered who Lord Avallone was and what had prompted him to offer her the hospitality of his home. And what he expected in return.

"Will there be anything else?" Mrs. Thornfield asked.

"No, thank you."

"Very well. If you should need anything, you have only to ring and someone will come to attend you."

So saying, the housekeeper left the library. Analisa

glanced around the room. Three of the walls were lined from floor to ceiling with bookcases, and every shelf was filled with books. She pulled one off the shelf nearest her and thumbed through the pages, anxious for the day when she would be able to read the words. She replaced the volume and took down another, and then another. Her father had always told her there was power in words. Soon, she would have the ability to read and write more than just her name, something her mother and brothers had never learned.

She walked slowly around the room, her fingertips trailing over the spines of the books. So many books. Old ones. New ones. Here and there she found scrolls that were yellow with age. Had the mysterious Lord Avallone read them all?

She stopped at the window and looked out. She was lucky to be here, lucky to be alive. She lifted a hand to her throat, wondering, as she had so often, what the hooded stranger had given her that had caused such rapid healing, such a miraculous cure, when she had been so close to death. Ah, well, she would probably never know.

She glanced at the bookshelves again, her gaze drawn to a slim volume bound in blood-red leather. Taking it from the shelf, she opened the cover and turned the page, stared at the grotesque black and white image on the paper. The drawing was of a skeletal creature with long, bony fingers, sunken eyes, and fangs. She turned the page, revealing another horror: a body lying in a crude wooden coffin. A man stood beside the coffin. He held a sharp wooden stake over the heart of the corpse. There was a mallet in his raised hand. The next page showed a fanged monster hovering over the bed of a small child.

She turned the pages, revealing one horrifying image after another, each one more grotesque than the last. She closed the book, wishing she could read the title. Perhaps she would ask Mrs. Thornfield later.

Leaving the library, she went into the parlor. At her request, Sally brought her a pot of tea and a plate of cheese and crackers. Analisa ate slowly, pretending the house was truly hers, that she really was the mistress of this fine manor, and not just some poor orphan allowed to stay on the sufferance of its owner.

Later, she wandered through the house. The servants' quarters were below stairs. The kitchen, pantry, parlor, and library were located on the main floor. The second floor held a number of bedrooms. She stopped counting after eight. All were furnished and immaculate; all had the feel of rooms long unused.

It was growing dark when she paused at the bottom of the stairway leading to the third floor. Dared she go up there? Mrs. Thornfield had assured her she could do as she pleased, go where she pleased, but, with each step she took, she felt a growing sense of unease.

There were no lamps to light the way on this floor. The only illumination came from a single narrow window to her right.

Chewing on the inside of her cheek, she took a few

steps down the corridor. She put her hand on the latch of the first door on her left, waited a moment, and then opened the door. It revealed a large empty room. So did the door across the corridor when she opened it. There was only one other room on the floor. It was at the far end of the corridor behind a set of imposing double doors. As she drew closer, she saw that each door had the head of a snarling wolf carved into the wood.

Analisa walked down the corridor, her steps slow, reluctant, yet she was unable to turn back. Her footsteps made no sound, muffled by the thick carpet. Her hand was trembling as she reached for the latch. The door opened into a large dark room. It was Lord Avallone's room—she had no doubt of that. An enormous bed covered with a quilted black spread was located directly across from the doorway. A large chest, the drawers intricately carved, stood to her left; an armoire that took up most of the wall was on her right. There was an enormous fireplace in the corner.

A large painting hung over the bed. She could just make it out in the faint light. It depicted a tall, dark-haired man gazing at his reflection in a quiet blue pool. The man in the painting bore an uncanny resemblance to the stranger she had seen in the hospital. Frowning, she took a step closer. The pool did not reflect the man's image but the image of a large black wolf with deep blue eyes. A whim of the artist, surely, for she had never heard of a wolf with blue eyes. But she had seen one, she thought, remembering the wolf she had seen running alongside the coach the night she arrived at Blackbriar.

A shiver swept down her spine and she turned away, suddenly eager to be out of the room, away from the painting.

She was hurrying down the corridor toward the stairs when she heard a voice call her name. It was a voice she could never forget, low and soft, dark as midnight. The voice of the stranger in the hospital. She paused in mid-flight and whirled around, expecting to see him standing in the hallway behind her. But no one was there. And then she heard it again.

Analisa.

She lifted a hand to her throat, troubled by a sudden image of the stranger bending over her, looking at her with the unblinking eyes of a wolf.

Filled with a sudden unreasoning fear, she flew down the stairs and ran into the parlor. Lamps blazed with light; a fire crackled cheerfully in the hearth. The air was filled with a wondrous aroma.

Breathing heavily, she sank down in a chair before the fire, her arms wrapped tightly around herself. She closed her eyes, willing her heart to stop racing, her breathing to return to normal.

A short time later, Mrs. Thornfield appeared to announce that supper was ready.

The next six weeks passed swiftly. Analisa spent an hour each afternoon in the solar with Mrs. Thornfield, going over the lessons she had learned the day before. Mrs. Thornfield seemed pleased with her progress and even complimented her a time or two. Analisa basked in her praise, sparse though it might be.

Analisa's admiration for Mrs. Thornfield grew immensely. The housekeeper was busy from dawn till dark. Under her rule, the household ran smoothly and efficiently. In addition to her household tasks, which included the making of jams, jellies, and candles, she also gathered flowers and herbs that were used for cooking, or for the making of fragrances or potpourri. She made lavender bags for the linen cupboards, and also made herbal drinks and pomades. Since Blackbriar employed no steward, Mrs. Thornfield was also in charge of the marketing, and settling Blackbriar's accounts with the local tradesmen.

The midday meal was served at noon. Analisa took her meal in the breakfast room, finding the huge dining room oppressive and lonely. It still amazed her that she had the freedom of such a grand house, that there were servants to wait on her, to fulfill her every wish, her every need.

She passed the hours until lesson time by doing needlework, or studying a little more. Sometimes she took a nap. Sometimes she wandered the grounds.

There was an ice house and a milk cellar, and on the far side of the barn there was a dovecote. She had heard of them but never seen one, and she spent one morning exploring it. The ground floor was used for storing grain and feed, the upper level was filled with nests. The birds, and there must have been hundreds of them, were let out during the day and flew home at night. She didn't like to think of them being raised for food, but Cook's pigeon pie was simply too good to refuse. Still, after seeing the lovely birds, she did not ask for it often.

She explored the barn, too, taking time to pet the beautiful horses. She always took a handful of carrots or a couple of apples to feed them. She was especially fond of a pretty little gray mare that whinnied a welcome each time Analisa entered the barn. There was a brown and white cow with big brown eyes, a half dozen curly-haired sheep, a pair of goats, dozens of chickens, an arrogant rooster.

At two, she met Mrs. Thornfield in the library to study the day's lessons. She took tea at four, and then went walking in the vast flower gardens if the weather was fair, or, if the day was stormy, she curled up in front of the fire, listening to the rain. She loved books, loved to take a new one from the shelf each day and slowly turn the pages, picking out the words she knew, trying to sound out the ones that were unfamiliar to her.

Evenings were sometimes difficult. Often, while sitting alone in front of the hearth, she thought of her parents and her brothers, wishing they could be there with her. It would have been so wonderful to see her mother clad in a fine dress, with servants to attend her; to see her father sitting at the head of the table, the lines of worry gone from his brow; to share her lessons with her brothers, see their delight as they learned their numbers and letters.

Her life would have been almost perfect had it not been for the nightmares that continued to plague her.

Every night she woke in a cold sweat, tormented by the sensation of being buried alive, of feeling the earth crushing her, of fighting for breath. She tried to brush it off, attributing it to being a stranger in a strange place, but the dream came more and more often, until she was afraid to close her eyes, afraid to go to sleep.

Mrs. Thornfield was the first to notice that something was wrong. "Are you ill, child?" she asked one morning.

"No," Analisa replied, smothering a yawn. "Why do you ask?"

"You have looked rather peaked these past few days. Are you sure you're quite well?"

"Yes, I'm sure."

"You must tell me if something is amiss," the housekeeper said, frowning. "My Lord Alesandro will be most displeased if he returns and finds that you . . ." She took a deep breath, as if she was aware of saying more than she should.

"I'm quite well, truly," Analisa said. "It's just that I haven't been sleeping well."

"The bed is not to your liking?"

"Oh, no, it's most comfortable. It's just that . . ."

"Yes?"

"Well, I've been having the most disturbing dreams."

"I shall bring you a cup of hot milk," Mrs. Thornfield said, obviously relieved that Analisa's wan look was the result of nothing more serious than a lack of sleep.

Later that night, after drinking a cup of hot tea

laced with milk and honey, Analisa sat in a chair by the window, gazing out into the night, wondering how long she would be allowed to stay before the master of the house returned. Where would she go then? Though she had been in the manor only a matter of weeks, she was rapidly growing accustomed to having servants wait on her. How easily she had grown used to being waited on, she mused; to having her meals prepared for her, someone to make her bed, draw her bath, dress her hair. She had no responsibilities, no duties, no worries. She had only to say she wished for something, and it was hers. But the master's return would quickly put an end to that, and she would be on her own again, with no place to go, and no one to care for her.

She shook off her melancholy mood. She was young. She was healthy and strong again, thanks to the stranger in the hospital, and the good food and care she had received at Mrs. Thornfield's hands. Other young women managed to survive on their own, and so would she. . . .

Analisa.

His voice. She heard it so clearly in her mind that she glanced over her shoulder, expecting to see him there, surprised to find she was alone in the room.

Analisa.

Hardly aware of what she was doing, she stood up, drew on her robe, and left her chamber.

Her slippered feet made hardly a sound as she made her way through the quiet house and out the back door. Compelled by an impulse she could not deny, she moved down the narrow stone-lined path that led through the gardens and around the decorative hedges, past the pretty little lake that shone like a dark mirror in the moonlight, past the maze, until she came to the far end of the property. Tall trees grew here, arranged in a wide circle, and in the center of the circle there was a raised tomb made of white marble.

A bright beam of moonlight shone down on it, illuminating the writing etched into the stone. She leaned forward, sounding out the words.

"Here lies Ale-Alesan-Alesandro de Avallone. Born the seventh day of June in the year of our Lord 1435. Left this world the twenty-second day of Jan-Janu-January, 1469."

Below that were the words "I am not an answer to a prayer—nor a whisper—nor a dare—I am but a thought—across time."

She ran her hand over the cold stone, wondering if the Alesandro who had so generously given her the hospitality of his house had been named for the man buried here.

"Alesandro." She murmured the name aloud, liking the sound of it.

"Analisa."

It had been no voice within her head this time, and she whirled around, her heart leaping into her throat when she saw a man standing in the shadows. A man she had seen before. A man she would never forget.

"You," she murmured.

He moved out of the shadows and into the moon's

light. He was as tall and lean as she remembered. Clad all in black as he had been in the hospital, he seemed to be a part of the night itself. A long cloak fell from his broad shoulders. Silver moonlight played over the sharp lines and angles of his face.

He took a step toward her, and she stumbled backward, afraid without knowing why.

His eyes burned with a familiar deep blue flame as he gazed at her.

He held out his hand. "Analisa." His voice was a whisper, a caress, a command.

Unable to help herself, she moved toward him even though every instinct she possessed screamed at her to run away.

And then she was standing in front of him, staring up at him, helpless to move, to resist. And he was bending toward her, his gaze swallowing her up, until she felt as though she were drowning in the heated blueness of his eyes. She felt her limbs grow weak, felt herself falling, falling, into the never-ending depths of his eyes. . . .

She was warm and pliant in his embrace, helpless to resist his call. He had told himself he would never do this again, yet, like her, he was unable to resist. Her life force had called to him every night she had been here, in his house. He had been deep underground, seeking the sleep of his kind, and yet her essence, her nearness, had permeated his soul. Even wrapped in the arms of the earth and trapped in the darkness, he had heard her footsteps as she walked his land, heard the rhythmic beat of her heart. The

siren song of her blood had called to him in soft tones
of desire and insistent hunger, until it had drawn him
from the depths of the earth to her side.

And now he stood poised above her, about to do
what he had vowed never to do again. His gaze held
hers captive while he listened to the seductive call of
her heartbeat. She was his, to do with as he wished.
His, for this night, or for every night as long as she
lived. His. He had but to take her.

"Analisa." He whispered her name, and it echoed
back to him on the wings of the night.

Analisa. Analisa. Analisa.

She stared up at him, mute, helpless, and he knew
he could not take her by force, knew that as much as
he craved her sweetness, as much as he needed it, he
did not want to take her life's blood by force or by
trickery. He wanted it as a gift, freely given.

One kiss, he thought; one kiss would do no harm.
Her eyelids fluttered down as his mouth sought hers.
Her lips were warm and soft and tasted of chamomile
and honey. She was so young, so alive; being this
close to her was like standing in front of a roaring
fire. She radiated life and goodness. It drew him like
a living flame, chasing the coldness from his being,
banishing the loneliness from his soul. His lips moved
over hers, ever so lightly. Desire surged within him
as, ever so tentatively, she returned his kiss.

Afraid of hurting her, afraid he could not for long
resist the powerful temptation of her nearness, he
lifted her into his arms, carried her swiftly into the
house, and put her to bed.

"Sleep, my sweet Analisa." He brushed a lock of hair from her brow, let his fingertips slide down the warm, sweet curve of her cheek. "Sleep and dream your girlish dreams," he murmured, "and I will make them come true."

Chapter Four

Analisa awoke late the next morning, feeling wonderfully alive and refreshed. For the first time in weeks, she hadn't been bothered by the nightmare that had been plaguing her. But she'd had another dream to take its place, a wonderful dream. She had seen him in the garden, the mysterious man who had come to her in the hospital, and he had kissed her, only a brief touch of his lips to hers, yet she had felt it in every fiber of her being.

She lifted her fingertips to her lips. Even though it had been only a dream, it seemed as though she could still feel his touch. Such a strange dream. She was certain she had actually gone walking in the gardens last night, yet she had no memory of returning to her room. Had she dreamed that, too? His voice seemed to linger in her mind. *Sleep and dream your girlish dreams,* he had said, his voice soft and low and strangely compelling. *And I will make them come true.*

Rising, she rang for Sally, who brought her a cup of cocoa and then went into the dressing room and laid out her clothes for the morning. At first, Analisa had felt rather uncomfortable having a maid wait on her, but Sally had quickly put her at ease with her cheerful chatter; now their morning routine had become a habit. While Analisa drank her cocoa, Sally filled a basin with hot water, then left the room for a few minutes so Analisa could wash up. When summoned, Sally returned to the room, lacing up Analisa's corset and arranging the folds of her dress over her petticoats.

She sat at her dressing table while Sally brushed her hair and then drew it up into a neat coil, leaving a few tendrils to frame her face.

Smiling her thanks, Analisa went downstairs to breakfast. She ate quickly, then left the house, hurrying down the flagstone path that led past the gardens and the lake until she came to the circle of trees.

She was breathing heavily as she stepped into the center. And the crypt was there, just as she remembered. It was made of white marble, shimmering in the sunlight, almost as if the marble were alive, breathing.

Analisa.

She heard his voice within her mind again, felt his presence there, within the grove, imagined she felt the touch of his lips on hers, the whisper of his breath against her skin.

She glanced around, certain he was nearby. "Where are you?" she asked plaintively. "Why are you hiding from me?"

But there was no reply, only the soft sighing of the wind through the trees.

She placed her hand on the head of the crypt. It was cold to her touch, and yet she felt a warmth in her fingers, a warmth that spread through her hand and up her arm. With a startled cry, she jerked her hand away. Filled with a sudden unease, she turned and ran out of the grove and didn't stop running until she was back at the house.

"Mercy, child, whatever is the matter?" Mrs. Thornfield asked as Analisa burst into the parlor. "You look as though you've seen a ghost."

Analisa put a hand to her chest. Her heart was fluttering like a wild bird trapped in a cage.

"Who . . . who's . . ." She drew a deep breath. "Who's buried in the crypt in the grove?"

The housekeeper frowned. "The first master of Blackbriar, I believe."

"He's dead?"

"I should hope so, child," Mrs. Thornfield said, displaying one of her rare smiles. "He died over four hundred years ago. Now, what is this all about?"

"Is Blackbriar Hall haunted?"

Mrs. Thornfield shrugged. "Rumors of ghosts are not uncommon in houses as old as this one."

"Have you ever seen one? Here? A ghost?"

"A ghost? No, child, I've never seen a ghost."

Analisa sank down on the sofa, her arms folded over her chest. She was cold, so cold.

"Have you seen something?" Mrs. Thornfield asked, her expression wary.

"I'm not sure. Last night . . . I . . ."

"What happened last night, child?"

"I'm not sure. I think it was a dream. But it seemed so real. I heard a voice calling my name, at least I think I heard it, and I went out into the gardens. I saw the crypt there. And a man . . . a man I've seen before . . ."

"I'm sure it was only a dream," Mrs. Thornfield said, her voice brisk. "You needn't worry. There are no ghosts at Blackbriar." She patted Analisa's arm in motherly fashion. "A good hot cup of tea is what you need." Pulling a warm throw from the back of a chair, she draped it around Analisa's shoulders. "I'll bring you one directly."

"Thank you."

With a nod, the housekeeper left the room. A few moments later, Sally came in to light the fire. She smiled uncertainly, bobbed a curtsey, and hurried out of the room. She returned a short time later with a tray bearing a cup of tea and a biscuit.

"Anything else I can get for you, miss?"

"No, thank you."

Left alone, Analisa stared into the fire. They probably all thought she was crazy, asking about ghosts. Now that she was sitting there with the sunlight streaming through the windows and a fire blazing cheerfully in the hearth, it all seemed like foolishness.

The rest of the day passed in a sort of a blur, as if she were seeing everything through a mist, as if she weren't really there at all. She picked at her dinner, causing Mrs. Thornfield to inquire after her health.

That night, getting ready for bed, she could scarcely remember how she had spent the day.

Sally came in to light the fire. Mrs. Thornfield brought her a hot cup of tea, and then she was alone. She drank the tea and put the cup on the bedside table, blew out the lamp, slid under the blankets, closed her eyes.

And heard his voice in her mind, soft as smoke.

Analisa.

She put the pillow over her head, hoping to shut him out even though, deep inside, she knew she had been waiting for this moment all day.

Analisa. Come to me.

She heard the need in his voice, the longing, and knew she could not resist, knew it was not his need that drew her, but her own.

Rising, she pulled on her robe, stepped into her slippers, and left the house.

The light of the full moon brightened her way as she followed the now familiar path to the crypt within the grove.

And he was there, waiting for her.

"Analisa."

No one had ever caressed her name the way he did.

She stared up at him. He was tall, so very tall. And dark. His hair, his clothing, all were black. As black as the night that surrounded them. "Who are you?"

"Alesandro de Avallone," he replied with a low bow. "Master of Blackbriar Hall."

"*What* are you?"

"One night perhaps I shall tell you."

"Why not now?"

"The time is not right."

"Have you come home to stay?"

He hesitated, and then nodded.

Analisa wrapped her arms around her middle. "Thank you for allowing me to stay here while you were away. I'll leave in the morning."

"No!" He made a slashing motion with his hand. "There is no need for you to go."

"But—"

"It is a large house, Analisa, and I am never in residence during the day. Please, continue to make my home your own."

She bit down on her lower lip, wondering if it was acceptable for her to stay in his house without a proper chaperone when he was in residence. But surely there were servants enough to keep gossip down. Although, except for the servants, she had no idea who would be gossiping about her. There were no other houses nearby, and except for Dr. Martinson, no one else knew she was here. Sadly, there was no longer anyone left to care what happened to her.

"Thank you, my lord," she replied. "I should very much like to stay." She looked up at him. "Why did you invite me to stay here?"

"Because you had nowhere else to go." It was the

truth, at least as much of the truth as he was willing to tell her. He held out his hand. "Come, walk with me."

She hesitated a moment, then put her hand in his. His skin was cool, his grip firm yet gentle. She could feel the latent strength in his grasp. For a time, they walked in silence. She was ever aware of him beside her, aware that his hand grew warmer in hers. He moved silently, his feet making scarcely a sound on the flagstone path. So silently that she glanced down to see if his feet were indeed touching the stones.

"You have a question you wish to ask me," he said, drawing her attention back to his face.

She looked up at him, startled. Questions? She had dozens, but how had he known?

"Ask them, child."

"Are you truly a doctor?"

Even in the dim light, she saw the shadow that passed over his face before he said, "Yes, I am." It was what he had been born for, to ease the suffering of others, until Tzianne came and stole his life from him.

"Why couldn't Dr. Martinson see you that night in my room?"

"It is as I told you. I did not wish to be seen."

"But you weren't invisible," Analisa insisted. "I saw you."

"It is a mind trick, child. Nothing more than that."

"A mind trick?"

"A form of hypnotism."

"Oh." She looked up at him. She had no doubt in

her mind that he could mesmerize anyone with those eyes. "Where have you been all this time?"

"Ah, you might say I was on holiday."

"Where did you go?"

A faint smile flitted across his face. "Not far."

"I've never been anywhere," she said. "Have you been to London? And Paris?"

"Yes, many times."

"Are they wonderful?"

"Yes," he said, and she heard a note of wistfulness in his tone. "Wonderful." He looked down at her and smiled. "Perhaps I shall take you there, one day."

"Would you? Truly?"

She looked up at him, her eyes glowing with excitement. He heard the increased beat of her heart, smelled the warmth of her skin. In spite of the fact that he had fed earlier, hunger stirred deep within him.

"Are you all right?" she asked.

"Yes, of course." He took a deep breath, calling on the strength of four hundred years to quell the hunger that burned through him like hellfire, a hunger that could be quenched so easily with just one taste. . . .

"My lord?"

"What is it, child?"

"You look so . . . are you ill?"

He turned his face away, knowing that soon his eyes would betray him for what he was, that she would see the hunger ever lurking just below the surface.

"My lord?"

He took a deep breath, felt the hunger curl in on itself until it was again under control. Only then did he turn to face her once more. "You need not worry about me, child. I am never ill. Come, I will walk you back."

He took her hand in his when they reached the back door. "Sleep well, Analisa."

"Aren't you coming in?" she asked. "It's late."

He glanced up at the sky, then shook his head. "Not for a while yet."

"Very well then. Good night, my lord."

He lifted her hand, brushed a kiss across her knuckles.

"Will I . . . ?"

Still holding her hand, his gaze met hers. "What is it, child?"

"Will I see you tomorrow night?"

"If you wish."

"I do," she said. "Very much."

Her words moved through him, warming him like the touch of the sun he had not seen in four hundred years. "Until tomorrow night," he said, and disappeared into the darkness.

Chapter Five

He was waiting for her at dusk the following evening.
Her heart seemed to skip a beat when she descended
the stairs and saw him standing there. He wore a
black jacket over snug black breeches. His shirt was
white, open at the throat.

"Come," he said, and ushered her into a room near
the back of the manor. She stood in the doorway
while he lit a fire in the hearth.

It was a large room, one she didn't remember seeing before. The walls were paneled in dark wood.
There were no pictures on the walls save one of a tall
masted ship riding a storm-tossed sea.

She moved toward a narrow bookshelf beside the
fireplace. Many of the titles were in languages unfamiliar to her. A few sounded like medical journals or

textbooks. She ran her fingertips over the volumes: *A Study of Hemophilia* by Dr. Jonathan Forsythe, *Diseases of the Blood* by Thomas Balderston, *Die Ehre des Herzogthums Krain* by Count Valvasor, *Faust* by Goethe, *In a Glass Darkly* by Joseph Sheridan Le-Fanu, *The Count of Monte Cristo* by Alexandre Dumas, *The Tibetan Book of the Dead.*

"You enjoy reading?"

She turned with a start to find him standing beside her. His nearness overwhelmed her.

"I've only just learned. Mrs. Thornfield has been teaching me every afternoon at two. She says I'm doing very well. . . ."

She stopped abruptly. She was babbling like a silly child, she thought. Indeed, she felt like a foolish schoolgirl standing there beside him. He was tall and dark and self-assured. She wondered suddenly how old he was. He might have been any age from twenty to forty. She wondered, too, why he wasn't married. Surely a man of his wealth and breeding could have any woman he fancied. And children. Surely he wanted an heir, someone to carry on his family name, to inherit his lands and wealth.

She felt a quiver of anticipation as he reached toward her, then a strong sense of disappointment as he reached past her to pull a book from the shelf.

"Come," he said, moving toward the high-backed sofa in front of the hearth. "Read to me."

She shook her head. "Oh, no, I couldn't."

"Of course you can." He sat down, looking at her over his shoulder. "Come, Analisa."

Trapped by his gaze, mesmerized by the smooth seduction of his voice, she went to sit beside him. He handed her the book, then sat back, one arm resting along the edge of the sofa, waiting.

Swallowing hard, Analisa opened the book and began to read. When she occasionally stumbled over a word, he supplied it for her. The story was titled *Carmilla*. It was a dark tale about a young girl named Laura who was attacked by a vampire. It told of Laura's childhood encounter with Carmilla, an incident near forgotten until years later when the vampire reappeared. In the end, the vampire was destroyed.

With a sigh, Analisa closed the book. "A troubling tale, my lord. I am glad that such creatures as vampires do not exist."

But exist they did, and he was not the only one. He thought of his ancient enemy. Would he be able to keep Analisa safe should Rodrigo learn of her presence at Blackbriar?

His dark gaze met hers, glittering strangely, a fact she ascribed to the light of the fire. "There have always been tales of vampires, Analisa. Every civilization has its own legends and myths. The *ekimmu* of Sumeria, the *chiang-shih* of China, the *vrykolakas* of Greece."

"Yes, my lord, but they are only stories told to frighten children."

"Are they?"

"Aren't they?"

"Of course." He plucked the book from her hand

and placed it on the table beside the sofa. "Come," he said, rising. "Your dinner is ready."

She was about to ask him how he knew when Sally rapped lightly on the door to announce that very thing.

Alesandro offered Analisa his hand. "Shall we?"

He escorted her into the dining room, took his proper place at the head of the table, indicated she should sit on his right. As usual, the table was covered with a lace cloth and laid with fine china, gleaming silver flatware, and crystal rimmed with gold. She thought the cost of one plate alone would probably have fed her family for a month.

Sally served dinner shortly thereafter: tender roast beef swimming in gravy, Brussels sprouts and mashed potatoes. And Yorkshire pudding.

Analisa frowned. "You're not eating, my lord?"

"No."

The look in his eye, the clipped tone of his voice, effectively stilled any further questions.

He requested a glass of dark red wine, which he sipped while she ate, ever aware of his deep blue eyes watching her.

"Tell me of your life, Analisa."

"There is nothing to tell, my lord. Were it not for your kindness, I should be quite lost."

"You have no family?"

"No, my lord. Nor any friends left."

"The epidemic?"

"Yes, my lord." She looked down at her plate. "Sometimes I wish I had died, as well."

"No! No, Analisa, one must never wish for death. Life is far too precious, and too fleeting."

"Have you lost loved ones, my lord?"

He nodded, his expression suddenly wistful. "Many." Far too many, he mused. His parents, his beloved sister, the friends and colleagues of his youth, so many deaths, until the pain had become too great and he had cut himself off from the world and the people in it.

"My lord?"

"Yes, child?"

"You seem very far away."

"I am afraid I was. Forgive me."

"Why do you call me a child? I'm ten and seven. Hardly a child."

"Ah, ten and seven. A vast age, to be sure."

"Are you mocking me, my lord."

"No, Analisa."

His voice moved over her, slow and sweet, like thick, dark honey. And his eyes, those blue, blue eyes . . . they seemed to see into her mind and heart. Indeed, into the very depths of her soul. Did they see the loneliness she felt? Her sorrow over the loss of her family? Her fear of the future? If he turned her out, she had nowhere to go, no one to turn to for help.

"Analisa."

"Yes, my lord?"

His hand cupped her nape and drew her closer, until she felt as though she were swimming in the blue depths of his eyes. His kiss, when it came, was excruciatingly tender, hardly more than a whisper across her lips, yet she felt it in every fiber of her being.

"You have nothing to fear from me," he said, hoping he spoke the truth. "My home is yours for as long as you wish." He kissed her again, ever so gently. "My life is yours."

She looked up at him, not knowing what to say, but knowing that, from this moment on, her life was irrevocably bound to his.

She dreamed of him that night, a dark, erotic dream that faded upon awaking, leaving her with only a vague memory of smoldering indigo eyes and his mouth on hers.

Feeling a sudden inexplicable urge to go to the grove, she slipped out of bed. Dressing quickly, she ran down the stairs and went out the side door.

Heavy gray clouds hung low in the sky; the grass was still damp with dew; the flagstones were cold beneath her bare feet.

She entered the grove, expecting somehow to find him there, disappointed to find herself alone. What was there about this place that called to her? Going to the crypt, she put her hand upon the cold stone, but it did not warm to her touch as it had before.

Because the crypt was empty?

She folded her arms over her breasts, wondering where such a ridiculous thought had come from.

Shivering, she ran back down the path to the house. Reentering by the side door, she hurried up the steps to the second floor, paused, and continued on up to the third floor.

Her heart was pounding erratically when she reached the room at the end of the hall. She stood there a moment, feeling foolish for what she was thinking. Hand shaking, she reached for the door-knob. The door was locked.

Turning away, she went downstairs to breakfast. If the crypt was empty, she mused, was it because the occupant was now asleep upstairs in the master's bed-chamber?

She was on edge all that day, waiting for him to come downstairs, waiting to see him again. But morning turned to afternoon, and still there was no sign of him. She spent two hours in the library with Mrs. Thornfield, but her mind kept wandering to the up-stairs bedroom and the man who was sleeping there.

"Analisa? Analisa!"

"What? Oh, I'm sorry, Mrs. Thornfield, did you say something?"

"I asked if you were ready to continue."

"Yes, of course." She bit down on her lower lip. "Where were we?"

"Your mind isn't on reading today," the house-keeper said, sitting back in her chair. "Is something amiss?"

"No, no . . . I was just wondering if . . . if Dr. Avallone . . . is he here?"

"Yes, I believe so."

"Oh. I was wondering . . . that is . . ."

"Go on."

Analisa shook her head, suddenly embarrassed. She had been disappointed when he hadn't joined her for breakfast. She recalled he had told her he was never home during the day. It was none of her business where or how Alesandro spent his days, but she couldn't help wondering.

"Analisa?"

"Nothing," she said, and picking up her book, she began reading again.

She had just finished her lesson when Sally burst into the library.

"Mrs. Thornfield, the constable is at the door."

"The constable!" Analisa exclaimed.

Mrs. Thornfield stood slowly. "I'll take care of it, Sally."

"What can he possibly want here?" Analisa asked.

"There's nothing for you to worry about," Mrs. Thornfield said. And so saying, she left the room.

Sally cast a worried look at Analisa, curtseyed, and hurried after the housekeeper.

Analisa sat there a moment, her finger tapping on the cover of the book. Laying it aside, she left the library. When she reached the parlor, she slowed, then stopped, careful to stay out of sight. She could hear the voices coming from the other room quite clearly now.

"When do you expect Dr. Avallone to return?"

"I'm not sure," Mrs. Thornfield replied. "He was called away on business."

"I see," said the same deep male voice. "He was away the last time we tried to contact him, as I recall."

71

"He travels extensively," Mrs. Thornfield said.

"So it would seem."

"Might I tell him why you wished to see him?"

"There was a murder last night. A right grisly one it was, too."

Analisa gasped, then quickly covered her mouth with her hand.

"A murder?" Mrs. Thornfield didn't sound shocked, only mildly curious.

"Yes, not far from here. When Dr. Avallone returns, tell him we want to see him."

"Yes, I will. Good afternoon, Constable."

"Good day to you, mistress."

Analisa released a breath she hadn't realized she'd been holding when she heard the door close. She flushed guiltily when Mrs. Thornfield entered the parlor and saw her standing there.

"You heard?" the housekeeper asked.

"Yes. A murder. How awful!"

"There's nothing to fear, Analisa."

"But—"

"You're in no danger here," Mrs. Thornfield said with a tight smile. "In fact, this is the safest place you could be."

Mrs. Thornfield had intimated that Alesandro was away, so Analisa did not expect to see him that evening. She wondered why he hadn't told her he was going away, though there was no reason why he should. He owed her no explanations for how he spent his time. Still, she couldn't help feeling hurt, and rather disheartened that she wouldn't see him that evening.

She had just finished dining on a succulent Cornish game hen and was sipping a glass of syllabub when he suddenly appeared in the room, silent as a shadow.

"My lord," she exclaimed.

He raised one black brow as he took the seat across from her. "You seem surprised to see me."

Sally hurried into the room carrying a bottle of wine and a crystal goblet on a silver tray. "Will there be anything else, my lord?"

He dismissed her with a wave of his hand, leaving Analisa to wonder how Sally had known he was in the house, or that he had wished for wine.

The girl bobbed a curtsey and left the room.

"Will you not have dinner, my lord?" Analisa asked.

"No. I . . . dined earlier."

"Oh. There was a constable here today, looking for you," she said. "Mrs. Thornfield told him you were away."

"I would not leave without telling you." His voice was soft and low, as intimate as a caress.

"She lied, then."

"At my request."

"But why?"

"I have my reasons for avoiding the constabulary."

She stared at him, astonished that he spoke of lying to the constable so easily, that he seemed so unconcerned. "But there was a murder . . ."

His expression grew dark. "Do they think me responsible?"

"I . . . I don't know," she stammered. "The constable didn't say."

"Do you?"

Her mouth went suddenly dry, and she clasped her hands in her lap to still their trembling, frightened by the way his gaze burned into hers, by the fine edge of anger she heard in his voice.

"No, my lord," she said, her voice no more than a squeak.

"You think me capable but not responsible?"

She stared at him, not knowing what to say, but knowing, deep inside herself, that he was capable of violence and, yes, even murder.

He lifted one brow, his grin mocking the growing fear in her eyes.

Analisa rose to her feet. "If you'll excuse me, my lord, I need to . . . to . . ." She searched her mind for some urgent matter of business. "To study my lessons."

In a lithe movement reminiscent of a cat intercepting a mouse, he stood, blocking her path.

He was tall, so very tall. She looked up at him, her heart pounding wildly. Mrs. Thornfield had told her she was safe here, but she didn't feel safe, not now, not with Alesandro standing so close. His eyes burned into hers, so dark they looked almost black. She wanted to look away, but try as she might, she could not draw her gaze from his.

His hands folded over her shoulders and slowly,

74

slowly, drew her closer, until she could feel his breath on her face.

"Please." Even as the word whispered past her lips, she wondered what she was trying to say. Please don't hurt me? Please don't let me go?

His head lowered toward hers, until all she could see were his eyes burning like blue fires into her own.

"Analisa. Yield to me."

His voice was soft yet rough, like velvet rubbed the wrong way. It surrounded her, wrapping her in seductive warmth, beguiling her senses. She didn't know what it was he wanted, knew only that, whatever it was, she yearned to give it him, to ease the pain underlying his command.

"Analisa."

Her eyelids fluttered down and her head fell back, exposing her throat. As from a great distance, she heard a low sound, almost a moan; felt his breath, hotter than any fire, along her neck; heard him swear as he released her.

Feeling dazed and disoriented, she looked around. Mrs. Thornfield stood in the doorway, a look of disapproval on her face.

"What is it?" Alesandro snapped.

"Judith Wentworth is here, Doctor. She's wanting you to come look at her grandmother."

He nodded curtly. "Get my cloak."

Mrs. Thornfield glanced at Analisa, then turned and left the room.

"Go to bed, Analisa," Alesandro said brusquely. "And lock your door."

Chapter Six

Analisa ran out of the room, aware of his heated gaze burning into her back. Ran out of the room and up the stairs, not stopping until she was in her bedroom with the door locked. But even as she turned the key, she feared that nothing as flimsy as a lock and a wooden door would keep him out.

Breathless, she pressed her forehead against the cool wood. There was something passing strange about the lord of Blackbriar Hall. She recalled the hackney driver asking her if she was daft when she'd told him where she wanted to go, remembered how quickly he had departed.

Pushing away from the door, she stood in the center of the floor, one hand pressed over her heart, remembering the night in her hospital room. She had asked Alesandro why Dr. Martinson couldn't see him, and he had replied, *Because I did not wish to be seen.*

What kind of man was he, that he could hide his presence from others? He had told her it was nothing more than a mind trick, but now she wondered if there wasn't more to it than that. Something dark and sinister.

She glanced around her room, her gaze probing the shadows. Was he here now, lurking in a corner somewhere? How was she to know? Who was he? What was he? Maybe it was time she left this place.

She jumped at the sound of a knock on her door. "Who . . . who is it?"

"Mrs. Thornfield."

"Oh." Relieved, Analisa opened the door.

"Are you all right, child?"

Analisa nodded.

"Shall I have Sally draw you a bath? You seem ill at ease. Perhaps a hot bath will relax you."

"Yes, thank you."

With a nod, Mrs. Thornfield turned to go, only to be stayed by Analisa's hand on her arm.

"What did he do to me tonight?"

A shadow passed over Mrs. Thornfield's face. "Do, child?"

"He did something to me. Did he bewitch me somehow? Put a spell on me? Is he a warlock?"

Mrs. Thornfield smiled indulgently. "Nay, child, he is not a warlock."

She should have been reassured by the housekeeper's words but, somehow, she was not. Analisa was certain the woman was hiding something, but what? "Who is Judith Wentworth?"

"One of the villagers. Her aged grandmother lives with her. It's her grandmother who has need of the doctor."

"What is wrong with her?"

"I'm sure I don't know. Rest now. I shall have Cook heat some water for your bath."

The water was warm, fragrant with scented oil. Analisa lay back, willing herself to relax, trying to tell herself that she was overreacting to what had happened, even though she wasn't exactly sure just what *had* happened.

She closed her eyes, trying to remember what she had felt when she looked into his eyes, but all she could recall was a sense of helplessness, as if she were trapped in a dream from which she couldn't awake.

She stayed in the tub until the water grew cool. Drying off, she slipped into her gown and robe, then went downstairs in search of a glass of warm milk.

There were no lights burning downstairs. That was odd, she thought, since it wasn't late.

She paused at the bottom of the stairs, wondering if she dared go into the kitchen. Cook was very fussy about anyone else being in his domain. She considered a moment, then decided against it.

She was about to go back upstairs when she sensed she was no longer alone.

"Who's there?" She turned slowly, her gaze searching the darkness. "Who is it?"

"Do not be afraid, Analisa."

"My lord?"

"Yes."

She turned in the direction of his voice. "Why are you sitting down here in the dark?" she asked. "Shall I light a lamp?"

"No. I think better in the dark."

"I shall leave you to it, then," she said, wishing she dared ask what it was he was thinking about.

"Stay."

A single word, yet it rooted her to the spot.

"Come," he said. "Sit with me."

She moved toward him blindly, felt his hand on her arm, drawing her down beside him on the sofa. She shivered as all her senses came alive at his nearness. "Your hand is very cold, my lord."

"Is it?"

"Y-yes."

"You could warm me."

"Me? How?"

He laughed softly, humorlessly, and she turned toward the sound, wishing she could see his face.

"My lord?"

"Will you warm me, my sweet Analisa? Will you give me what I need, what I crave?"

"If I can."

"Oh, you can, there is no doubt of that. But will you? Would you?"

His voice, low and seductive, moved over her like silk sliding against bare skin. She leaned toward him, hardly aware that she was doing so, felt his arm slide around her shoulders to draw her even closer.

She swallowed hard, her mind whirling. "Were you able to help Miss Wentworth's grandmother, my lord?"

He laughed softly. "Yes, I had just what she needed." He had healed the old woman's wounds, taken sustenance from her in return, but it had not satisfied his eternal hunger, nor stilled the damnable craving that was ever waiting just below the surface of his cool demeanor. He took a deep breath, inhaling the warm, sweet scent of the woman beside him. Her nearness intoxicated him. Her humanity drew him like a roaring fire on a cold night. One sip of her pure, virginal blood would warm him for days, fill the empty hollows in his damned soul, satisfy the hellish need that burned through him, relentless, insatiable.

His arm tightened around her as he whispered her name. He unleashed his power, letting it surround her. "Analisa."

"Yes, my lord?" Her voice was quiet, toneless.

He looked deep into her eyes, and knew she was his for the taking. The hunger moved through him, hotter than the fires of the unforgiving hell that awaited him when his existence came to an end. It clawed at him, demanding to be satisfied.

He whispered her name again, watched her eyelids grow heavy as her head fell back, exposing the pulse beating in her throat.

His lips drew back, his fangs lengthening in response to her nearness and his own overwhelming need. . . .

* * *

She awoke in her bed the next morning with no memory of how she had gotten there. Awoke feeling wonderfully refreshed. Alesandro . . . she had dreamed of Alesandro. Strange dreams. Dark dreams. Frightening, at times. He had loomed over her, larger than life, his deep blue eyes blazing, glowing with an otherworldly light. He had touched her, his hands cool against her heated skin, and an image of the crypt in the garden had flashed through her mind. In her dream, she had pried the lid from the crypt . . . and that was when she awoke.

She jumped when Sally knocked on the door.

"Mornin', miss," the maid said brightly. She placed a tray on the table beside the bed, then crossed the floor to draw the drapes. "Lovely day."

Analisa squinted as the room was flooded with sunshine. "What time is it?"

"Half past eleven." Sally smiled at Analisa. "You must have been havin' some lovely dream, to stay abed so long."

Analisa sat up. "Yes, lovely." She reached for the cup of cocoa on the tray and took a sip. Cook made the most delicious chocolate she had ever tasted. She had once asked Mrs. Thornfield what his secret was, but the housekeeper insisted it was a recipe known only to Alfred and his deceased mother.

"Will you be wantin' breakfast?" Sally asked.

"Yes, I find I'm famished this morning."

"Very well, miss," Sally said, bobbing a curtsey. "Will you break your fast here, or downstairs?"

"Here, please. Sally?"

"Yes, miss?"

"Is Lord Alesandro at home?"

"I don't believe so, miss. Is there anything else you need?"

"No, thank you. Sally, wait," she called as the girl turned to leave.

"Yes, miss?"

"Sit down, won't you?"

Sally's eyes widened. "Oh, no, miss, I couldn't."

"Please."

Wringing her hands together, Sally glanced at the door, obviously uncertain as to whether she should obey or not.

Squaring her shoulders, Analisa forced herself to remember she was the lady of the manor, at least for the time being. Pointing to the small chair near the window, she said, "Sally, sit down."

The young maid did so with alacrity, her hands folded tightly in her lap. "Yes, miss?"

"Have you worked here long?"

"Going on three years now," Sally replied. "And right good years they've been."

"Have you ever seen anything . . . singular?"

"Singular, miss?"

"You know, anything strange? Anything out of the ordinary?"

"Why, no, miss." The maid leaned forward a little, her eyes widening with curiosity. "Have you?"

"No, not really."

Sally sat back, looking relieved.

"You have seen something, haven't you?"

The maid shook her head vigorously. "No, miss, but . . . well, I have *felt* something."

"What? When?"

Sally glanced at the door. "You won't tell anyone?" She meant Mrs. Thornfield, and they both knew it.

"No," Analisa replied quickly, "of course not."

"When I first come here, I went into the master's room late one night," Sally confided, her voice low, "to clean up, you know, because I'd forgotten to do it earlier in the day, and I . . ." She shook her head. "You'll think me mad."

"Go on."

"I felt like there was someone, or something, in there, watching me." The maid's laugh was high-pitched, nervous. "Gave me quite a fright, it did."

"Was that the only time?"

"Yes, miss. I never forgot to clean in there again, I can tell you that."

"Thank you, Sally."

"You're welcome. Is that all, miss?"

"Yes, thank you."

"I'll bring your breakfast directly," the maid said. Rising, she left the room.

Sipping her cocoa, Analisa tried to recall the details of her dream. She remembered that it had been pleasant in some parts and disturbingly frightening in others.

Sally brought her breakfast a short time later. For all that she was hungry, Analisa hardly tasted what was placed before her.

When she finished eating, she dressed and went downstairs. She read for a while, then spent two hours at her lessons with Mrs. Thornfield.

"You're doing wonderfully, dear," the housekeeper said, offering Analisa one of her rare smiles. "I think we're ready to move on to the next level."

Analisa basked in the housekeeper's praise. She loved being able to read, loved knowing how to write, though she had no one to correspond with. But perhaps she did, she thought, and dipping her pen in the ink well, she began to write:

Dear Doctor Martinson: I take pen in hand to write and let you know that I am doing well. Lord Alesandro has returned, and he has been most kind. His housekeeper, Mrs. Thornfield, is teaching me to read and write. I hope this short letter finds you well.
Sincerely, Analisa Mathews

She examined it critically, pleased that there were no unsightly blots. When the ink was dry, she folded the paper neatly and left it on the desk. Tomorrow, she would ask Mrs. Thornfield to post it for her.

Picking up her book, she read for half an hour, then put the book aside and left the house. It never failed to amaze her that all this land belonged to Alesandro. Acres and acres of grass and trees, ferns and flowers. It was like a wonderland, a fairy land, with trees cut in the shapes of elephants and giraffes and bears, ferns that grew in wild green splendor, a clear pond where colorful fish swam in lazy contentment. Winding paths lined with neatly trimmed hedges led into the gardens, where flowers in brilliant shades of red and pink and yellow and purple grew in abundance.

She wandered further away from the house than she ever had before. The grounds were not so carefully tended here. There were weeds in the grass; the hedges weren't trimmed. The path she was following gradually disappeared. She heard the sound of a waterfall up ahead, and followed it into the forest that rose up to her left.

As she went deeper into the forest, the trees grew taller, thicker, their branches rising upward, entwining, so that very little sunlight penetrated through the foliage to the forest floor. Sparrows flitted from tree to tree. Once, she saw the white flash of a deer's tail.

Enchanted, she walked faster, and then, as if by magic, the waterfall appeared before her, cascading over a high granite cliff, falling into a large pool that emptied into a river. A rainbow shimmered in the spray.

"Oh," she breathed. "It's beautiful."

Hurrying forward, she sat down on the grass. Taking off her shoes and stockings, she put her feet in the water. And immediately took them out again. The water was icy cold.

She sat there for a long while, watching the birds flutter back and forth from tree to tree, listening to the music of the waterfall.

She glanced up as the sky grew dark, surprised to see gray clouds gathering overhead. Moments later, it began to sprinkle. Grabbing her shoes and stockings, she put them on; then, flinging out her arms, her face turned up to the sky, she twirled round and round and round until dizziness overcame her and she dropped to the ground, breathless. She sat there until the world stopped spinning.

The rain was falling harder now.

"Time to go back," she muttered, and stood up.

Chilled to the bone, she hurried down the path, only to come to an abrupt halt as there was a blinding flash of lightning. A moment later, the tree in front of her burst into sizzling flame.

With a shriek, she threw her hands in front of her face as sparks and bits of bark exploded before her eyes. The storm was raging now, the skies black, the wind scattering sodden leaves and small branches. Thunder rumbled like distant drums across the heavens.

Turning, she ran through the forest, heedless of her direction, ran until the trees were far behind and she found herself in the middle of a small meadow.

She stopped abruptly, peering through the rain's gray haze. Was she imagining things? Wrapping her arms around her waist, she stared at the sight before her. At first glance, there appeared to be a small cottage made of gray stone at the far edge of the meadow. Only she had never seen a round cottage before, or one that had no windows and no chimney. The roof, also made of stone, was peaked, reminding her of one of the turrets at the manor house. The door to the cottage was made of iron instead of wood.

Shivering from the cold, she moved closer, taking shelter from the wind and the rain under the slight overhang that extended above the doorway. What manner of place was this? she wondered. Certainly no one would live in a dwelling without windows or a fireplace. Perhaps it had once been used as a jail, or a storage shed.

Convinced that she wasn't about to intrude on someone's home, she reached for the latch. She was still reaching when the door swung open of its own accord. She hesitated a moment, then stepped warily inside.

There was a whoosh of air as the door closed behind her, plunging her into complete and utter darkness.

And the realization that she was not alone.

Chapter Seven

She was there. He had sensed her presence the moment she entered the forest. It had been the sweet musical rhythm of her heartbeat that had aroused him. He had lain there, his body heavy, unmoving, trapped in the death-like lethargy that possessed him by day, yet still aware of her nearness. She was forever bound to him by the blood he had taken; a bond that could not be broken, except by her demise, or his.

Her scent, as fresh and clean as the rain, was carried to him on a breath of air. Her skin was almost as cold as his own. The fear coursing through her was a palpable entity as the heavy iron door to his lair whispered shut behind her.

She was right to be afraid, he mused, for he was in

desperate need of blood to heal his wounds, to satisfy the voracious hunger that was clawing through him, ravenous as a wild beast. Until his hellish thirst had been quenched, nothing living that crossed his path would be safe.

He fought back the need raging inside him, his senses probing the surrounding area. It was not yet sunset, but the heavy clouds hanging low in the sky gave the appearance of dusk. The woman was the only living creature in the vicinity. His presence had long ago frightened away the wildlife that had once inhabited this part of the estate.

He lifted a hand to his throat, his fingertips exploring the bite marks left by the other vampire. The wounds had not healed; even now they burned with fervent heat, the pain spreading downward, sending fingers of flame sizzling inside his heart and lungs, through his arms and legs, draining him of strength. Was his old enemy suffering the same agony? It had been a brief and bloody battle fought in near silence. If Rodrigo had known how badly he had wounded his opponent, he would not have fled the scene. Alesandro's last attack had been born of desperation and a deep-seated instinct to survive. And now he was paying the price.

Blood. He needed blood to regain his strength, to conquer the pain, and Analisa's called to him like no other, warm and sweet, virgin blood, so pure that it would take only a little to heal him. The urge to go to her was strong, yet fear for her safety held him back. Weak as he was, he doubted his ability to stop before he took too much, before he drank her dry and left nothing but an empty husk behind.

Yet even as he fought the hunger, he was rising, drawn by the pulsing beat of her heart, by the glow of her life's force. He moved swiftly up the narrow winding staircase to the top of the landing, silent as a dark shadow. A wave of his hand opened the thick stone doorway that was invisible from the other side. It was the only entrance to the lair below.

She whirled around at the faint whisper of stone sliding against stone. "Who's there?"

He saw her clearly though there was no light at all in the room; her face was pale, her eyes wide and scared. The pulse in her throat beat wildly as she peered into the darkness. Raindrops clung to her hair and skin.

He moved silently across the cold stone floor until he stood directly behind her. For a moment, he basked in the glorious heat radiating from her body, letting her warmth banish the cold that was so much a part of him, a cold that emanated from deep within his being. Closing his eyes, he took a deep breath, his fangs lengthening in response to the scent of her blood, the promise of relief.

"Who's there?"

He heard the quiver in her voice, the terror she couldn't hide.

"Do not be afraid, Analisa."

He heard the catch in her breath as she recognized his voice. "Lord Alesandro, is that you?"

"Yes."

"What are you doing here?" she asked, relief evident in her tone. "What is this place?"

"What are *you* doing here?"

"I was out walking and I got caught in the rain," she said. "I can't see you. Can we light a lamp?"

"There are no lamps here."

"Oh."

Unable to help himself, he placed his hand on her shoulder.

She flinched at his touch. "You're very cold, my lord."

Cold didn't begin to describe it, he thought, releasing her. He ran his tongue over his fangs. Relief was near, so very, very near. Relief from the cold that engulfed him, the seething hunger that clawed at every fiber of his being, relentless, insatiable. A four-hundred-year-old thirst that could be appeased but never quenched.

He groaned low in his throat, a primal, animal-like growl that made her shiver.

"Are you ill, my lord?" she asked tremulously.

"Yes." He ground the word out between clenched teeth.

She turned toward the sound of his voice. "Is there anything I can do?"

Would she willingly offer him what he craved, what he so desperately needed? In four hundred years, no one had done so. Dared he hope? Dared he ask? Pain twisted inside him like a hellish flame that threatened to burn away what was left of his self-control, urging him to take her, to drink and drink until the pain was gone.

"My lord?"

"I need . . ."

"My lord . . . Alesandro, are you in distress?"

The fingers of his right hand curled over her shoulder. "Yes."

"Let me help you."

"Analisa . . ." He took a deep breath, his left hand curling into a tight fist as he fought to control the beast that raged within him. "Analisa, go! Now!"

"Only tell me what to do, my lord, and . . ."

She gasped, the words dying in a throat gone dry. He turned his head away, but it was too late. In the blackness that surrounded them, she had glimpsed the hunger that burned like twin flames in his eyes. He could hear her heart hammering in her breast as she backed away from him, only to be brought up short by his hand, still clutching her shoulder.

"Don't," she whispered. "No. Oh, no . . . please . . . don't . . ."

But it was too late to let her go. The pain of his wounds, his excruciating need for nourishment, her nearness, even her fear, beckoned to him, refusing to be denied.

With a low growl, he drew her up against him. Her body was hot against the chill of his own. His hand brushed her hair away from her neck, his tongue skimmed over the smooth skin beneath her ear, tasting rain, and then his fangs pierced her flesh and he drank . . . Ah, the sweetness, the purity. He closed his eyes, feeling the warmth of her life's force flow through him, strengthening him, easing his pain. And mingled with the relief was disgust for what he was, for what he was doing.

Her thoughts drifted into his mind, borne to him on a flood of hot, sweet crimson. Sheer terror thrummed through her every vein, fear of what she had seen, fear of what he was doing. The fear of the unknown. Of death.

Ah, Analisa, there are worse things than death. . . .

The demon within him fought for control, urging him to take it all, to savor every drop, to drink as he had not done since he was a newly made vampire. To drink until he was sated and nothing remained of his prey but a dry empty shell. And it was tempting. Far too tempting.

As his pain eased, he became aware of two things simultaneously: Her heartbeat was slow and faint, and her skin had grown cold. Alarmed by what he had almost done, he lifted his head. His tongue slid over the marks left by his fangs, and then, with a savage cry that was almost a howl, he thrust her away from him. A thought opened the cottage's outer door.

"Leave me," he said, his voice harsh.

She staggered toward the doorway, stepped out into the rain, stumbled and fell to her hands and knees in the mud. Head hanging, she didn't move, hardly seemed to be breathing.

With a curse, he was at her side. Sweeping her into his arms, he hurried back inside. Closed the door. And carried her down into the bowels of his lair.

* * *

The shivers that wracked her body had nothing to do with being wet and cold and everything to do with the stark terror that embraced her. If she lived to be a hundred, if she lived past this day, she would never forget the eerie, inhuman glow blazing in his eyes, never forget the sharp prick of his teeth at her throat. Never forget the almost sensual pleasure that had followed, pleasure that had been frightening in its intensity.

She had faced death in the hospital, but it had not been as terrifying as the look in this creature's eyes.

He carried her effortlessly across the room, his feet making no sound on the stone floor as he carried her down a long, winding flight of stairs. She was lost in a dark world, terrified beyond words. Her breath came out in short, shallow gasps. She tried to pray, but the words were trapped in her throat, caught in the web of her fear.

It took her a moment to realize he had stopped moving.

"A light." The words whispered past dry lips. "Can we not have a light? Please."

The words had barely been spoken when several candles sprang to life, filling the room with a soft amber glow. Afraid to look at him, she glanced at her surroundings. The floor was of smooth, dark earth, the walls were of pale gray stone. A large bed covered with a dark quilt stood in the center of the room. There was a single high-backed chair, a small square table made of rough-hewn mahogany. There were no windows, but then, they were far below the ground. Like being buried alive in a tomb made of stone, she thought, and shivered.

He carried her to the bed and placed her on it.

She immediately rolled to the far side and stood up, putting the bed between them. Only then did she risk a look at him. His eyes were no longer a hellish red. Had she imagined it?

"Who are you?" she asked tremulously. "*What* are you? What is this place?"

He bowed from the waist. "It is as I told you. I am Alesandro de Avallone, and this is my home. As for what I am, have you not guessed, my sweet Analisa? No?" He took a deep breath. "I am a vampire."

He watched her eyes widen as the words registered, saw the color drain from her face . . .

He caught her before she hit the ground.

She swam to consciousness through thick layers of cotton, fighting it all the way, not wanting to face what would be waiting for her when she awoke.

She kept her eyes closed as full consciousness returned, waiting, listening. She was lying on something soft. The bed? Where was he?

"I am here, Analisa." His voice broke the stillness, as deep and dark as death itself "And I know you are awake."

She opened her eyes, afraid of what she would see. He was standing beside the bed, gazing down at her.

No monster now, but the man she knew. Or thought she knew.

She shook her head. "It can't be true."

"You know it is."

She shook her head again, not wanting to believe, yet knowing, in the deepest part of her, that it was true. Perhaps she had always known. "Are you . . ." She swallowed hard. "Are you going to kill me?"

"No, Analisa."

Her eyes widened. "You're not going to make me . . . what you are?"

"No."

She lifted a hand to her neck. "You . . ." A shudder of revulsion ran through her. "You drank my blood."

"Yes. I am sorry."

"Sorry?" She felt a bubble of hysterical laughter rise in her throat. "Sorry!"

"You should not have come here. What were you doing wandering around out in the rain?"

"I told you. I went for a walk." She sat up, her cheeks flushed with anger. "I didn't know it was going to rain!"

Surprised by her outburst, he felt himself grinning.

"Well, it's true!" she said, annoyed by his reaction.

"Ah, Analisa," he murmured. "You are so young. So very young."

She wanted to deny it, but couldn't summon the words. She felt young. Vulnerable. And afraid. So afraid. "What . . ." Her mouth was suddenly dry. "What are you going to do with me?"

He ran a hand through his hair, then shook his head. "I wish I knew."

"Please let me go. I won't tell anyone what you are. I won't tell anyone about this place, or what happened here today. I swear it." Who would she tell? she thought frantically. Who would believe her?

"Young," he murmured again. "So very young. There are many who would believe you." He looked past her, his thoughts turned inward. "Many who are searching for me, even now."

"People are looking for you?" She started to ask why, and then realized there was no need. If he was really a vampire, there were undoubtedly many people hunting for him. To destroy him. She remembered the night in the library, his words echoing in her mind.

There have always been tales of vampires, Analisa. Every civilization has its own legends and myths. The ekimmu *of* Sumeria, *the* chiang-shih *of China, the* vrykolakas *of Greece.*

She had been so certain then that stories about vampires were only fables, tales told to frighten children. "But I thought . . . you said you were a doctor."

"I am."

"Who would go to a doctor who was a vampire?" she asked skeptically.

"Those who have been bitten. Those who are dying, without hope."

She lifted a hand to her throat. "You bit me in the hospital, didn't you?"

He nodded.

"And I got better. Dr. Martinson was amazed by my sudden recovery." She looked thoughtful, and then she frowned. "Why would your biting me make me better?"

He lifted one dark brow. "Why, indeed?" he said, and waited for her to make the obvious connection.

Her fingers plucked at the quilt that covered her and then stilled. "You gave me your blood," she said, her voice a whisper of disbelief. "You did, didn't you?"

"Yes."

"And it saved my life? You saved my life. Why? You didn't even know me then."

"I heard your voice calling for help the night I came to you."

"But I wasn't calling for you. And even if I had been, how could you have heard me? And why would you help a stranger who could not pay for your . . . your treatment?"

"But you did."

She touched her throat again. "You took my blood, in payment?"

"A life for a life, sweet Analisa."

The thought of his drinking her blood, of taking his in return, made her stomach clench.

"Would you rather be dead?" he asked quietly.

"Of course not. Why did you invite me to come here?"

He drew in a deep breath. "Because you had nowhere else to go."

"I don't believe you."

"It is the truth." Part of the truth, at any rate, he thought.

"You wanted my blood, didn't you?" she said, her voice filled with accusation. "A ready supply."

He did not deny it. How could he?

Her eyes widened with horror. "You gave me your blood. Am I . . . will I become"—she couldn't say the word—"what you are?"

He shook his head. "No. I did not give you enough to bring you across."

"Am I your prisoner, then?"

"Have you been treated like a prisoner?"

"No. You've been very kind. Very generous."

"A small price, for what you have given me."

She looked up at him. He stood there, unmoving, his gaze fixed on her face. He looked as he had when she first saw him, tall and dark and lean, shrouded in shades of mystery. Had his eyes truly burned with that hellish fire, or had it been her imagination?

She lifted her hand to her throat. "How often do you have to . . . ?" She paused. Did he call it eating or drinking? The whole idea suddenly seemed ludicrous, so why did she feel like crying?

"Do you really want to know?

She shook her head. "You said I'm not a prisoner?"

"Yes."

"Then I'm free to go?"

"Is that what you wish? To leave this place?" The words *to leave me* hung unspoken in the air between them.

"I . . . I don't know." She stared at him a moment,

then frowned. "How have you managed to keep your secret from Mrs. Thornfield?"

"She knows."

"She knows!" Analisa exclaimed. "I don't believe it." Her eyes widened. "Is she a vampire, too? But, no, she couldn't be, could she?"

"No, my dear."

"Does everyone know what you are except me?"

"No. Only Mrs. Thornfield."

"And you trust her?"

He nodded. "With my life. The rest of the staff knows nothing." He stared at her, his gaze fierce. "And you will not tell them."

"No, I won't. Were you ill before? You looked strange, and sounded . . . odd."

He blew out a breath that seemed to come from the very depths of his soul, and then he sat down on the edge of the bed.

"I am a vampire, Analisa. Much of what people say of my kind is untrue. What is true is that I must have blood to survive. I cannot bear the light of the sun, and I am vulnerable during the hours of daylight. I am constantly at war with what I am, constantly struggling to survive. We are predators, hunters. Killers."

She clasped her hands to still their trembling. "Why are you telling me this?"

"I do not know. I have never told anyone else, save Mrs. Thornfield."

"How long have you been a . . . a vampire?"

"Just over four hundred years."

She stared at him. "Four hundred years!" She shook her head, unable to comprehend such a thing. "You must have had many wives in that time. And children."

"I have never married."

"Never? Why not?"

"I never found a woman I wished to marry when I was mortal, and now . . ." He shrugged. "What woman would marry a vampire?"

"But . . . but surely there's been someone in four hundred years."

"Of course. I am a vampire, not a monk."

"You found no one you wanted to marry in all that time?"

"None I dared trust with the truth."

She looked at him, startled by his admission. Startled and afraid. "And yet you've told me." Did he mean to kill her? Was that why he felt comfortable telling her the truth?

"Yes."

She swallowed hard. "Why?" she asked again, though she was afraid to hear the answer. "Why have you told me?"

He shook his head, then took her hands in his. "Perhaps because, after four hundred years, I have found the woman I have been searching for."

His expression was usually as impassive as stone; now it revealed the surprise that was surely etched on her face, as well.

"Me?" she asked, her voice hardly more than a squeak. "You don't mean me?"

He nodded. "Do you deny the attraction you feel for me? The yearning?"

She looked down at her hands, clasped in his. He had only to touch her, and her whole body came to life. She shook her head slowly. She couldn't deny what she felt for him any more than she could stop her heart from beating.

"It is very real, my sweet Analisa. Never doubt it. I could bend your will to mine if I wished, make you feel desire for me, but I have not. What you feel is true. As is what I feel for you."

She stared up at him, mute.

"And now, you must tell me what you want."

"What do you mean?"

"Do you wish to stay here, with me? If you do not wish to remain, Farleigh will take you wherever you wish to go." He squeezed her hands. "You do not have to decide now. The sun is down. I shall take you home."

She had thought he meant to walk her back to the manor. Instead, he picked her up in his arms. A moment later, they were in her room. Dazed, she glanced around. "How did we get here?"

"A bit of vampire magic."

It was all too much. The loss of blood, combined with his confession of what he was, the miraculous way they had arrived in her bedchamber . . . too much, she thought. The room seemed to tilt and spin out of focus, carrying her down, down, into a whirlpool of oblivion. . . .

She was floating in darkness. Suspended. Separated

from the rest of the world by a crimson haze. Being consumed by a pair of blazing blue eyes.

"Drink." His voice was, low, mesmerizing, filled with power and authority.

In her dream, she had no control over her own actions, and she did as she was told.

"Isn't that too much?" Was that Mrs. Thornfield's voice sounding so worried and uncertain? So concerned?

And his voice, assuring the housekeeper that, after four hundred years, he knew what he was doing. . . .

Chapter Eight

She awoke late the next morning, wondering, hoping that her walk in the woods and all that had happened afterward had been a nightmare. And even as she hoped it had been nothing but a dream, she knew, deep in her heart, that it was all too real.

Alesandro de Avallone, Lord of Blackbriar Hall, was a vampire.

He had asked her last night if she wanted to stay with him. She didn't want to leave him, but, knowing what she knew now, did she really want to stay? And if she stayed, what would it mean? Would she be nothing more than a source of . . . of nourishment, or . . . Warmth crept up her neck and into her cheeks. Would he expect to share her bed, as well?

A knock at the door scattered her thoughts as Sally arrived with her morning chocolate.

The day had begun.

She drank her cocoa, bathed and dressed, then went downstairs to breakfast. She looked at the food on her plate—poached eggs and ham, scones and marmalade—and thought of Alesandro, who hadn't eaten real food in over four hundred years.

Later, walking through the rose gardens, she thought of him yet again. How awful, to be surrounded by such beauty and unable to enjoy it in the light of day, to spend every waking moment in darkness, to be unable to feel the warmth of the sun on one's face or enjoy a cup of hot tea on a cold winter night. And yet . . . how wonderful, to never grow old, never know sickness, or have to endure the ravages of disease and death.

All that day, she pondered what it would be like to live as a vampire, to crave the blood of others. She was aware of the passage of time as never before as she waited for dusk, both excited and apprehensive at the thought of seeing him again.

She dressed with care that evening in a gown of pale blue wool, brushed her hair until it gleamed.

She was nervous all through dinner, waiting for him to come to her, but the clock chimed the hours with annoying regularity—eight, nine, ten—and still he did not appear.

She was sitting in the library, a book on ancient vampire lore in her lap, when the clock tolled the hour of midnight. With a sigh, she closed the book and placed it on the table beside her. He wasn't coming. She didn't know whether to be relieved or disappointed. She didn't really know anything about him, she admitted. Not where he spent his evenings, not what he did to pass the long hours before dawn when the rest of the countryside lay sleeping. What a lonely life it must be, she thought, to be awake when everyone else was abed.

And that was where she should be. Upstairs, in her bed, but she was too restless to sleep.

Where was he? Why hadn't he come to her?

Unbidden came an image from the book she had read earlier, its lurid photograph burned into her brain—the image of a vampire lying in a coffin surrounded by men carrying knives and torches. And underneath the photograph, the words *There is only one sure way to kill a vampire. Take the head and the heart and burn the body.*

And hard on the heels of that ghastly image came the echo of Alesandro's voice in her mind. *There are many who are searching for me, even now.*

Had his enemies found him? She had a sudden, horrifying image of Alesandro being set upon by the townspeople during the day when he was helpless.

Grabbing her shawl, she wrapped it around her shoulders and went out into the garden. The night was cloudy and cold. A chill wind stirred the leaves on the trees and tugged at the hem of her skirt.

Why had he avoided her? Did he need to satisfy his hunger every night? And if so, had he gone elsewhere?

She was shocked by the rush of jealousy that consumed her at the mere idea of his going to another woman for nourishment.

Where was he!

Hardly realizing what she was doing, she walked to the crypt and placed her hand upon the cold stone marble, wondering why she felt his presence there so strongly when his resting place was in a small stone fortress in the woods.

"You should not be out here, my sweet Analisa. There is the smell of rain in the air."

She didn't move, didn't turn, only closed her eyes and let the sound of his voice move over her, embracing her.

He glided up behind her. Though he said no word, made no sound, she knew he was there, so close that if she leaned back she would be touching him. And that was what she wanted, she thought, to touch him. And be touched in return.

"Analisa. Look at me."

She shook her head, suddenly afraid. Of him. Of her own tumultuous feelings.

"Analisa."

She could not resist the pleading in his voice, any more than she could resist the siren call of her own desires.

She turned to face him and he drew her slowly into his arms, as if he was afraid he might frighten her away if he moved too fast.

"I waited for you all night," she admitted quietly.

"I know."

"You didn't come."

His arms tightened around her. "Analisa, you are so young, and I am so afraid of hurting you. You are so tempting, so fragile. I could crush you with a thought, destroy you with a touch. Why do you not run screaming from my presence?"

"Is that why you came here tonight? To frighten me away?"

"No. I came because I could not stay away from you any longer." He placed his finger beneath her chin, tilted her head back, and kissed her ever so lightly. "I came because I have been lonely for so long. Because, even though you are afraid of what I am, you do not flee from me in terror. Because you let me do this," he murmured, and kissed her again, more deeply this time. Her lips were soft and sweet and warm, so warm. "Ah, Analisa."

She gazed up at him, her heart pounding, her body aching in places coming alive for the first time. "Are these feelings my own? Or am I under your spell?"

"No, my sweet Analisa, it is I who am under your spell."

"What spell is that?"

"Love, my sweet one. Dare I hope you are caught in its web, as well?"

"I don't know." Was it love she felt, this fluttery feeling in the pit of her stomach, the happiness that bubbled up from the deepest part of her whenever he was near? "I've never been in love before."

"Nor I. Perhaps we will discover its joys together, if you are not afraid."

"Will you kiss me again?"

"As often as you wish," he murmured, and claimed her lips with his own. She fit into his arms as if she had been made for him, and him alone. He heard the increase in her heartbeat as he drew her closer still, sensed her anxiety, her eagerness. She was so young, so innocent, he was afraid of defiling her with what he was, and even more afraid of yielding to the sweet temptation of her lips, to the hours of forgetfulness to be found within her embrace.

With an effort, he drew back. "Will you stay here with me, Analisa? Can you trust me enough to stay?"

"Yes, Alesandro."

"Will you do whatever I say?"

"What do you mean?"

"What do you see when you look at me?"

"A man, my lord. What else?"

"But I am not a man, Analisa, and if I tell you to go to your room and lock the door, you must do so immediately, without question."

"All right. Will you tell me why?"

"There are times when my control is tenuous at best. At those times, it will not be safe for you to be near me. Do you understand?"

"Like last night, you mean?"

"Yes. If I have not fed for several days, or if I have been wounded, the hunger can be overpowering."

"What happened to you last night? You were in pain. Were you injured?"

"There is another vampire roaming in the vicinity. . . ."

"And he hurt you?"

Alesandro nodded. "He has no right to be here. I have held this territory for almost four hundred years. . . ."

"You were fighting with him? Over who has a right to be here?"

"Yes."

"You were badly hurt. Is he stronger than you are?"

He shrugged. "Perhaps. But these are my people. It is my land. He will not have it."

"Why does he stay?"

"He is preying on the people of the village."

"Isn't that what you do?"

"Yes. But he is taking too much, leaving his victims on the brink of death, or killing them outright." His expression grew hard. "It is not my way."

"But you've killed."

He did not deny it. "I do not want to hurt you, Analisa. I have not taken a life in over two hundred and fifty years, except to defend my own."

She leaned back a little in his arms and looked up at him through guileless eyes. "Will I be safe in my room?"

"I hope so."

"You hope so?" she exclaimed softly. "Don't you know?"

"The truth is, my sweet Analisa, that there is no way for you to be truly safe from me, not so long as you dwell within my house."

"But . . . what about crosses, and . . . and holy water?"

"Daylight is the only thing that will keep you truly safe. A silver cross will burn me, as will holy water, but they will not keep you safe."

She shivered in his embrace. "Why are you telling me this? You ask me to stay, and then try to scare me away."

"I am afraid for you," he said solemnly. "And afraid for me."

"What are you afraid of?"

"I have never loved anyone before." He ran his knuckles back and forth across her cheek. "I am trusting that I can control the hunger, that I can keep you close and keep you safe. If I am wrong, if I hurt you, it will destroy me as surely as the touch of the sun."

"We must be very careful, then," she said solemnly.

"You are not afraid to stay?"

"I am more afraid of being without you."

He gazed deep into her eyes, charmed by her innocence, captivated by her beauty. Though he knew she could not be his forever, it was enough that she was here now, that, for a short time, he would have the company, the comfort, only a mortal woman could give.

"If you ever wish to leave, you have only to tell Mrs. Thornfield. She will see you safely gone."

"Are we to be"—her cheeks turned scarlet—"lovers?"

He laughed softly. "No, my sweet Analisa, it is enough that I take your blood. I would not steal your virginity, as well. You must save that for the man you will someday wed."

"You don't want to marry me?" she asked, confused. "But I thought . . . you said you loved me."

"I do."

"But—"

"It is because I love you that I will not defile you. Your virginity is a prize you must save for the man who will be your husband. We can have no lasting future together, Analisa, you must realize that. In six months, a year perhaps, I shall send you away."

"What if I don't want to go?"

"We will burn that bridge when we come to it. For now, let us be happy together."

She smiled up at him, her thoughts as familiar to him as his own. She would not argue with him now. She would bide her time, certain that eventually she could convince him to change his mind.

Their new life together began the following evening. He appeared at dusk clad in black broadcloth. His shirt was snowy white, his boots polished. A black cloak fell from his broad shoulders.

"Good evening, my sweet Analisa," he murmured, and bowed low over her hand.

"Alesandro. How handsome you look."

He smiled his pleasure. "You must change quickly, my sweet one. We are going to the opera."

Her eyes widened. "We are? Where?

"At the Royal Opera House in Covent Garden."

"Covent Garden! London!" She had heard of it,

but never dreamed she would go there. "But it will take hours to get there." She glanced down at her dress. "I've never been to London, or the opera. I don't have anything to wear."

"It will not take hours," he assured her. "And a new gown awaits you upstairs."

The dress was the most beautiful creation Analisa had ever seen. Made of mauve-colored silk, it had long sleeves, a square neck, and a modest train. Looking in her mirror, she felt quite elegant, though she felt she was looking at a stranger. Sally had done her hair up in a loose coil, leaving one long curl to fall over her left shoulder. Sally had insisted on adding a bit of rouge and a touch of powder to her cheeks.

Analisa sighed. Her mother would have fainted if she could have seen her daughter now. Ann Matthews had considered paint and powder to be tools of the devil.

Alesandro was waiting for her at the foot of the stairs. Heat flared in the depths of his eyes when he saw her, flowed between them until her cheeks grew warm beneath his gaze.

He took her hand in his and raised it to his lips. "You are more beautiful than sunlight," he murmured. The sight of it, the feel of it, was something he had almost forgotten, until now. Had the sun glowed as brightly as Analisa's smile, or warmed him as much?

He placed her shawl around her shoulders. "Are you ready?"

She had no sooner nodded than she felt herself swept into the same vortex she had experienced once before. It was a sensation beyond words, a feeling of being swept through time and space that left her momentarily disoriented.

When she opened her eyes, she was in a box at the opera house with Alesandro. She sat down, waiting for her breathing to return to normal, and then leaned forward, her eyes wide. There was so much to see. Men in stylish evening attire, women in elegant gowns, the musicians tuning up in the pit, the conductor, the theater itself with its lavish scrollwork, plush carpets, expensive murals and paintings, the fresco on the ceiling. The prevailing colors were a rich dark red and gold. The pillars of the proscenium were made of veined marble. Alesandro told her that the first theater, built in 1732, had burned down in 1808. It had been built again, and burned again in 1856. The current theater had been built in 1858.

No sooner had he finished speaking than the curtain went up and the opera began.

She tried to take it all in, the singers on the stage, the costumes, the sets, the music. She had never heard an orchestra before, never heard such singing. It brought tears to her eyes; she tried to wipe them away without letting Alesandro see, and failed. He leaned toward her, his thumb catching a tear, and then he handed her his handkerchief.

She applauded wildly when the curtain came down.

"I take it you enjoyed the production?" Alesandro said dryly.

"Oh, yes, it was wonderful. Thank you so much."

"I shall bring you again, just to see you smile."

"Really?"

"Really. Are you ready to go home?"

She hesitated before nodding.

"What is it?" he asked.

"I've never been to London before."

"It is a grand city. I wish I could show it to you."

"Couldn't we see it tonight?"

"Would you not rather come during the day with Mrs. Thornfield?"

She laid her hand on his arm. "I'd rather see it with you."

Her words warmed him. "As you wish, my sweet one."

He was as good as his word. He hired a carriage and they spent the rest of the night driving through London. They saw Buckingham Palace, which had been built in 1703 by John Sheffield, the first Duke of Buckingham.

"Have you ever seen the Queen?" Analisa asked as she gazed at the palace.

Alesandro shook his head. Victoria had been in seclusion ever since her husband died in 1861. She no longer resided at Buckingham Palace, but lived at Windsor or Balmoral instead.

They drove around Hyde Park. Alesandro told her it had been a royal deer park during the reign of Henry VIII. He told her that the famous bridle path known as Rotten Row was located there.

They went to London Bridge, which, until the

Westminster Bridge had been built in 1760, had been the only thoroughfare across the Thames River. He told her there had been houses, shops, and a church built on the original bridge, but they had been removed in 1763. He even described them to her. In 1831 the old bridge had been replaced by a granite one designed by John Rennie.

They drove past Newgate Prison. It had been destroyed in the great fire of 1666 and rebuilt, he told her, and then destroyed again during the Gordon Riots of 1780, and rebuilt.

They stopped at St. Paul's Cathedral and she stared up at it, enthralled by its age and beauty.

"It was built by Christopher Wren," Alesandro remarked. "Before St. Paul's, there was an old Gothic church here, but it too was burned in the fire of 1666. It took thirty-six years to build St. Paul's."

"It was time well spent," Analisa murmured. She glanced up at Alesandro. He had been alive when the original church burned down.

It was near dawn when they returned to the carriage.

She was better prepared for the journey home. When Alesandro took her arm, she closed her eyes and held her breath, and when she opened her eyes again, she was in her own bedroom

Chapter Nine

The next month passed in a blur. Analisa had thought living at Blackbriar Hall to be the epitome of elegance and luxury, but Alesandro showed her a world of opulence and grandeur she had never dreamed existed. They went to the ballet, and to the opera again. The music never failed to sweep her away, and Alesandro was there to interpret the words for her, to explain what she did not understand. They saw *Le Siege de Corinth* by Rossini, *La Muette de Portici* by Auber, *Robert Le Diable* by Meyerbeer, *Faust,* of course, and *Le Prophete,* which to her utter amazement featured roller skating. They dined in the finest restaurants in London and Paris.

One night after the opera he took her to a small private club that was frequented by actors and singers. Analisa could only stare as the tenor she had seen on stage earlier that evening rose to his feet and began to sing. Alesandro asked if she would like to meet him, but she shook her head.

He took her to Westminster Abbey. She looked at him askance as they entered the Gothic style church.

"Never fear, my sweet," he had said with quiet reassurance. "I will not go up in a puff of smoke."

It was a place that inspired awe. She had knelt in a pew, her eyes wide as she looked around. Kings had been crowned here. Notables were buried here.

One night they passed through Covent Garden, which was the main fruit and vegetable market in London. Located near Charing Cross, not far from the theater district, it was also a favorite haunt of prostitutes, a few of whom were plying their trade that night, their skirts tucked up.

"It is the badge of their calling," Alesandro told her.

Analisa saw a heavily painted prostitute approach a well-dressed young man. Eyes wide with the curiosity that chaste women always had for their fallen sisters, Analisa watched the prostitute and the young man strike a bargain, and then the prostitute went off, arm in arm, with her "escort" for the evening. It was a life Analisa could not imagine, being intimate with a complete stranger for a few shillings, especially when Alesandro told her that many of the women were mistreated, or died of diseases that decent folk did not discuss.

As time passed, Analisa found herself adapting her

life to Alesandro's, sleeping far into the afternoon so she could stay up with him late at night. If Mrs. Thornfield and the rest of the household found the sudden change in her hours odd, they refrained from making any comment. She was the mistress of the house, after all.

As much as she loved seeing the sights, she especially liked the nights they stayed at home.

One evening after supper, Alesandro took her into the ballroom. At his look, the candles in the crystal candelabra overhead sprang to life. Another look, and the music box on a small octagon table in one corner began to play, filling the air with the strains of "Greensleeves." Making a courtly bow, he offered her his hand. "May I have this dance, my lady?"

"I can't . . . I don't know how . . ."

"Then it shall be my pleasure to teach you," he said.

Her body seemed to pulse with new life as he drew her into the circle of his arms. Lost in the depths of his eyes, every fiber of her being aware of his nearness, she found it difficult to concentrate on the steps of the waltz.

He smiled down at her, as if he knew perfectly well the devastating effect he was having on her senses.

"Relax, Lisa. Listen to the music. Follow my lead."

Follow his lead, she thought dreamily. She would have followed him anywhere.

He sang along with the music. His voice was deep and rich, as entrancing as his gaze. He held her close, his body brushing against hers in a most scandalous

119

manner as he whirled her around the floor.

"To make it easier for you to follow my lead," he murmured, amused by her shocked expression.

She loved waltzing with him. It was exhilarating, being held so close in his arms, being twirled around the floor. He was so light on his feet, so graceful, she felt like a clumsy child in comparison, and yet they danced together perfectly, dipping and swaying and turning as if they had waltzed together for years.

Once she gained a little confidence, she had time to notice her surroundings. Placed at intervals around the room, were a number of chairs and settees covered in a rich green and gold damask stripe, as well as several low tables made of rich dark wood. Heavy velvet drapes hung at the windows. A delicate crystal chandelier hung from a thick silver chain. For softer light, there were candles in silver wall sconces. Mirrored panels set in the walls reflected the candlelight.

She smiled when she saw her image in one of the mirrors as they twirled about the room. Her gown swirled around her ankles. Her hair gleamed in the light of the fire. Her eyes were shining with pleasure . . . she felt her smile wilt when she realized that he cast no reflection.

She stopped abruptly, staring at the mirror.

"What is it?" Alesandro asked with a faint smile. "Have I made you dizzy?"

"No." She pointed at the single image reflected in the glass. "I . . . you . . . you don't . . ."

He followed her gaze, his smile fading.

She glanced at him, at the mirror, at him again. "Why?"

"Did no one ever tell you? Vampires cast no reflection."

"Why not?"

He shrugged. "Some say it is because vampires have no soul."

She stared up at him. Vampire. Sometimes she forgot what he was. She saw the pain in his eyes, and even though he made no move, she felt him withdraw into himself.

Not wanting to spoil the mood of the evening, she placed her hand on his arm and said, "Shall we finish our dance?"

One evening, sitting on the sofa in front of the hearth in the parlor, she asked him about the collection in the cabinet. "Are they things from your childhood?"

"In a way." He glanced over his shoulder. "The jade animals belonged to my mother. The books belonged to my father. My sister gave me the bird's nest. The seashell and the stone are souvenirs of home."

"And the heather?"

"It was given to me by a witch in Scotland. She said it would bring me luck." He gazed into her eyes. "I did not believe her at the time, but now . . ." He brushed a kiss over her lips. "Perhaps she was right, after all."

Several times during the month, Alesandro was called away from the house by those needing aid. She worried each time he was called away, knowing that he was going out to treat those who had been attacked by the other vampire, afraid that he might be attacked again, that he would be destroyed.

And late one night the constable came calling again.

Analisa followed Mrs. Thornfield to the door, listened quietly as the housekeeper informed the constable that Dr. Avallone had been called away on an emergency.

"Bit of a coincidence, don't you think? His being absent every time I arrive?"

"I wouldn't know, sir," Mrs. Thornfield answered, her voice cool.

"And who might this be?" the constable asked. Removing his hat, he turned his attention to Analisa.

"This is Analisa Matthews," Mrs. Thornfield replied in the same cool tone. "She is a friend of the doctor's, recently come to stay with us."

The constable's gaze moved over Analisa, missing nothing. Clad in a gray uniform and a brown overcoat, he was of medium height, with sharp brown eyes, a bald pate, thin lips, and a nose that was too large for his face.

"I don't suppose you would be knowing where the good doctor might be found this evening?" the constable asked.

Clenching her hands to still their trembling, Analisa shook her head.

The constable nodded. "I believe I'll just wait for his return."

"He may not be back for quite some time," Mrs.

Thornfield remarked, her tone and expression making it clear the man was not welcome in the house.

"That's quite all right," the constable said. "I'll wait."

"Very well," Mrs. Thornfield said, a note of exasperation in her voice. "You may wait in the library. Come along, I'll show you the way."

Analisa waited in the parlor while the constable followed Mrs. Thornfield into the library.

"What do they want with Alesandro?" she asked when the housekeeper returned.

"They suspect he is guilty of the murders in the village."

"But why?"

"He keeps strange hours, is never seen during the day. There have always been rumors about him. The villagers fear him."

"But I don't understand. If they're afraid of him, why do they come to him for help?"

"They only come to him when they've nowhere else to turn."

"Alesandro told me there was another vampire in the area, that he was the one responsible for the deaths."

Mrs. Thornfield nodded, her expression somber. "His name is Rodrigo. He is a wicked, evil creature, as old as Lord Alesandro. He is a very powerful being."

Analisa's eyes widened. "You know him?"

"I only know of him."

"Is Alesandro in danger from this other vampire?"

Analisa asked, and even as she did so, she remembered that night in the rain. Alesandro had been hurting then, in desperate need of blood because of Rodrigo's attack.

Mrs. Thornfield nodded. "They have been enemies for four hundred years."

"Why?"

"Lord Alesandro has never seen fit to confide in me. Perhaps—"

"Mrs. Thornfield, perhaps you should take some tea in to our guest."

Analisa's heart seemed to skip a beat at the sound of his voice. Turning, she saw him striding across the floor, his long black cloak billowing behind him.

"Yes, doctor," Mrs. Thornfield said. "Analisa, would you care for a cup?"

"No, thank you." Analisa smiled at Alesandro. "Good evening, my lord."

"Lisa." He brushed a kiss across her lips, then turned his attention to the housekeeper once more. "What does the constable want now?"

"There's been another murder," she replied.

"Yes," he replied curtly. "I have seen the body."

"You couldn't help?"

"No, I arrived too late." Removing his cloak, he handed it to the housekeeper. "Thank you, Mrs. Thornfield, that will be all."

With a nod, the housekeeper left the room.

Analisa looked up at Alesandro, her gaze searching his. "Was it Rodrigo?"

"Yes, damn him!"

"That night you were hurt, did he . . . ?"

He nodded. "Yes, he attacked me."

"Has it happened before?"

"Many times. Do not worry, Lisa, you are safe here." A dark shadow passed behind his eyes. "As safe as you can be with a vampire in the house."

"I'm not worried about myself," she said.

You should be. She heard the words as clearly as if he had spoken them aloud.

His hand caressed her cheek. "Go have some tea with Mrs. Thornfield while I speak to the constable."

"But—"

"I won't be long." He silenced her questions with a wave of his hand. "Go along now. Have some tea and cookies with Mrs. Thornfield."

With a little "humph" of pique, Analisa turned and flounced out of the room. She was a woman, for goodness sake, not some child to be sent off to another room while the grown-ups talked.

She paused at the end of the hallway. She stood there a moment and then she turned and tiptoed toward the library. Holding her breath, she pressed her ear to the door, frowning as she strained to hear what was being said.

"Good evening, Constable Drummond." Alesandro's voice came to her, strong and deep, filled with self-assurance.

"Dr. Avallone."

"Please, be seated."

"No, thank you."

She could almost visualize the two of them, facing

each other in front of the hearth, the constable as short and squat as a mushroom, Alesandro tall and elegant.

"You wished to see me?" Alesandro sounded faintly bored.

"Yes, I would like an account of your activities tonight."

"I was treating the butcher's wife." Alesandro's voice turned soft, mesmerizing. "She cut her hand on a knife and lost a great deal of blood."

"Yes," the constable repeated, his voice strangely flat. "The butcher's wife."

"I was with her most of the evening," Alesandro went on in the same hypnotic tone. "She will be on her feet again in a few days. As soon as her condition was stable, I came home. You were waiting for me. We took tea together in front of the fire. Mrs. Thornfield brought us a tray of bread and cheese. You questioned me quite thoroughly."

"Yes, thoroughly," the constable repeated.

"My answers satisfied you completely."

"Completely," the constable agreed.

"There is no reason for you to come here again."

"There is no reason for me to come here again."

"I trust there are no further questions," Alesandro said briskly.

"What? Oh, no. No further questions. Thank you for your time, Dr. Avallone. And don't worry, we'll catch this madman, whoever he might be."

"Yes, of course you will," Alesandro said. "Come, I will see you out."

Lifting her skirts, Analisa turned and ran down the hallway toward the parlor.

"Heavens, child," the housekeeper exclaimed as she burst into the room. "Are you being chased?"

"No, of course not." Blowing out a breath, she turned and peeked out the door in time to see Alesandro bid the constable a final good night.

Alesandro stood there a moment, staring out into the darkness before he shut the door, and then he was striding toward her.

"My lord," she murmured as he entered the room.

"Come with me." He didn't wait for an answer; didn't look to see if she followed him.

She trailed in his wake, her gaze fixed on his back. How tall and broad he was. Elegant. Handsome. Forbidding, at times.

He opened the door to the library, held it for her, then closed it firmly behind him.

"So," he said abruptly. "What did you hear?"

She looked up at him with feigned innocence, her heart pounding erratically. "Hear, my lord?"

"Do not play childish games with me, Analisa. I know you were listening at the door."

A guilty flush warmed her cheeks. "What did you do to him?"

"I merely planted a suggestion in his mind."

"You hypnotized him?"

He shrugged. "It is fortunate that his mind is susceptible to suggestion. I had no wish to kill him." He spoke as if it were a matter of no consequence, but his eyes belied his calm demeanor.

127

She bit down on her lower lip. He had told her before that he had killed in defense of his own life, but to hear him speak of it so openly chilled her to the marrow of her bones.

"I have distressed you."

"Oh, no . . . well, yes. I mean . . . would you really have killed him?"

"If I thought it necessary. Do not be fooled, Analisa. As I told you, I am a killer by nature, a predator."

"Alesandro—"

"It is late," he said quietly.

It wasn't that late, she thought. He was just giving her an excuse to leave the room. And, coward that she was, she took it.

"Yes, it is," she said. "Good night."

"Good night, Analisa."

She didn't see him the next night, or the next. As always when he wasn't there, she felt a keen sense of loss, of emptiness. She picked at her food, couldn't concentrate on her lessons, slept poorly. She had disappointed him in some way she didn't quite understand, she thought. He had told her the truth, told her from the beginning that he was a predator, a killer, but she had been too caught up in going to the opera and the ballet, in seeing the beauty of Paris and London, to think about the rest. She had been so mesmerized by the magic of what he was, by the powers he possessed, that she had blocked out the rest of it, refused to see the danger, the ugliness, that was also a part of what he was.

On the third night, she went upstairs to her chamber early. Unable to sleep, she paced the floor.

Alesandro, come to me.

Again and again, she called to him in her mind.

Come to me, come to me, come to me . . .

She felt his presence. She turned as a whisper of air brushed her cheek, and then he was there. Tall and dark, his hair tousled. He wore a loose-fitting white shirt open at the throat, snug black breeches, and knee-high black boots.

"You came," she said.

"Did you think I would not?"

"I don't know what to think." She looked up at him, wanting to feel his arms around her, but lacking the courage to ask him, or to move toward him. "I disappointed you. I'm sorry."

He shook his head, his eyes filled with pain. "I forget how young you are, how innocent. How vulnerable. I am afraid I expect too much of you."

"Where have you been the last three nights?"

"Nearby."

"Alesandro . . ."

She gazed up at him, all her longing, her confusion, visible in the depths of her eyes.

"Analisa," he murmured. "What am I to do with you?"

Hold me.

She didn't speak the words aloud, but he heard

Amanda Ashley

them clearly in his mind, knew that if he took her in his arms now, their relationship would somehow be irrevocably altered. The smart thing, the best thing for both of them, would be to send her away. He did not deserve her, did not deserve the light she brought into his dark existence. Her mere presence in the house had added color to his bleak life. He had never intended to keep her with him forever, only long enough to ease his loneliness. He could salve his conscience by sending her away with enough money to live on for the rest of her life. And that was what he would do, he thought, until he saw the single tear glistening in the corner of her eye. He watched it slide down her cheek. One single tear. It was his undoing.

Murmuring her name, he drew her into his arms.

She leaned into him, so young, so vulnerable. How could he send her away?

He carried her to a chair and sat down, cradling her in his lap. It was heaven to hold her in his arms, to hear the soft beat of her heart, to feel her skin beneath his hand, the touch of her hair against his cheek.

Curled against him, she fell asleep in his arms, as trusting as a child. Time passed. Her scent filled his nostrils, awakening a myriad of emotions within him. Desire. Hunger. Lust. A need to protect her, to see her smile, hear the merry sound of her laughter.

He brushed his lips across the crown of her head,

130

breathed in the scent of her hair, her skin, and knew he was lost, knew that, no matter what the future held, no matter what the cost, he would never willingly let her go.

Chapter Ten

He bent over the woman. Caught in his grasp, she looked up at him, mesmerized by the preternatural power of his unblinking stare. He could smell the stink of her fear, hear it in the rapid thudding of her heart, see it in the depths of her clear brown eyes. She stared at him and knew him for what he was, but, like a mouse impaled on the claws of a lion, she was helpless to escape.

Her terror filled him with excitement. He loved the thrill of the hunt, the unbridled excitement when his prey was brought to its knees, the surge of power that spiraled through him in that moment when his victim realized death was inescapable.

He smiled, letting her see his fangs, letting the

bloodlust that was raging through him shine clear and bright in his eyes.

She knew what he was. Oh, yes, she knew.

She would have screamed, wanted to scream, but she could not move. Could only watch, helpless, as he slowly lowered his head until she saw nothing but his eyes, and his fangs, sharp and white, descending toward her throat.

Another victim for you, my dear Dr. Avallone.

The thought made him smile in the midst of drinking.

It was a game he played, finding a victim, draining her to the point of death, then leaving her where she was sure to be found. Sometimes the good doctor reached his victims in time; sometimes he did not.

Did the doctor keep score? he wondered. By his reckoning, the doctor had fallen a little behind in the past year. Lives he had saved: 23; lives he had lost: 29.

How did Avallone know? he wondered. How was it that he arrived so often in time to save the poor foolish women who were Rodrigo's favorite prey? Silly mortals. So easily tricked, so easily lured to his side. More often than not, he did not even have to use his preternatural power. A bit of flattery, the promise of a pretty bauble, and they hastened to him, eager to be in his arms. And they were sweet, sweeter than anything he had tasted in mortality.

He drew back, his body filled with stolen warmth, the taste of the woman's blood lingering on his lips.

She sagged in his arms, her head lolling back, her complexion pale, waxy, her lips turning blue. A bit of blood oozed from her throat. Leaning down, he slowly wiped it away with his tongue.

The good doctor would have to hurry, Rodrigo thought as he lowered the woman's limp body to the ground, for this one was nearly gone.

Alesandro caught the scent of the Other on the night wind, and with it the knowledge that a woman lay dying. It was his gift, and his curse. A thought carried him through the dark night, across the hills and valleys, to the woman's side. The stink of the Other was all around. His evil laughter rode the wings of the night as Alesandro knelt beside the woman, his dark cloak spread around them, shielding them from the sight of any who happened to be passing by.

Too late this time, Dr. Avallone. Too late . . . too late . . .

He could hear Rodrigo's voice, taunting him.

The woman was on the brink of death, her breathing shallow, labored, her skin pale. Her heartbeat was faint, the merest flutter, barely audible even to his enhanced hearing, but she had a strong will and reason to live. She had three small children at home, a husband who was ill. He drew on his power, felt his fangs lengthen. He tore a gash in his wrist, held it to her lips.

Drink, woman! Drink!

She was weak, so weak, but not so far gone that she could resist the power in his voice. Her mouth fastened onto his wrist, her throat working convulsively as she swallowed the life-giving fluid.

Gradually, the color returned to her cheeks. Her eyelids fluttered open. She stared up at him in horror.

He could not blame her. He knew how he must look, his eyes burning red, his face a monster's mask. He had seen the lust for blood burning in Tzianne's eyes when she forced the Dark Gift upon him, had seen it in Rodrigo's eyes on more than one occasion. It was a look to strike terror into the heart and soul of any mortal.

She shoved his arm away, struggling to free herself from his grasp.

Be still, woman! His mind spoke to hers in a tone that demanded obedience.

"Please, sir," she whispered. "Please, let me go."

"All in good time," he murmured.

He was bending over her, needing to take back a little of what he had given her, when the first blow came, driving him to his knees and away from the woman. He rolled onto his back, raising his arm to block Rodrigo's next attack, so that the vampire's fangs, aimed at his throat, ripped a deep gash from his wrist to his elbow instead.

Alesandro scrambled to his feet. Blood poured from the wound in his arm.

"Coward!" Alesandro spat the word.

Rodrigo laughed. Teeth bared, he hurled himself toward Alesandro a third time.

It was a silent, bitter battle. With fangs and claws, they fought like two great cats, slashing viciously at one another, the hatred that flowed between them a living thing.

The woman watched in horror and then fled into the night.

Alesandro fought as best he could, but the blood flowing from the wound in his arm weakened him. For all their preternatural strength, vampires were fragile creatures. The loss of the blood he had given the woman weakened him still more. Though it galled him to do so, he dissolved into mist and disappeared deep into the earth.

"Who's the coward now?" Rodrigo taunted.

The sound of the vampire's mocking laughter followed Alesandro underground.

Chapter Eleven

Four days, and she'd had no word from him. Where was he? Time and again Analisa sought out Mrs. Thornfield, begging the housekeeper to tell her where Alesandro was if she knew, but Mrs. Thornfield only shook her head.

"Try not to worry, child. He'll be home when he is able," was all the housekeeper would say.

When he was able. The words conjured horrible images in Analisa's mind; images of Alesandro lying helpless and alone in the dark, weak and in pain.

Her studies came to a standstill. She ate but little and slept less. Too worried to read, too restless to concentrate on needlework, she paced the floors of the manor.

"You'll wear out your slippers," Mrs. Thornfield

chided, but Analisa knew the housekeeper was as worried as she.

On the eighth night, overcome with exhaustion, she went up to his room. Going to the wardrobe, she opened the doors and ran her hands over the coats hanging inside. They were all fashioned of expensive cloth, most in dark colors. It comforted her a little, to see them there, to touch something he had worn. With a sigh, she crawled under the covers of his bed. His scent surrounded her, soothing her even as it reminded her of what might be forever lost. Alesandro . . .

She sat up, her heart pounding in anticipation when the door opened, but it was only Mrs. Thornfield.

"I brought you a nice cup of tea," she said, "to help you sleep."

Analisa knew that her disappointment was evident as she thanked the housekeeper.

"Try not to worry," Mrs. Thornfield said. "I'm sure he'll be back soon."

Analisa nodded.

"Good night, child."

"Good night."

She sipped the tea, grateful for its warmth. Putting the cup on the table beside the bed, she slid under the covers once more.

She was almost asleep when she heard his voice in her mind.

Analisa . . .

"Alesandro!" She bolted upright, her gaze searching the darkness. "Where are you?"

Come to me . . .

Slipping out of bed, she left his chamber. Heedless that her feet were bare and she wore nothing but her nightgown, she left the house, following the narrow, winding path that led to the crypt in the grove. The wind whipped her nightgown around her ankles, sent chills down her spine.

She was shivering when she reached the crypt. "Alesandro? Alesandro, where are you?"

"Here."

She whirled around, her eyes widening when she saw him. He was pale, his skin almost as white as the marble tomb. She reached for his hand, and he jerked it away, but not before she touched him. He was cold, so cold. The words *cold as death* whispered through her mind.

"What's happened?" she asked. "You look . . ."

"Rodrigo," he said, and told her, in a voice empty of emotion, what had happened.

"You need blood, don't you?"

He nodded. He looked down at her, hating himself for his weakness. He should not have called her here. Had he any honor, he would have gone elsewhere to assuage his hunger, but it was her blood he craved, her blood that called to him, sweeter, more satisfying, than any other.

" 'Lisa . . ." He gazed into her eyes, not wanting to ask, knowing he could take what he needed by force, knowing, just as certainly, that he would not.

In silent invitation, she tilted her head to one side, brushed the hair away from her neck, and waited.

He told himself to leave her, to take his hellish thirst elsewhere, but he could not deny his need. Quietly cursing the hunger raging through him, he took her into his arms and bent over the slender curve of her neck.

She moaned softly when his fangs pierced her skin, a soft sound of mingled pain and pleasure as she surrendered to his vampire kiss. It should have repelled her, she thought. Why did she find it somehow arousing instead of abhorrent? Why did she find the thought of his going to another so distressing? But none of that mattered now. Closing her eyes, she surrendered to his need. And her own.

Strength flowed through Alesandro, chasing away his lassitude. The demon within urged him to take more than he needed, to bury his fangs deep in her soft flesh and take it all. He fought the impulse to do so, taking only what he needed to ease his pain, and then he put her away from him.

She looked up at him, her eyes unfocused.

"Analisa?" He stroked her cheek with the back of his hand.

She sagged against him, her eyelids fluttering down, her cheek resting on his chest, her face pale. Sweeping her into his arms, he carried her up to the house, settled her onto the sofa, covered her with a blanket. A wave of his hand summoned a fire in the hearth. Feeling unworthy, he sat beside her, his senses lightly probing hers.

With a sigh, she looked up at him. She had beautiful eyes. If they were indeed the windows to the soul, then her soul was as pure as that of a newborn babe.

Muttering an oath, he looked away, unable to meet her gaze. "I am sorry, *cara mia*. Forgive me for my need, my weakness. It is beastly. Unforgivable." He shook his head. "Irresistible."

"There's nothing to forgive, Alesandro," she said quietly. "I'm fine, truly I am. It's quite pleasurable, you know."

His gaze moved over her, noting the dark shadows under her eyes, the faint hollows in her cheeks. "Are you well?" he asked.

She nodded. "I'm fine. Except . . . well, I've not been sleeping very well the last few nights."

"Is something troubling you?"

"You trouble me."

He smiled faintly. "Not nearly as much as you trouble me."

"Who is Rodrigo? What's between the two of you?" His arms suddenly felt like steel around her. "I'm sorry," she said quickly. "I didn't mean to pry."

"It is all right. You, of all people, have a right to know. He is what people expect a vampire to be," Alesandro said quietly. "He revels in what he is, in the power he has. He delights in killing."

"He tried to kill you, didn't he?"

"Yes."

"Why?"

"We were friends once. We grew up together, practiced medicine together, such as it was those days. Rodrigo was in love with my sister, Serafina. They

141

planned to marry. A few months before the wedding, Rodrigo and I went into the city. We had been drinking heavily. When we left the tavern, we saw a woman. A beautiful woman. Rodrigo decided to follow her, and I followed him.

"When we reached the lane that led to her house, she turned and beckoned us to follow. Rodrigo did so, but I held back. He was in there for a long time, and I began to worry. I crept up to one of the windows and peered inside."

He paused, seeing it all again in his mind.

"They were on the bed. At first, I thought they were making love, but then the woman turned toward me, and I saw the blood smeared on her mouth. Her eyes were red and glittering. She hissed when she saw me.

"I turned away in terror and began to run, but she caught me easily. I fought her, my terror adding to my strength, and yet I was helpless against her. She threw me to the ground, and I felt her fangs tear at my throat. She was angry that I had spied on her, and there was no gentleness in her."

Analisa's eyes grew wide, her face pale.

"She carried me back to her house and left me there, with Rodrigo. I watched in horror as he died before my eyes, and then it happened to me, as well, and when we woke the next night, we were new creatures."

"But how . . . how was it done?"

"The transformation? She took our blood, drained us to the point of death, and then gave it back to us.

That night, we died as mortals and were reborn as vampires."

"But you gave me your blood, and I'm not a vampire."

"It is not just the giving of blood, 'Lisa. To bring you across, I would have to take your blood, all of it, and then give it back to you."

"Have you ever made another vampire?"

"No."

"Go on," she said. "What happened next? Were you terribly afraid when you woke the next night?"

He nodded. "The woman was gone. I never saw her again. Rodrigo and I washed away the blood and went home, not certain what had happened to us, knowing only that we were different somehow. My family was relieved to see me, apparently safe and well. Little did they know. The days that followed were like a nightmare. Eventually I realized I could not stay there, could not pretend that nothing had changed. Could not put the lives of my loved ones in danger. As a new vampire, the hunger was strong within me, impossible to resist. At first, Rodrigo and I hunted together, but that did not last long. Vampires, we learned, are territorial by nature. We could not share the same hunting grounds. It was a difficult time.

"Rodrigo gloried in the killing. I did not, and yet I killed because I could not control the hunger inside me, because the pain of not feeding was beyond bearing. Because I did not know, then, that I did not have to kill to survive."

"But, to drink blood . . ." She shuddered. "Wasn't it . . . isn't it horrible?"

"I am a vampire, Analisa. It is natural for me, as natural as drinking water is for you."

She considered that a moment. "Didn't your family wonder why they didn't see you during the day anymore?"

He shook his head. "No. I had rarely been home during the day. They assumed I was seeing patients."

"Go on."

"Rodrigo was still planning to marry my sister. I told him he could not, but he laughed and said I could not stop him, that he intended to marry her and bring her across. Nothing I could say would change his mind.

"I tried to talk to Serafina, to tell her that Rodrigo had changed, that he was no longer fit to be her husband, but she refused to listen. I told her what he had become, but she did not believe me. In desperation, I told her that it had happened to me, too, and when she still refused to believe, I showed her what I was."

He grew silent, his features twisted with agony.

"Alesandro?"

"She was a delicate creature, my sister, my Serafina. Fragile. She took one look at me, at the monster I had become . . . it was too much for her to bear. She went quite mad. No one knew what had happened to her, of course, and I dared not explain. My father could not bear to send her away. He locked her in a room in the attic to keep her from hurting herself and to protect my younger sisters."

He stared into the distance. "It did no good. A month later, Serafina hanged herself. I left home that night, never to return. I came here, had this place built, and when I learned to control the hunger, I tried to redeem myself by helping others."

"And the crypt in the grove?"

"I cannot stay in one place too long lest people notice that I do not age. I had the crypt made and then I left the country for a time. When I returned, I posed as the son of the first Alesandro."

It was a charade he had played out numerous times in each country where he maintained a residence.

"And then, two hundred years ago, Rodrigo found me in Spain. He has never forgiven me for what I did. But then," he said quietly, "neither have I."

"Alesandro, I'm so sorry."

"You should leave here," he said. "Now. Tonight."

"No!"

"I have been a selfish fool to think I could keep you safe."

She caressed his cheek. His skin was cool, taut. "I'm not afraid."

"You should be."

"You said Rodrigo preys on the villagers. He does that to hurt you, doesn't he?"

"He has no regard for human life, and he considers it a weakness that I do, that I have not completely forsaken my humanity, as he has. It is a game he plays, following me wherever I go, draining his victims almost to the point of death, seeing if I can save them before it is too late."

"That's cruel!"

His gaze moved over her face. "No more cruel than it is of me to keep you here."

"But you're not keeping me here. I want to stay."

His arm tightened around her, threatening to cut off her breath. " 'Lisa."

Leaning forward, she kissed him lightly, one hand cupping his cheek. "You must put the past behind you, my lord, and think only of the future."

"I have tried. Believe me, I have tried."

"Then we must try again."

We. How very much he liked the sound of that.

"Is there no way to stop him?" she asked. "No way to end this hatred between you?"

"He will not stop until one of us has been destroyed."

Her eyes widened in denial. "Then let's go away from here! Someplace where he can't find us."

"I do not know if such a place exists, Analisa. He is a powerful vampire."

"More powerful than you?" she asked incredulously.

"Yes."

"How can that be?"

"Killing makes a vampire strong, 'Lisa. The hunger feeds on itself. When a vampire kills, he takes not only the blood of his victim, but his strength as well. It is a potent combination."

And Alesandro had not killed for over two centuries, Analisa mused. "Please, let's go away from here. Maybe he won't find us. Maybe he won't try."

He smiled down at her, knowing that he would grant her anything she desired. "Where would you like to go?"

"I don't know."

"I have a small estate in the north. We can go there, if you like."

She nodded, her dark eyes eager, hopeful.

"Very well. I shall have Mrs. Thornfield make the arrangements. I will meet you at Gallatin Manor two nights from now."

Alesandro was as good as his word. Two days later, the house at Blackbriar was locked up and Analisa and the staff were packed and ready to go.

Farleigh handed Analisa, Sally, and Mrs. Thornfield into the Avallone carriage, then climbed on top and took up the reins. Cook and Dewhurst rode topside with him. Annie Cullen and Elton would remain behind to look after the house and the livestock. No easy task, Analisa thought, even with most of the Hall's occupants away.

Analisa sat back against the seat, excited by the thought of a journey. She had seen so little of the world. Until the epidemic, she had never left the small village where she had been born.

"Is Gallatin Manor as grand a place as Blackbriar?" she asked.

"Gallatin is a bit smaller," Mrs. Thornfield replied. She drew her shawl more closely around her shoulders. "It's a grand place, though."

147

"And Robert is there," Sally murmured, and then blushed to the roots of her hair.

"Who's Robert?" Analisa asked.

Mrs. Thornfield fixed Sally with a stern look before replying, "Robert Mason. He is the caretaker at Gallatin Manor. Quite a handsome young man. And quite a ladies' man, if you take my meaning."

Analisa glanced at Sally, who met her gaze briefly before looking away.

"I'm afraid I don't understand," Analisa said. "Is there something wrong with Robert?"

"Married help is frowned upon," Mrs. Thornfield said stiffly.

"I had assumed *you* were married," Analisa remarked, frowning.

"In my case, Missus is a title of respect," Mrs. Thornfield replied. She glanced at Sally. "Not that Robert is a marrying man. I daresay he's had his way with every maid in the county."

"That's not true!" Sally exclaimed, then covered her mouth with her hand.

The coach fell silent after Sally's outburst. Analisa knew little of what was expected of servants. She had heard that it was a hard life, that they were paid little, and granted little time off save for half a day on Sundays, one evening out each week, and one day off each month. In truth, she found it hard to feel sorry for them. At home, she had worked harder than any servant employed at Blackbriar. At home, there had been times when there was no wood for a fire, days when she'd had nothing to eat but a piece of dry bread. Blackbriar's servants at least were assured of a warm place to sleep and food to eat. As housekeeper, Mrs. Thornfield had the most enviable position, and the most authority. She was responsible for hiring and firing and was in charge of the other servants.

Analisa gazed out the window, her thoughts turning toward Alesandro. Where was he now? Already at the Manor? Or sleeping in his lair back at the Hall, waiting for nightfall? She frowned, wondering if he had a place to spend the days at the Manor, or if he would return to the stone cottage at Blackbriar each morning before dawn. She wondered why he slept in the cottage and not in his bed at the Hall. Surely the servants would not approach his room if he told them not to. All he need do was lock his chamber door and instruct the staff to stay away. Or was it that he didn't trust them? Would she, if she were in his place? He had told her he was vulnerable during the daylight hours. Did that mean he was helpless as well?

She watched the scenery pass by, gently rolling hills green from the last rain, spring flowers blooming on the hillsides. They passed a small herd of sheep, and she smiled at the antics of the lambs. The sun played peekaboo with a handful of fluffy white clouds. It was such a beautiful day, it was hard to imagine any ugliness in the world, hard to imagine that a creature like Rodrigo was causing such terror in the village, hard to believe that Alesandro was a vampire. . . .

She lifted a hand to her neck, felt a little flare of heat from the place where his teeth had pierced her skin. Hard to believe that an act that should fill her with fear and loathing should be so pleasurable.

She closed her eyes as the rolling motion of the carriage lulled her to sleep.

He was asleep in the stone cottage in the woods, his head resting on a feather pillow covered with a black pillow slip, his body unmoving in its death-like sleep. He did not dream, and yet her image, vague and shadowy yet still recognizable, moved through his mind. . . .

She woke with a start as the carriage came to a halt.

"Are you all right, miss?" Sally asked, leaning toward her.

"Yes, of course. Why do you ask?"

"You look right pale, you do."

"Do I?" Analisa glanced out the window. "Where are we?"

"The Hare and Hound Inn. We've stopped to rest the horses and get a bite to eat."

"Oh."

A moment later, Farleigh opened the door and handed Analisa out of the carriage. She started toward the inn, stopped when she realized only Farleigh was following her. She turned to speak to Mrs. Thornfield. "Aren't you and the others coming?"

"No, child." Mrs. Thornfield gestured at a table in the shade of the inn. "We'll eat out here."

"Oh." Of course, Analisa thought, servants weren't in the habit of sitting at table with the lady of the house.

"Farleigh will act as your footman," Mrs. Thornfield explained.

Analisa nodded. Ladies did not travel about unaccompanied, just as unmarried ladies under the age of thirty were never to be in the company of a gentleman without a chaperone.

Still, she didn't like the idea of eating at a table by herself while Farleigh looked on. "Farleigh, you and Dewhurst go and get us all something to eat and bring it out here." She reached into her bag and handed the coachman some money. "That should be enough, shouldn't it?"

Farleigh glanced at Mrs. Thornfield, his expression uncertain.

Mrs. Thornfield shook her head. "Miss Analisa, 'tisn't proper for you to eat out here with the help."

"Well, I don't want to eat alone." She held up a hand, cutting off the housekeeper's protests. "I shall eat out here."

"Very well, miss."

Analisa sat down at the table, and after a moment, Sally, Cook, and Mrs. Thornfield joined her. It was odd, she thought, that no one ever called Cook by any other name.

Though she had lived at the Hall for months now, an awkward silence settled over them. Analisa thought it strange. She supposed she had come to think of the servants at the Hall as her friends; it was obvious they did not feel the same. Having been poor all her life, Analisa had never had servants, never realized the social barrier between master and servant.

151

She could understand the distance between Alesandro and the staff. After all, he was the lord of the manor. But she was nothing more than a guest, an orphan with no place else to go. In truth, her social standing was more equal to the staff's than to the master's.

Farleigh and Dewhurst returned with the food a short time later. Dewhurst ate quickly, then went to check on the horses. Farleigh and Cook excused themselves not long after that.

The ladies visited the necessary, and then they all piled into the coach again.

Analisa fastened her attention on the passing countryside. She wasn't cut out to be lady of the manor, she thought. If not for Alesandro's kindness, she would probably be working as a servant herself. She drifted off to sleep with that thought in mind.

They traveled until dusk, then took shelter at another inn. Analisa had a room of her own. Mrs. Thornfield and Sally shared a room; the men occupied another.

As always, Alesandro had been most generous and their rooms were large and well furnished.

After a hot bath, Analisa crawled into bed, weary from the long journey. Tomorrow night, she thought as she closed her eyes; tomorrow night she would see Alesandro.

Chapter Twelve

Gallatin Manor was set amidst a broad expanse of lush green grass and ancient oaks. A long, winding drive led up to the house, which was made of dark red brick and stone. Even in the gathering dusk, Analisa could see that the Manor was of a much sunnier disposition than Blackbriar Hall.

The coach came to a stop; a moment later, Farleigh opened the door and handed her out. Analisa stretched her arms and shoulders as she glanced around. It was by far the prettiest place she had ever seen, with the house sitting like a ruby in a field of jade.

Lifting her skirts, she hurried up the stairs to the beautifully carved front door, opened it, and stepped inside.

The entryway wasn't nearly as large or as dark as that at Blackbriar. Analisa hung her bonnet on a hook, ran a hand through her hair, and made her way into the front parlor. It was a large, square room furnished in light oak. A sofa covered in a dark blue print stood in front of a red brick fireplace. There was a collection of colored bottles on the mantel. A pair of overstuffed chairs covered in the same fabric as the sofa were placed on either side of a square table. Several lamps were placed around the room, all lit in anticipation of their arrival. A large seascape commanded one wall.

On the ground floor, there were a small dining room decorated in shades of green, a cozy drawing room, and a library whose walls were lined with shelves filled with books. There was also a breakfast room on the east side of the house with a large window that looked out on the side lawn, as well as a conservatory filled with greenery and flowers, and a servants' hall where the staff ate together. She was surprised by the size of the pantry. It was a large, cream-colored room lined with glass-fronted cabinets. It was here that the butler (if they'd had one) would keep the plate and fine china and give directions to the other male servants. There was a wooden tub for washing the dishes, a rack for drying. A large, square table ringed by several high stools was in the center of the room; there was another table for pressing cloths. A large clock hung on one wall, a picture of Queen Victoria on another.

There was also a room for the housekeeper, where

she could make preserves, keep the household accounts, and look after the affairs of the housemaids.

Analisa was climbing the curved staircase when she heard Mrs. Thornfield's voice. There would be no rest for the servants, Analisa mused, for the housekeeper was already issuing orders to Cook and Sally, saying that they must take an inventory of the household goods. The bedding must be washed, the rooms aired.

There were five bedrooms upstairs, all similar in nature save for the largest chamber, which obviously belonged to Alesandro. Like his room at Blackbriar, the furnishings here were of heavy dark wood; the covering on the bed was a deep blue that was almost black. Heavy draperies covered the windows, shutting out the sunlight.

Climbing the stairs to the second floor, she found a nursery and a schoolroom.

The third floor held the servants' quarters, which also had a separate set of stairs at the rear for the servants to use.

Gallatin Manor seemed to be a much newer house than Blackbriar Hall.

She was about to return to the main floor when she heard someone talking. She paused, recognizing Sally's voice. At first, she thought Sally was looking for her, but then she heard another, deeper voice.

"How long will you be staying, love?"

"I don't know," Sally replied. "Lord Avallone didn't say."

"Then we must make every moment count, mustn't we?" the man replied, his tone low and suggestive.

Tiptoeing toward the sound of the voices, Analisa peeked around a corner of the hallway, stifled a gasp when she saw Sally fall into the arms of a tall, blond-haired young man. Analisa stared, noting the way they clung to each other, the way the man's hands moved over Sally's back and buttocks, his touch familiar, possessive. It had to be Robert, she mused. No wonder Sally was so smitten with the man. He was quite handsome, though not as handsome as Alesandro.

Alesandro. She glanced at the window, felt her heart flutter when she saw that the sun was going down.

Turning away from Sally and her young man, Analisa hurried down the stairs. Alesandro would be here soon. She needed to wash up, brush her hair, and change out of her traveling suit.

She found her belongings in the room next to the master's chamber. It was a nice room, decorated in deep mauve and white, but she hardly noticed her surroundings as she removed her clothing. Someone, Mrs. Thornfield, no doubt, since Sally was otherwise occupied, had laid a fire in the fireplace and left a basin of hot water on the commode. She washed quickly, dried off, slipped into a dress of maroon kerseymere. After brushing her hair, she tied it back with a matching ribbon, stepped into a pair of low-heeled slippers, took a last look at herself in the mirror, and went downstairs.

The lamps in the parlor were lit, a fire burned in the hearth. Too restless to sit, she walked around the room, admiring the painting on the wall, the colored bottles on the mantel.

Where was he?

She went into the study. A lamp, turned low, burned in here as well, as though awaiting the master's arrival. There was a fire in the hearth. The furniture in this room was dark and heavy and sparse—only a large desk, a comfortable chair, a small sofa, and a bookcase that took up all of one wall from floor to ceiling. Every shelf was filled with books.

Rounding the desk, she sat down in the chair, imagining that she could smell Alesandro's scent in the rich dark leather.

She was tempted to open the desk drawers, curious to see if she could learn more about the mysterious man she had fallen in love with, but she stayed her hand, afraid he would know somehow that she had been snooping where she didn't belong.

Where was he? He had said he would meet her here tonight. Had something happened to detain him?

Her imagination was running wild with all sorts of horrible possibilities when suddenly he was standing before her. Just looking at him sent a thrill of excitement running through her. He was tall and dark and broad-shouldered, and power emanated from him like the heat radiating from the hearth, invisible but undeniable. She felt small and helpless in the face of such strength.

"Analisa."

"Good evening, my lord."

He held out his hand, and she rose to her feet and rounded the desk.

"I was afraid you weren't coming."

"I said I would be here, did I not?"

She nodded, her gaze caressing his face as she moved into his arms. "I missed you."

He drew her close, holding her tight in the circle of his arms. He brushed a kiss across the top of her head, inhaling her scent. Only two nights without her. It had seemed much longer.

"How do you like it here?" he asked.

"It's beautiful, my lord."

"It suits you far better than Blackbriar." The Hall was a dark, forbidding place. His Analisa deserved better. He closed his eyes a moment. He had spent the past two nights trying to convince himself to let her go. Even if he could keep her safe from the darkness that was so much a part of his life, there were other dangers in being associated with him.

She gazed up at him. "Will you not kiss me, my lord?" she asked shyly.

Desire rose within him, melding with his hunger, burning through him like the heat of the sun. Lowering his head, he claimed her lips in a kiss that left them both shaken and breathless.

She stared at him for the space of a heartbeat, and then she smiled. "I missed you too, my Alesandro."

"'Lisa!" A shudder ran through him, and he closed his eyes as if he were in pain.

"Alesandro, what is it?"

With a deep sigh, he released her and took a step

back. "Go to your room, Analisa. Now."

Once, she would have fled the room with alacrity, but not now. Not when he was in such obvious pain, such blatant need. It glowed from the depths of his eyes, throbbed in the taut line of his jaw, in the way his hands clenched and unclenched at his sides.

She heard the door open behind them. Without knowing who it was, she said, "Leave us!" in a voice she hardly recognized as her own.

Sally murmured, "Yes, miss," and closed the door.

"Analisa, go to your room," he said.

She could not bear to see him in such pain, could not abide the thought of his taking what he so desperately needed from someone else.

"I won't let you send me away." She lifted her hair away from her neck. "Take what you need, my lord. It is freely given."

" 'Lisa, you make me ashamed of what I am." But he was moving toward her as he spoke, his eyes alight. He drew her down on the sofa and gathered her into his arms.

She trembled in spite of herself as he bent over her. She felt his breath warm upon her throat as he muttered an oath, and then she felt the prick of his fangs. His hands tightened on her shoulders, holding her in place. She moaned softly, but it was a sound born of pleasure, not pain.

She whimpered in protest when he drew away. He never took very much, yet it always left her feeling weak and a little disoriented.

He looked down at her for a moment, then crushed

her to him. She wasn't sure, but as she drifted to sleep, she thought she heard him crying.

Drawing her cloak tightly around her, Sally tiptoed down the back stairs. Outside, she ran lightly along the path that led to the stables, her heart pounding in anticipation as she hurried to meet Robert. If Mrs. Thornfield discovered her absence, it could mean dismissal, but she didn't care. It didn't matter. Nothing mattered but Robert, waiting for her in the barn.

She slowed to a walk as she drew near, smoothed a hand over her hair, pinched her cheeks to give them some color. He had left one of the big double doors slightly ajar. Taking a deep breath, she slipped through the narrow gap. A lamp, turned low, hung from one of the overhead beams.

The barn smelled of horses and hay and pungent manure, of leather and oil. She made a slow circle. "Robert? Robert, are you here?"

She gasped as he stepped out of the shadows. "Oh, Robert, you frightened me!"

"Sorry, love." His blue eyes danced with merriment and mischief as he held out his arms. "Come here."

She flew across the floor into his embrace.

"Miss me, love?" he asked.

"You know I did." Her gaze moved over him. He was the handsomest man she had ever seen. His hair was the color of sun-ripened wheat, his eyes as clear and blue as the sky on a midsummer's day, and when he smiled at her, she felt as though her heart would burst with happiness. "Tell me you missed me, too."

"I'll do better than that." Taking her by the hand, he led her into his room in the back of the barn. "I'll show you," he said, and closed the door.

Chapter Thirteen

Analisa slept late the following day and woke with a smile on her lips. Lifting her hand, she ran her fingertips over her neck, felt a familiar warmth where Alesandro's fangs had touched her skin. Strange, that something she should fear, something that should make her stomach turn with revulsion, filled her with such pleasure. Last night, after she had roused, Alesandro had read to her from a book of poetry, and then he had told her a little about his childhood. There was so much about him she didn't know, so much she yearned to discover.

Sitting up, she rang for her maid, and a short time later Sally entered the room.

"Afternoon, miss," the maid said cheerfully, and

Analisa noticed that Sally also wore a smile. "Will you be wanting breakfast?"

Analisa nodded. As always after satisfying Alesandro's hunger, she was famished.

"Very well, miss. I'll tell Cook you're awake. Will you be wanting anything special?"

"No, anything he makes will be fine. Just bring me lots of it." She sat up, stretching her arms over her head. A glance out the window showed it was a rare, clear day. Throwing the covers aside, she got out of bed.

"You look well rested and happy," Sally remarked as she handed Analisa her robe.

"I am." Analisa slipped into her robe, then hugged herself. In a few hours, she would see him again. "You look quite happy yourself," she remarked, noting the color in her maid's cheeks and the sparkle in her eyes.

"Oh, yes, miss, I am. Shall I fetch you some hot water?"

Analisa nodded.

"Very well, miss."

Sally practically floated out of the room, making Analisa wonder if the girl's cheerful mood had a source similar to her own. Just thinking of Alesandro made her smile inside and out. She loved him, she thought, loved him with all her heart and soul. He was a man sorely in need of loving after so many years of solitude. It pleased her when she could make him smile. Alesandro. He was truly a man like no other. Dark and dangerous, yet capable of such gentleness, such tenderness. She wondered if Sally's feelings for Robert ran as deep and wide as her own for Alesandro.

The maid returned with a bucket of hot water a short time later. "Breakfast will be ready when you're finished here," Sally said. "Shall I bring it up, or will you eat in the breakfast room?"

"I'll come down."

Sally bobbed a curtsey, laid out a dress and clean underwear, and left the room, humming softly.

Analisa took off her robe and nightgown and quickly washed her hands, arms, and face. She dressed quickly, brushed her hair, and then, humming the same tune as her maid, she went downstairs.

The breakfast room was awash in sunlight when she stepped inside. A tray was placed before her as soon as she sat down. Breakfast was delicious, as usual, but, staring out the window, her thoughts on the coming night, she was hardly aware of what she ate.

Mrs. Thornfield entered the room as she was finishing her morning meal and laid out a place setting at the opposite end of the table.

"What's that for?" Analisa asked curiously.

"Lord Alesandro wishes you to know how to behave at a proper dinner."

"I don't know what you mean."

"Come," Mrs. Thornfield said, her hand tapping the back of a chair, "sit here."

When Analisa was seated, the housekeeper pointed

out what each knife, spoon, and fork was used for.

Analisa looked up at the woman, confused. Meals at Blackbriar and here at the Manor were always informal. After all, there was little need for proper protocol when Analisa ate her meals alone, or occasionally with Alesandro for company.

"Lord Alesandro feels you need to know how to conduct yourself in society. At a large gathering, you can expect to be served as many as ten courses—"

"Ten?" Analisa squeaked.

"Yes. You might expect to have soup, a turbot of lobster and Dutch sauce, perhaps some red mullet or oysters. A sweetbread. Lamb cutlets served with asparagus or peas, venison or mutton or stewed beef, perhaps a duckling. There might also be sardines and plover's eggs in aspic. You can expect chocolate for dessert, or perhaps a cherry ice, as well as whatever fruit is in season. And there will be wine, of course. Sherry with soup and fish, port with venison and cheese, claret with roast meat, and Madeira with sweets."

"I don't understand," Analisa said. "Alesandro and I have never been invited out, nor is it likely to happen."

"I'm only doing what I was told, miss," the housekeeper said, and for the next two hours, she schooled Analisa in proper etiquette.

A lady who was unmarried and under the age of thirty was never to be in the company of a man without a chaperone except for a walk in the park in early morning, or when walking to church. A lady did not wear pearls or diamonds in the morning. A lady never danced more than three dances with the same gentleman. A lady never called on a gentleman except on a matter of business. A lady never "cut" someone after meeting them socially. A lady should always rise to offer her hand. A lady must never lounge or sit timorously on the edge of her chair. Her feet should scarcely be seen and never crossed. A lady always left something on her plate.

Analisa's head was fairly spinning when the lesson came to an end, though she was no less confused than she had been at the beginning. What need did she have to know such things? Alesandro did not go visiting, nor did he have company at his home, and there was little chance that she would be invited anywhere without him.

"Anyone would think he was trying to make a lady out of me," she muttered.

Feeling suddenly tired, she went upstairs to take a nap. Sleep came quickly. Her dreams were erratic. One minute she was sitting at an enormous table surrounded by dozens and dozens of dishes while faceless people looked on, waiting for her to choose the right fork, and the next minute Alesandro was there, his eyes blazing red with the lust for blood. "This is the correct fork," he said, and with an insane laugh, he plunged it into her throat.

She woke with a start, her heart pounding wildly. Scrambling out of bed, she ran out of the room and out of the house.

It was near dusk, and cool. The setting sun set the

sky ablaze with vibrant shades of crimson and scarlet. The colors of blood. Shivering, she scrubbed her hands over her arms, and then, needing a distraction, she walked toward the barn.

Robert was outside, currying a pretty gray horse. Dewhurst sat on a bench nearby, mending a harness.

"Evening, miss," the caretaker said, tipping his hat.

"Hello, Robert."

" 'Tis a lovely night for a ride, miss." He patted the horse on the shoulder. "I could saddle Old Bess for you, if you like."

"Oh, no," Analisa replied, shaking her head. "I don't know how to ride." At home, they had been far too poor to own a horse and had made do with a donkey, which was far cheaper to buy. She had, on occasion, ridden the animal bareback, but she had been a child then. She had no idea how to ride side-saddle.

"As you will, miss."

"Is it all right if I look around?"

"You've no business asking my permission," Robert said, obviously taken aback.

Analisa flushed. She kept forgetting she was supposed to be the mistress of the manor.

Head high, she lifted her skirts and walked into the barn. She stopped in the doorway, letting her eyes grow accustomed to the dim interior, and then wandered down the center aisle. There were large box stalls on either side. The carriage horses whickered softly as she drew near. She stopped in front of the first horse and ran her hand over its neck. She paused

167

a moment in front of the adjoining stall, giving equal attention to the second horse, and then moved on down the row to the end where a big black horse eyed her suspiciously. It was a beautiful animal, with fox-like ears and a long, silky mane. The stallion blew through its nostrils and shook its head, its ears going flat at her approach.

It could only belong to Alesandro, she thought, for certainly only a man unafraid of death would have the nerve to ride such a fearsome beast.

She kept her distance, put off by the wild look in its eyes, gave a start when she felt a hand on her shoulder. She whirled around, smiling with surprise. "Alesandro!"

He wore black breeches and knee-high black boots of soft leather. His shirt, of fine white lawn, was open at the throat, the perfect foil for his black hair. As always, just looking at him made her breath catch in her throat.

"What do you think of him?"

"He's yours, isn't he?"

He made a soft sound of assent.

"He's beautiful, but how did you ever get the nerve to ride him?"

"It wasn't easy." Alesandro moved past her to stroke the stallion's neck. "I've had him since he was a colt. Horses have an instinctive fear of my kind. It took a long time to win his trust. But we're friends now, aren't we, Deuce?"

The stallion made a soft snuffling sound, pushing his nose against Alesandro's chest. With a faint smile,

Alesandro drew a cube of sugar from his pocket and offered it to the stallion.

Analisa smiled as the stallion plucked the cube from Alesandro's hand, then tossed its head up and down in what could only be a gesture of equine approval.

"Why do you keep him here instead of at Blackbriar?"

"Robert has been breeding him to some of the local mares." Alesandro scratched the stud's ears, then turned to face Analisa. "Come and meet him."

She shook her head vigorously and took a step back.

"Come, 'Lisa," Alesandro insisted. "He will not hurt you."

"Are you sure?" Keeping one wary eye on the horse, who seemed to be keeping one wary eye on her, she walked toward Alesandro. She gasped as the stallion lowered its head to sniff her hand.

"Shall we go for a ride?" Alesandro asked.

"I don't know how."

"You can ride double with me."

She hesitated a moment, torn between her fear of the horse and her desire to please Alesandro.

In the end, Alesandro won. Ten minutes later, she was sitting on the back of a mountain of black horseflesh with Alesandro's arm tight around her waist. She detected no movement, heard no command, but the stallion moved forward, his long strides carrying them quickly out of the barn and into the yard.

Robert and Dewhurst bowed as they rode by.

Once clear of the yard, Alesandro put the horse into a slow canter.

Analisa went rigid, her arms folded over Alesandro's, her hands clutching at his biceps.

"Relax, 'Lisa."

She nodded. Leaning back against him, she took a deep breath, telling herself there was nothing to fear, not with Alesandro's arm fast around her waist. A short time later, the stallion's pace increased.

The stallion had a smooth, even gait and they fairly flew across the ground. It was exhilarating, unlike anything she had ever experienced before—the hard press of Alesandro's arm around her waist, the motion of the horse, the cool breeze in her face. Laughter bubbled up inside her. How could she have ever been afraid? She cried out with delight as the stallion jumped a trio of small hedges.

She glanced over her shoulder. "Can we go faster?"

Alesandro chuckled. A moment later, the stallion stretched out in a full gallop.

They rode for miles through the lowering darkness, until the stallion's inky black coat was dotted with foamy lather. Gradually, Alesandro slowed the horse to a trot, then a walk. A short time later, he reined the stallion to a halt in a small clearing surrounded by towering trees. The leaves whispered together in the evening breeze.

Dismounting, he lifted her from the horse's back.

Analisa extended her arms and twirled around. "Oh, but that was wonderful! Thank you, Alesandro." She smiled up at him. "You are so good to me."

He returned her smile. She was so like a child, so eager to learn, to experience life.

"I don't know where I'd be if it weren't for you," she said, suddenly serious. "I've learned so much since you took me in. How to read and write. How to behave like a lady. How will I ever repay you?"

Alesandro shook his head. "I will hear no talk of repayment. You have given me far more than I could ever hope to give you. Not just your blood, Analisa, though that is sweet indeed," he said, reading the question in her eyes. "You have given me hope for the future, a new zest for living." He caressed her cheek, his touch heartbreakingly gentle. "Something to look forward to when I awake."

His words nestled deep in her soul. Not knowing what to say, she spread her hands against his chest, rose on her tiptoes, and kissed him. She'd meant it to be just a light touch, a press of her lips to his, but his arms closed around her and he was kissing her back, a hot, desperate kiss that sent her senses reeling and curled her toes.

He drew his mouth from hers, his gaze burning into her own like a bright blue flame. She gasped his name, and then he was kissing her again, his arms so tight around her she could scarcely breathe. His breathing sounded ragged and uneven, and when he took his mouth from hers, she saw the glint of his fangs.

A long shudder wracked his body. Muttering an oath, he put her away from him and turned his back,

171

but not before she saw the haunted expression on his face.

"Alesandro." She placed her hand on his back, felt him flinch at her touch. "Alesandro, don't turn away."

"I do not want you to see me like this." He laughed, a hollow sound tinged with pain. "I am not at my best."

"I've seen you before. I'm not afraid."

He whirled around, his hair whipping about his face, his eyes blazing and tinged with red. "And do you like what you see?" He could feel the hunger stirring within him, rising up to engulf him, feel it clawing at his vitals, demanding to be fed.

He bared his fangs. "Not afraid?" he said. "Well, you should be."

She stepped backward, the movement instinctive, hardly aware she had done so. "Alesandro, please, don't do this. I love you."

"No!"

She stared up at him, not knowing what to do, or what to say. She hated it when he was like this, steeped in anger and filled with despair. She placed her hand on his arm; the muscle felt like steel beneath her fingertips.

He wrenched his arm away. Grabbing her around the waist, he lifted her onto the stallion's back and thrust the reins into her hand.

"Go home!" he said. "Now!"

Before she could argue, before she could protest that she was more afraid of riding the horse alone

172

than she was of staying with him, Alesandro slapped the stallion on the rump and the horse turned and headed back the way they had come.

She clung to the reins with one hand and the stallion's thick mane with the other. Fear rose up within her as she fled through the night. Fear that she would tumble off the horse and break her neck. Fear that Alesandro's dark side would overcome his affection for her and she would fall prey to the horrible hunger that tormented him.

She glanced over her shoulder. Was he coming after her even now?

Alesandro stared after her, his hands clenched into tight fists at his sides. He had been so proud of himself, of his ability to control his hunger. What was happening to his self-control? He laughed softly. Analisa had happened. In the beginning, a few drops of her life's blood had had the power to satisfy his hellish hunger, but lately . . . he raked a hand through his hair. For some reason he did not understand, it was getting harder and harder to control his need.

The need that burned through him even now.

A thought took him to the city, to the dark alleyways frequented by lightskirts and pickpockets and drunks looking for salvation in a pint of ale.

The woman was old for her line of work, worn down by life, her eyes dull. He drew her into his gaze, his mind overpowering hers. He grimaced as he bent her back over his arm. She smelled of sweat and old lust, and he closed his eyes, thinking of Analisa, who always smelled of soap and flowers.

He took what he needed and then, disgusted with himself, he lowered the woman to the ground. He tucked several coins in her pocket, then left her there, her mind wiped clean of all that had happened.

Filled with anger and rage and a growing sense of helplessness, he walked the dark streets until it was almost dawn. Analisa. He yearned for her, hungered for a single drop of blood, craved the feel of her body pressed to his, the sound of her laughter, the light of her smile. Analisa . . .

He was at her bedside between one heartbeat and the next, her name whispering past his lips. "Analisa." A hope unspoken, a longing he dared not acknowledge, a prayer for salvation.

His hand stroked a wisp of hair from her brow. How beautiful she was! Her skin was fair, unblemished. Her hair spread across the white linen pillowcase like a splash of black ink. She lay on her side, one hand tucked under her cheek, a cheek stained with tears.

The sight was like a dagger in his heart. He had put those tears there. He swore softly. Hurting her was the last thing he wanted to do. Closing his eyes, he took a deep breath. Her heat, her scent surrounded him. He had to let her go, he thought, before it was too late. For both of them.

She would never want for anything. He would give her the Manor and a yearly allowance that would allow her to live comfortably. With land and money of her own, she would have no trouble finding a husband to protect her.

A growl rose in his throat at the thought of her with another man.

"Alesandro?"

He opened his eyes to find her staring up at him.

She sat up, the covers falling away. She wore a demure gown of white lawn that did little to hide the sweet curve of her breasts.

"'Lisa."

"Are you all right?"

"No."

"What is it?" she asked, her brow furrowed with worry. "What's wrong?"

"Us," he said flatly.

She shook her head. "I don't understand."

"I am a vampire."

"Yes." A faint smile tugged at her lips, surprising him. "I know."

"I am afraid for you, afraid I cannot keep you safe any longer. I want you, Lisa."

"I'm here."

"All of you."

She stared at him a moment, and then her eyes widened with understanding, but she didn't flinch, and she didn't turn away. "I'm still here."

He swore softly. "You do not understand!"

She rose up on her knees and reached for him.

He backed away as though burned by the sun. "No!"

"I am not afraid," she said, but he heard the tremor

175

in her voice, the uncertainty she could not disguise.

"I will not defile you! I . . . will . . . not!"

"Will you not love me, Alesandro, as I love you?"

"I cannot." He groaned deep within himself. "Lisa, Lisa, we have been together for so long, and still you do not understand, do you?"

"I understand that I love you. And I think maybe you love me too, a little."

A little? He loved her with every fiber of his being, loved her in ways she would never understand. And that was why she had to leave.

"I know what you are," she said, as if divining his thoughts. "I've seen what you are. I know what you do. It doesn't matter, Alesandro. I'm not afraid. You saved my life. It's yours to take."

"No!" He raked a hand through his hair. "You cannot mean that!"

"But I do. I would have been dead long ago if not for you."

She stood and moved toward him. He backed away, afraid of her touch and his own weakness, backed away until he came up against the door.

"Analisa, no . . ."

Standing on tiptoe, she leaned against him, her hands reaching up to cup his face. "I love you. All of you. Promise me," she said, her gaze intent upon his, "promise that you won't send me away."

"It is for the best."

"Promise me."

176

"I promise," he said, his voice hoarse. Taking hold of her arms, he put her away from him. Turning, he opened the door. "Go back to bed," he said gruffly, and closed the door behind him.

Chapter Fourteen

As she feared, Alesandro avoided her the next day, and the next. She took comfort in his promise not to send her away until she realized she should have made him promise that *he* would not leave the Manor, that he would not hide away from her.

She knew he was afraid that he would lose control and hurt her, but it was a chance she was willing to take in order to be with him. She knew he had killed in the past, that he was capable of killing again, knew that being in his presence was dangerous. And yet, she had faith in him, in his ability to control the hunger that drove him. Hadn't he already proved that he was stronger than the darkness that dwelled within him?

On the third night, she put on her cloak and left

the house. She wandered through the gardens, hoping he would seek her out. When he didn't, she called his name aloud and in her heart, hoping he would come to her, but to no avail.

Discouraged, she walked back to the house, pausing when she heard the sound of muted laughter. Curious, she followed the sound, smothered a gasp when she saw Sally and Robert sitting on a bench, locked in each other's arms. Sally's skirts were hiked up to her thighs. Her bodice was open. Even more shocking was the sight of Robert's hand cupping Sally's breast. For a moment, Analisa simply stood and watched, too stunned to move, as the couple kissed and fondled each other with complete abandon.

Unable to watch any longer, Analisa turned on her heel and ran back to the house.

"Ah, there you are," Mrs. Thornfield said as she entered the parlor, breathless. "Dinner is ready. Have you seen Sally? I asked her to take care of something for me an hour ago and haven't seen her since."

"I . . . oh . . . yes . . . I mean, no," Analisa stammered, and hurried into the dining room.

She sat there, picking at her food, vivid images of Sally and Robert running through her mind. It was wrong, terribly wrong, for Sally to behave so brazenly, and yet Analisa couldn't help feeling envious of the love they shared.

Leaving the table, she went into the library, hoping Alesandro might be there, but the room was dark and empty. Feeling lost and alone, she went into his bedchamber and closed the door. A fire burned in the hearth, lit each night in case he should return. She warmed herself at the fire, longing to be in Alesandro's arms, to kiss him with abandon, the way Sally had kissed Robert, to touch Alesandro and have him touch her. . . .

The thought made her shiver with longing, with a sense of fear that she was loath to admit. But it was there nevertheless, lurking deep within her, a primal fear of the unknown. The undead.

Feeling suddenly chilled in spite of the fire, she folded her arms over her breasts. How could she be afraid of the very man she claimed to love? *But I am not a man.* His words echoed in her mind.

She glanced around the room. His chamber here was also furnished with dark wood. A thick dark blue comforter covered the bed. There was a large armoire, a small dresser, a table, a chair. And over the bed, a large painting reminiscent of the one in Alesandro's chamber at Blackbriar Hall. This, too, was a powerfully haunting piece. Had Alesandro posed for it? Eyes narrowed, she took a step closer. He must have posed for it, she mused, for the resemblance was far too strong to be mere coincidence. Instead of looking into a pool, the man in this painting was standing in a dark room gazing into a mirror. Again, instead of seeing his own reflection, a black wolf stared back at the man, a wolf with hungry eyes and fangs stained with blood. Were the paintings symbolic? Did the wolf represent Alesandro's dark side?

With a shake of her head, she turned to stare at the fire. Where was he?

The warmth of the flames made her drowsy, and she climbed onto his bed and closed her eyes. . . .

The wolf ran though the night, his senses filled with sights and sounds unknown to mortals. He reveled in the feel of the earth beneath his feet—sensitive feet that felt every blade of grass, every rock, every twig. The wind filled his nostrils, carrying the scent of coming rain, trees, grass, the blood of another's kill. He ran on, caught up in the sheer joy of running, unfettered, through the dark.

A deer sprang from its hiding place, the scent of its fear arousing his instinct to give chase. He brought the animal down easily, stood over it, tongue lolling, fangs bared, blue eyes aflame with the lust for blood. . . .

Analisa woke abruptly, a cry of panic erupting from her throat as she found herself staring up into the wolf's eyes.

" 'Lisa, what are you doing in here?"

She blinked, and blinked again. "Alesandro? Oh, Alesandro, please don't leave me again!" she cried, and threw her arms around his neck. "Please!"

Sitting down on the edge of the bed, he drew her onto his lap. "Shh, 'Lisa, do not cry." The sight of her tears made him ache deep inside. His hand moved over her back. She was small and slender, as delicate as a flower.

She looked up at him through eyes swimming with tears. "I love you," she whispered.

" 'Lisa."

"Every time we . . ." She bit down on her lip, not

knowing how to say what she wanted to tell him. "Every time we seem to get close, you go away from me."

He didn't deny it. How could he? But she was far too tempting for his peace of mind. Love and lust, hunger and desire, all warred within him, so closely interwoven it was difficult to separate one from the other.

"You do love me a little, don't you?" she asked shyly.

"You know I do."

"Tell me."

"I love you, Analisa Matthews. Never doubt it."

"Won't you kiss me, then?"

He stared at her, a silent battle raging within him as the man he had once been struggled with the monster he had become. But neither man nor monster could resist the invitation in her eyes, the temptation of her lips.

Muttering an oath, he cupped her head in one hand, his mouth slanting over hers. Warm. Sweet. Soft as velvet. He groaned low in his throat as he deepened the kiss, hoping on some deeper level that his intensity would frighten her, send her running from the room before it was too late. Instead, she snuggled against him, her arms lifting to twine around his neck. Her heat engulfed him, her scent intoxicated him, her lips . . . there were no words to describe their effect on him, and he drank from their sweetness like a man too long deprived of nourishment.

He kissed her until she was breathless and then, mustering all the self-control he possessed, he drew back, knowing that if he didn't stop now, he would never stop.

She stared at him, her lips swollen from his kisses, her eyes cloudy with passion. "Don't stop," she whispered, and leaning back, she drew him down until his body covered hers.

She moved beneath him and desire exploded through him. How long, he wondered, how long since he had made love to a woman?

He kissed her again, and yet again, his hands lightly caressing her, each touch filling him with both pleasure and guilt. How could he make love to her, defile her? How could he not?

And then, to his relief, the decision was no longer his to make. He could sense the dawn's approach, feel the promised heat of the rising sun, the sudden heaviness in his arms and legs.

One last kiss, and he drew back, sitting up.

She reached for him, but he stood, eluding her.

"What's wrong?" she asked, her gaze searching his.

He didn't answer. Instead, he swung her into his arms and carried her swiftly through the house to her room.

"What are you doing?" she asked. "Alesandro, answer me!"

"It's almost dawn," he said, depositing her on her bed. "I must go."

She wanted to argue, to scream her frustration, but

one look at his face stilled her voice. He looked haunted, tortured.

"Where do you spend your days?" she asked, unable to restrain her curiosity any longer.

"You know where."

"Is there some reason why you must . . . must sleep there?"

"No."

"Then why do you not stay here?"

"I have never rested near the presence of others, or trusted anyone to know where I take my rest."

"But . . . I know."

"You are the only one. I must go."

"Tomorrow night," she said. "I'll see you then?"

He nodded once, curtly, started to turn away, then bent down and kissed her gently, tenderly. "Until then, *cara mia*," he whispered, his voice thick, and he was gone.

She didn't awake until after two that afternoon, woke remembering the heat of Alesandro's lips on hers as the sun chased the moon from the sky. She sat up, smiling. He had said he loved her. Excitement rippled through her. Alesandro loved her!

A moment later, there was a knock at her door. "Are you awake, miss?"

"Yes, come in, Sally."

Analisa watched the maid as she opened the drapes, laid out a change of underwear. It was easy to see that Sally was deeply in love. Her eyes glowed; she smiled all the time now, was often lost in a world of her own.

Analisa grinned, wondering if her own eyes held the same glow.

"Will you be wanting breakfast this afternoon?"

"Yes."

"Anything in particular?"

"No. Tell Cook to surprise me. Sally, we need to talk."

"Is something wrong?"

"Mrs. Thornfield was looking for you last night."

"Oh?" Sally's voice was suddenly wary.

"Sally, please be careful. I should hate for you to be dismissed."

"I've done nothing wrong," the maid said defensively, but there was no mistaking the guilt in her eyes or the flush that stained her cheeks.

"I saw you, Sally. With Robert."

"You didn't tell Mrs. Thornfield?"

"No, but—"

"Please don't tell her." Sally dropped down on her knees beside the bed. "Please, miss. I've no place to go if she sends me away! I love Robert, and he loves me. Here, at the Manor, is the only place we can be together."

"Of course I shan't tell her," Analisa said. "But she already knows how you feel, and she's not blind."

"Oh, bless you, miss."

"You must be more careful."

Sally nodded. "You're right, I know. But we have so little time together."

"Perhaps I could speak to Lord Alesandro," Analisa suggested. "I'm sure he could arrange for the two of you to be together."

Tears filled the maid's eyes. "You'd do that for me? Oh, miss, I don't know what to say."

"You don't have to say anything. People in love should be together."

Sally grabbed Analisa's hand and squeezed it. "Thank you, miss." Rising, she blinked back her tears. "I'll go get your cocoa and tell Cook to prepare your breakfast."

Rising, Analisa washed her hands and face. Sally came back a few minutes later. Analisa sipped her cocoa while Sally brushed her hair and then helped her dress, and all the while Sally thanked her over and over again for not telling Mrs. Thornfield about her rendezvous with Robert the night before.

When she finished dressing, Analisa went downstairs to breakfast, leaving Sally to make the bed and tidy up the room.

Analisa loved the Manor. It was so much brighter, so much more cheery, than the Hall. The grounds outside the window were all green and gold.

She ate slowly, wishing Alesandro were there with her, that they could share the day together, go for a walk in the sun. . . .

Overwhelmed by a sense of guilt for even wishing such a thing, she quickly put the thought from her mind. Giving up walks in the sun was a small sacrifice to make. She would give up much more just to be with Alesandro. He was the most fascinating man she had ever known, even though he had told her time and time again that he was not a man at all.

She spent an hour in the library with Mrs. Thornfield, who declared she had made such wonderful progress in reading and writing that there was nothing more she could teach her and suggested that Lord Alesandro might hire a tutor for her if she wished to pursue her education further. But Analisa had no interest in furthering her education. It was enough that she could read and write. When Mrs. Thornfield went to see to her other duties, Analisa perused the bookshelves. It was mind-boggling, the number of books Alesandro owned. Two libraries filled with books, and no two volumes the same. Of course, she mused, he'd had many, many years to collect them. As at Blackbriar, there were books here in many languages—medical books, history books, ancient texts and scrolls, books on art and music. And on vampires.

She plucked one of the books about vampires from the shelf, then made herself comfortable in his chair in front of the fireplace. She thumbed through the pages, reading a paragraph here, a paragraph there, fascinated by the various facts and myths. Some people believed that crossroads were unhallowed ground and therefore travelers should not approach them at night, as they were meeting places for vampires, ghosts, witches, and other supernatural creatures like trolls and demons. In some parts of England, suicides were buried at the crossroads.

Reading on, she found a chapter on how to destroy

a vampire. Driving a stake through the heart or cutting off the head were considered the most efficacious methods. Both thoughts left her feeling slightly sick to her stomach, especially when she imagined such a thing happening to Alesandro. Fire was another option, as was immersing the vampire in water. She frowned at that. Alesandro bathed, didn't he?

Another chapter gave opinions on how one became a vampire, such as being born the seventh son of a seventh son, or being born on a holy day or when there was a new moon, though why that should cause one to become a vampire was beyond her comprehension. Being a werewolf, practicing witchcraft, eating a sheep killed by a wolf, or committing suicide could lead to becoming a vampire. It was also believed that a person might turn into a vampire if he died by drowning, or if he was killed by a vampire, or if a cat jumped over his grave, or a candle was passed over his corpse.

Analisa shook her head. Did anyone really believe such things?

She turned one page after another, pausing when she came to a section on the supernatural powers of vampires. Could Alesandro do all these things? She knew he was capable of transporting her from one place to another in the blink of an eye, but could he turn into mist? Control the elements? Transform himself into a bat? Or a wolf?

She frowned, remembering the black wolf that had run alongside the carriage when she arrived at Blackbriar, the wolves in the paintings in Alesandro's bedchamber here and at Blackbriar. She had heard the howling of a wolf late at night from time to time. Could that have been he? Perhaps tonight she would ask him.

On another page, she found several drawings of what vampires were supposed to look like. They were depicted as hideous creatures, with sunken eyes, enormous fangs, long fingernails, hairy hands, and pointed ears.

Distressed by the sight, she closed the book and set it aside. Alesandro was not like that. He wasn't the spawn of the devil. He wasn't a ruthless killer . . . and yet she couldn't shut out the memory of his voice, or his words, the night he had told her what he was.

"I am a vampire, Analisa. Much of what people say of my kind is untrue. What is true is that I must have blood to survive. I cannot bear the light of the sun, and I am vulnerable during the hours of daylight. I am constantly at war with what I am, constantly struggling to survive. We are predators, hunters. Killers."

Feeling suddenly chilled, she went outside and stood in the sun, letting its warmth seep into her bones. How beautiful the sun was! How good it felt on her skin. She walked along the narrow path that wove through the gardens. It was hard to imagine there was evil or ugliness in the world on such a bright and beautiful day. Poor Alesandro! To think he had not seen the sun or felt its touch in over four hundred years. She sat down on a bench, the same bench Sally had shared with Robert, and stared into the distance, thinking of all the things Alesandro could no longer enjoy, like watching a flower lift its face to the sun, the taste of rich, warm cocoa on a cold night, bread fresh from the oven, one of Cook's airy soufflés, a glass of cold buttermilk. Poor Alesandro. How had he survived so long? How had he endured the loneliness?

She sat there for a long time, thinking of him, of the night he had first come to the hospital. For all that he considered himself to be a monster, if not for him she would be dead now. She knew he had killed in the past, but she could not hold him guilty. She couldn't imagine how horrible it must have been for him to accept what he had become, nor could she imagine the awful hunger that drove him. But, as bad as it was, he had overcome it, learned to control it, even learned how to use his powers to help others. She considered the blood he took from her a small price to pay for regaining her life.

Her Alesandro. He was a hero in her eyes. Not like that fiend, Rodrigo, who killed for the love of it.

A sudden chill made her realize the sun was going down. It would soon be time for dinner. And then Alesandro would come to her. Alesandro.

Rising, she hurried back to the house, eager to see him again.

Chapter Fifteen

Analisa sat at her dressing table while Sally brushed out her hair, then swept part of it up in a thick coil on the top of her head, leaving the rest to fall in waves down her back. She knew without asking that Sally was planning to meet Robert later that night. She could tell by the way the maid's hands trembled, the way she jumped when the clock chimed the hour.

"How's that, miss?" Sally asked, her head cocked to one side as she admired her handiwork.

"It looks fine, thank you."

Rising, Analisa shrugged out of her robe and stepped into her dress. It was a deep green watered silk with fitted sleeves, a square neck, and a slim skirt gathered in back to fall in graceful folds to the floor. She turned her back so Sally could fasten it. Biting down on her lower lip, she tried to decide whether she should say anything to Sally about sneaking off to meet Robert. Was it even her place to do so? Aside from Mrs. Thornfield, Sally was the closest thing she had to a friend and she didn't want to say or do anything to ruin that.

Analisa frowned. If she was the mistress of the house, and if she didn't see anything wrong with Sally meeting Robert, then maybe it was all right. Or maybe she should talk to Alesandro about it. It was really his decision, after all.

She smiled at her reflection in the mirror. She would talk to him tonight, and let him decide what should be done.

He was waiting for her when she descended the stairs. He smiled at her, a light burning in his deep blue eyes as his gaze swept over her.

"Good evening, my lord," she murmured, feeling her cheeks flush under his frankly admiring gaze.

" 'Lisa, you grow more beautiful each time I see you."

"Thank you. Will you sit with me while I dine?" she asked, slipping her arm through his.

"You will be dining out tonight."

"I will? Where are we going?"

"I have decided it is time for you to meet your neighbors. You spend far too much time alone."

She shook her head. She had no desire to mingle with anyone. And if she occasionally felt lonely, well, there were worse things than being lonely. She would

never fit in with her neighbors. They were people who had been born to wealth and position, who always knew the right thing to say whatever the situation, people whose manners were beyond reproach. She had been born in a poor part of the country and she had no desire to let others discover just how ignorant she was.

"You are far too young to spend all your time alone, hidden away here at the Manor or at Blackbriar," Alesandro said in a reasonable tone. "One day you will wish to marry and . . ."

She shook her head again, more vigorously this time. "No, my lord, I will not."

" 'Lisa, listen to me—"

She took her arm from his. "No, my lord. *You* listen to *me!* If you will not have me, I will not marry at all."

"You are being foolish and stubborn."

She glared up at him, her hands fisted on her hips. "No, it is you who are being foolish and stubborn. I love you. You say you love me, yet you stand there and speak of my marrying someone else, as if you didn't care at all!"

He might have laughed at her impertinence if they had been discussing a subject less serious. "It is because I care that I wish for you to find a young man, one who can share your whole life, give you children, one who can grow old with you."

"But I—"

He stilled her protest with a wave of his hand. "Do you honestly think this is easy for me?" he demanded.

"To think of you being with another man, bearing his children? I may be a monster, 'Lisa, but not so great a monster that I would keep you by my side and deprive you of the life you deserve."

"You promised! You promised you wouldn't send me away!"

"I am not sending you away. You may stay here until you find a man who suits you. I will give you a generous dowry and a wedding you will never forget."

She shook her head, her eyes burning with unshed tears. "You can't make me get married, Alesandro. You can't make me fall in love with someone else." She took a deep breath, her arms falling to her sides in a gesture of defeat. "If you don't want me, I'll leave here tomorrow and you'll never have to see me again."

" 'Lisa!"

She stared up at him, her hands fisted in the folds of her gown, her heart hammering as she waited to see if he would call her bluff. And if he did, what then? What would she do? Where would she go?

He was looking at her as if he had never seen her before. It was the first time she had known him to be at a loss for words.

"Very well, I'll leave in the morning," she said, and turned toward the stairs, her tears falling freely down her cheeks. She had gambled, and she had lost.

"Analisa." Just her name, spoken ever so softly, the way a man whispered the name of the woman he loved.

Heart pounding, hardly daring to hope, she turned to face him.

He held out his hand. "Come to me, 'Lisa."

She walked slowly toward him and placed her hand in his, aware that, from this moment forward, things would be forever different between them.

His hand curled over hers, his skin firm and cool, his touch gentle, belying the preternatural strength he possessed.

"Never doubt that I want you," he said quietly. "You will never know how difficult it is for me to leave you when dawn approaches."

"And I want you, Alesandro. You must know that."

He nodded, his dark eyes filled with anguish, his expression troubled.

Going up on her tiptoes, she pressed her lips to his. In an instant, his arms were around her and he was crushing her body to him, his mouth quickly taking control of hers. She could feel the hard press of his desire, taste it in his kisses, in the rapid pounding of his heart against her own. He had never kissed her quite like this before. It was frightening, exhilarating. Her body's response was immediate. Heat flowed through her, hotter than a brushfire, burning away every other thought but the need to touch him and be touched in return.

Muttering an oath, he swept her into his arms and carried her to his bedchamber. The door opened as if by magic, and he carried her swiftly inside.

The door closed behind him.

A fire sprang to life in the hearth.

He crushed her close, murmuring her name, raining kisses over her face, her throat, the curve of her shoulder, the hollow between her breasts.

She moaned softly as his tongue slid over her skin.

He lifted his head and gazed down at her, his deep blue eyes ablaze. "Are you sure this is what you want, Analisa? If you are not, you must say so now, before it is too late."

"Make me yours, Alesandro," she whispered tremulously. "Now. Tonight."

He carried her to the bed and laid her down upon it. His eyes never left hers as he removed his cloak and tossed it over the back of a chair. Slowly, deliberately, he began to undress.

She watched his every movement. No one else moved the way he did. Like smoke, she thought, fluid, graceful. He made hardly a sound as he removed his cravat, his shirt, removed his shoes and socks, to stand before her clad in nothing but a pair of black trousers. The firelight caressed his broad shoulders and chest, cast red highlights in his hair. His eyes burned hotter than the flames in the hearth.

He was beautiful, magnificent. She could feel his power fill the room, feel it flowing over her like the sizzle in the air before a storm.

He moved toward the bed. Her heart pounded ever faster as he removed her shoes and unfastened her gown. She shivered with anticipation as his fingers, so long and strong, whispered over her skin, sliding her gown over her shoulders, down her arms. He tossed her dress on top of his shirt. Her petticoat and drawers came next, and then he unfastened her garters and removed her stockings, first one, then the other, his hands sliding sensuously down her thighs, her calves. When she wore nothing but her chemise, he stretched out beside her and drew her into his arms.

She trembled at his touch, wanting more, and yet afraid of what she wanted at the same time. She knew nothing of intimacy or what went on between a man and a woman, knew only that she wanted Alesandro to be the one to teach her.

She placed her hand on his chest, her touch shy and uncertain, until he covered her hand with his own, urging her to explore to her heart's content. His skin was cool, smooth, unblemished. His stomach was hard and unyielding; his muscles rippled at her touch. She leaned over him, measuring the breadth of his shoulders with her hands, running her fingertips over the corded muscles in his arms, thinking that his biceps were larger than her thighs. There was a fine sprinkling of curly black hair on his chest that narrowed to a fine line until it disappeared beneath the waistband of his trousers. She traced it with her finger, slipped her hand beneath the cloth.

He groaned softly as she continued her exploration.

She stopped, her gaze searching his. "Am I hurting you?"

"In ways you cannot imagine," he said, his voice thick, and then, before she quite knew how it happened, she was lying naked beneath him. He bent his head. She shivered when she felt the brush of his fangs against her throat.

Alesandro went still as only a vampire can be still. Lifting his head, he gazed down at her, his eyes probing the very depths of her soul.

"It's all right," she said, knowing somehow that if she changed her mind now, he would be lost to her forever.

And still he hesitated. She read the torment in his eyes, his fear of hurting her. Murmuring his name, she cupped his face in her hands and kissed him. At the first touch of her lips to his, he lost whatever battle he had been waging within himself. He surrendered with a groan that was part pleasure, part pain.

He shifted his weight. His trousers vanished as if by magic, and then his body covered hers and she was lost, caught up in a maelstrom of emotions, every sense heightened and alive, every fiber of her being yearning toward his, in tune with his. She felt the prick of his fangs at her throat, a sudden sharp pain in the deepest part of her as his body meshed with hers. She clutched his shoulders, felt the tremor that ran through his arms as he waited, poised above her, while the pain receded and her body grew accustomed to his. After a time, he began to move slowly, ever so slowly, within her.

Pleasure flowed through her, hot and liquid, as the world came to vibrant life. Colors were brighter, deeper. The candle's flame seemed alive. She was acutely aware of the texture of the soft wool blanket beneath her, and even more aware of the man whose body was now a part of hers. His skin was moist and warm against her own, his hands played over her body, showing her what pleasure was, teaching her how to give him pleasure in return. He whispered love words in her ear, speaking to her in French and Spanish, in the ancient language of his people, and though she did not understand the words, she understood the fervent tone of his voice, the tenderness in his eyes, the exquisite gentleness of his touch.

She writhed beneath him, her hands moving restlessly over his broad shoulders, up and down his back, her nails raking his skin. She closed her eyes as he moved within her; she was searching for something elusive, afraid she would never reach it. Higher and higher still until, at last, it was within her grasp. She cried his name, gasped as sunlight exploded within her, filling her with warmth and love and a contentment she had never known.

A moment later, a long, shuddering sigh rippled through Alesandro. She felt the coiled tension flow from his body as he rolled onto his side, drawing her with him so they lay facing each other, bodies still joined together, her head pillowed on his arm.

He brushed a lock of hair from her forehead. "Did I hurt you?"

She shook her head, her eyelids heavy. "No," she murmured. "It was wonderful. I love you, Alesandro."

He closed his eyes, letting her words wash over him, words he had never expected to hear from her lips or any other.

His arms tightened around her. "And I love you," he said, but when he opened his eyes, he saw that she was already asleep.

His gaze moved over her. He was humbled by her love, her absolute trust, ashamed that he had taken her virginity. She was so young, so innocent, even now. What right did he have to defile her with what he was? But after so many years in hell, surely even a monster deserved one night in paradise. Just one night to know a woman's love, to feel like a man again.

He took a slow, deep breath, inhaling the fragrance of her skin, the heady, musky scent of their lovemaking. She had fed both his hungers as no one else ever had, or ever could. For the first time in centuries, he was content, at peace within himself.

He held her close all through the night, listening to the soft sound of her breathing, the small sounds she made from time to time. He let his mind brush hers, knew she was dreaming of him. He ran his hand over her hair, dreading the time when he would have to let her go, when dawn would force him to take refuge in his dreary underground lair. If only he could hold her close through the long, empty hours of daylight.

The loneliness of four hundred years pressed down on him. Four hundred years without the sun. Four hundred years of hiding from the world. Four hundred years of darkness . . . until now. He stroked her hair, an aching tenderness stirring deep in his heart as she snuggled closer to him. What would it be like to wake up with her beside him, to have her face be the first sight that greeted him upon rising? He grunted softly. No doubt she would run screaming from his presence if she saw him then, when the hunger was fast upon him. And yet, he owed her a debt he could never repay. She was like a tiny ray of light, and in the total darkness of his being, one tiny ray shone as bright as the sun. Ah, the sun.

He lifted his head, drew a deep breath. He could smell the dawn, feel the sudden painful tightening of his skin as the sun's light began to chase the darkness from the sky.

Reluctantly, he let her go, drew the covers over her. "Rest well, my sweet one." He kissed her lightly; then, dissolving into mist, he fled the house.

Chapter Sixteen

Analisa woke with a smile on her face. Alesandro loved her, she thought dreamily. He loved her! And he had made love to her. Had ever a woman been loved so gently, so completely? Drawing the covers up to her chin, she giggled like a silly child. She closed her eyes and took a deep breath. Alesandro! His scent was all around her. She felt her cheeks grow hot as she recalled how brazenly she had surrendered to him, how eager she had been for his touch. She should be ashamed, she thought, and wondered why she wasn't. She had been taught that intimacy before marriage was a sin, but it hadn't felt like a sin. It had felt right somehow, as if she had found the other half of her soul. Did vampires have a soul? Or were they forever damned? She wouldn't, couldn't believe that.

For all that he was cursed to dwell in darkness, Alesandro wasn't evil. Not like Rodrigo, who went about killing for pleasure.

She thrust the thought of the other vampire from her mind, refusing to let thoughts of that depraved monster spoil the day, or her memories of the night before.

Sitting up, she placed her hand on the pillow beside hers, wishing Alesandro were there, wishing she could kiss him good morning, but of course he couldn't be here with her now. She thought of him sleeping in the bowels of the strange round cottage in the woods.

Rising, she went to the window and drew back the curtains. She was wondering what time it was when she heard the downstairs clock chime the hour. She smiled because it was a quarter after three. Only a few hours until she would see him again.

Feeling suddenly famished, she pulled on her robe, stepped into her slippers, and left the room, wondering why Sally hadn't come in to light the fire in the hearth.

She felt it as soon as she descended the stairs, a tension in the air, a strange hush, as if the house were holding its breath.

She looked into the parlor, the library, the dining room, the pantry, even went upstairs to check Mrs. Thornfield's room, but there was no one about. Gathering her courage, she even peeked into the kitchen, her concern growing when she saw that there was nothing cooking on the stove.

Growing more alarmed, she went out the back

door into the yard. There was an unnatural silence here, too. She hesitated a moment, and then, without knowing why, she started down the path toward the barn.

Her footsteps slowed as she neared the entrance to the barn. A sudden chill engulfed her, coupled with a deep sense of foreboding. She stared at the barn. One of the big double doors stood open. She paused and ⋯, feeling as though she were walking through a thick fog, she stepped into the building. As she did so, she heard Mrs. Thornfield call her name, a note of panic in her voice.

The warning came too late.

Farleigh whirled around as Analisa entered the barn, and in doing so, he let her see the very thing the housekeeper had tried to spare her.

Sally lay on her back on the floor, her face drained of color, her eyes empty of life. Her throat had been savaged; dark crimson streaks stained her skin, her bodice.

Robert lay beside her, a great gaping hole where his heart had been.

Analisa turned and stumbled out of the barn. Retching violently, she dropped to her hands and knees. She was dimly aware of Farleigh kneeling beside her. As from a great distance, she heard Mrs. Thornfield calling her name.

And then she heard nothing at all.

She didn't want to wake up, didn't want to face the memory of the horror she had seen. She told herself it hadn't been real. Couldn't be real.

She heard Mrs. Thornfield's voice, soft, worried; heard Farleigh's hushed reply, the sound of hurried footsteps as he left the room.

"Analisa? Child?" Mrs. Thornfield patted her hand, laid a cool cloth on her brow. "Analisa, can you hear me!"

Tears slid down Analisa's cheeks. "Tell me it isn't real."

"I wish I could."

Analisa opened her eyes to find herself on her own bed. Mrs. Thornfield removed her slippers, then covered her with a quilt. "Who?" she asked. "Who would do such a terrible thing?"

"Rodrigo."

"He was here?"

The housekeeper nodded. "Yes."

"He was in the house?"

"No. Farleigh found Mary and Robert deep in the woods."

Analisa choked back a sob. The lovers had met in secret far from the house, away from disapproval and prying eyes. "Have you notified the constable?"

"No. Here, sit up and drink this," the housekeeper said, taking a cup of tea from Cook's hand.

Analisa took a swallow, and nearly choked. "What's in this?"

"Only a bit of brandy," Mrs. Thornfield said. "Drink it. It will make you feel better."

Analisa did as she was told, though she doubted that anything would make her feel better. "Poor Sally."

205

"Don't think of it now." Mrs. Thornfield took the cup from her hand. "Rest now."

"Will you stay with me?"

"Yes, child."

Lulled by the brandy, the first she had ever tasted, she was quickly asleep.

She woke screaming, images of blood and eyes glowing with a fiendish light lingering in her mind.

"It's all right, child. You're safe."

"I had the most terrible dream." She looked up into Mrs. Thornfield's pale face. "But it wasn't a dream, was it?"

"No." There were tears in the housekeeper's voice. "Try not to think about it now."

Not think about it? Analisa doubted she would ever get her last glimpse of Sally out of her mind. The look of stark horror on the girl's face, the awful wounds in her throat. The blood . . .

A vampire had done that.

She looked at the window. It was dark outside. Alesandro would be up by now. Did he know what had happened? She closed her eyes. Of course he would know. She wished he were there to comfort her, and yet . . .

Vampire

The word slithered through her mind, malevolent, insidious, conjuring images of darkness and blood. And death.

But Alesandro was not like that! Not her Alesandro. He had ever been kind to her. He had sheltered

her in his house, clothed her in fine silks, shown her
a world she never dreamed existed . . .

And taken her blood on more than one occasion.

A chill ran down her spine. He had warned her
several times that she was not safe in his house.

Mrs. Thornfield left the room, returning a short
time later with a cup of warm broth, but Analisa had
no appetite.

"Will you be all right alone for a time, child?" the
housekeeper asked. "I must go and see to . . . to the
bodies. We will bury them later tonight."

Analisa nodded, grateful that she could stay in her
room, grateful that she would not have to look again
upon the horror Rodrigo had wrought. She stared at
the lamp burning beside the bed, at the half-dozen
candles Mrs. Thornfield had thoughtfully set around
the room to keep the darkness, and her fears, at bay.

What would happen now? And where was Alesandro?

He lingered in the shadows of her room, aware of the
fear that engulfed her, conscious of her every thought.
He had seen what was left of Sally and young Robert
Mason. Seen the bodies, smelled the fear that clung
to them, even in death. Smelled the dried blood on
their skin, and cursed the hunger the sight of it had
aroused in him. How could he fault Rodrigo for what
he had done when he himself was plagued with the
same evil? And yet Rodrigo had dared to come here
and kill two people in his employ and under his pro-
tection. They had not been killed to satisfy the vam-

pire's hunger. The deaths had been a challenge, boldly given, and perhaps more than that. Perhaps a warning that the vampire intended for Analisa to be his next victim. Rodrigo had sworn to be avenged for his loss. What better vengeance than to destroy the woman his enemy held dear?

Alesandro's gaze moved over Analisa. He had been a fool to keep her in his company. And a bigger fool to fall in love with her. And careless to bring her here. He should have known Rodrigo would find them. Should have known the other vampire would never stop looking for him.

Analisa slept restlessly, tossing and turning, her hands clutching at the blankets. It was an easy thing, to slip into her mind, into her dreams. She was running through a dark maze, running from hell-red eyes and gleaming fangs dripping blood. Running from a vampire. But was it Rodrigo she ran from in stark terror? Or himself?

If he went to her now, would she seek comfort in his arms, or cry out in horror?

He had never considered himself a coward. A vampire who was a coward would not have survived four hundred years. But he was afraid, afraid of what he would see in her eyes if he went to her now.

She cried out in her sleep, bolted upright, her gaze darting around the room. "Alesandro?" His name was a whisper on her lips as she clutched the blanket to her breast. "Alesandro, are you there?"

"I am here," he replied quietly, but stayed hidden from her sight.

She turned toward the sound of his voice. "Where are you? Show yourself."

Taking on form and substance, he stepped out of the shadows. " 'Lisa."

She stared up at him, apprehension and longing reflected in the depths of her eyes.

"You fear me now?"

She heard the sorrow in his voice and wished she could deny it.

"Shall I send you away, 'Lisa? Do you wish to leave here and find some place where you will be safe from me?"

"Is there such a place, my lord?"

"No." There was no place she could go where he could not find her. She could leave the Manor, leave the country, sail away to the other side of the world, but he would always know where she was.

"Did you see . . . ?" she began.

"Yes."

A tear glistened in her eye. "Poor Sally. She was so in love. All she wanted was to be with Robert."

"They are together now," he said quietly.

"Yes. But to die so horribly. So needlessly . . ."

He winced at the pain in her voice, in her eyes. Even though he wasn't the one who had taken their lives, their blood stained his soul. They had been his people. He should have protected them, should have detected Rodrigo's presence—and he would have, he knew, if he had not been caught up in the wonder of making love to Analisa. But he did not tell her that, did not want her burdened by the guilt that weighed him down.

"Tell me what you want," he said. "If you wish to leave, I will send you away."

"You said there was no place where I could be safe."

"There is no place where you will be safe from me, Analisa. I will always be able to find you wherever you go. But I can send you away. Keep you safe from Rodrigo. If that is your wish, you have only to tell me. I will buy you a house, give you the money to furnish it as you see fit, provide you with a comfortable income for the rest of your life, whether you marry or not."

"You would do that for me?"

"Yes, if you wish it."

"And Rodrigo would never find me?"

He closed his eyes, wondering what madness had possessed him to offer her such a choice. "No, he will not find you."

"And would you come after me?"

He opened his eyes to find her watching him intently. "No."

"You would let me go, just like that?"

Could he let her go? Could he go back to the dark existence he had known before she came into his life? Could he keep her here against her will?

"Alesandro?"

"I will let you go, if you wish it."

"And if I wish to stay?"

For the first time in four hundred years, a mortal

had truly surprised him. He looked at her, not daring to believe what he had heard.

"Alesandro?"

"You do not mean it. You cannot mean it." He shook his head. "I can smell your fear, read it in your eyes."

"Love is stronger than fear," she murmured, and held out her hand.

He closed the distance between them. Sweeping her into his arms, he crushed her close. " 'Lisa!" Weak with relief, he closed his eyes and breathed in her scent, let it fill him, surround him. He had not lost her.

"Alesandro," she gasped. "I can't breathe."

"Forgive me." He loosened his hold on her, brushed his lips across the top of her head.

She looked up at him, love and confusion replacing the fear in her eyes. "Is something wrong?"

" 'Lisa." He sat down on the edge of her bed and drew her into his lap. "I have been alone for four centuries. When I found you . . ." He shook his head, wondering how to make her understand.

"Go on."

"It was like finding a light in the darkness. I have taken blood from hundreds of women, but none is as . . . as sweet, as satisfying, as yours. Having you in my home, seeing you each evening, I began to have hope. And when I knew you loved me . . ." His arms tightened around her again. "With you in my life, the darkness of my existence no longer seemed such a curse. I almost did not come to you tonight. I was afraid of what I would see in your eyes, afraid I would stand condemned with Rodrigo."

"Oh, Alesandro!" She hugged him to her. "I admit, I was afraid. It's the first time I've ever seen what a . . . a vampire can do. It was so horrible! Poor Sally." Tears filled her eyes. "It's all my fault. All my fault. I knew she was going to meet Robert. I should have told her not to go, but I wasn't sure if it was my place." She sniffed back her tears. "I was going to talk to you about it. . . ."

"The fault is mine, love, not yours. I should have given them permission to marry. Had I done so, they would not have been forced to arrange clandestine meetings in the woods."

"Why didn't you let them marry?"

He shook his head. "I fear I am a selfish creature, 'Lisa, concerned only with my own needs, my own survival. Mortal concerns have not been mine, until you came here. You must not go outside after dark, 'Lisa. He can prowl the grounds of the Manor at will, but he cannot enter the house uninvited. I will instruct Mrs. Thornfield that no one is to answer the door after dark."

"You didn't take such precautions at Blackbriar."

"It was careless of me, but I did not think he would be so bold as to trespass on my property." He paused, listening. "Mrs. Thornfield is coming."

A moment later, there was a knock on the door. "My lord?"

"Yes."

"We're ready to inter the bodies."

"Very well. We will be down shortly."

"Yes, my lord. Does Miss Analisa need help dressing?"

"I will see to it."

There was a pause before the housekeeper replied, "Yes, my lord, as you wish."

"Alesandro? Mrs. Thornfield said the constable hasn't been notified. Shouldn't we call him?"

"No. Save for Mrs. Thornfield, no one in my employ has any family, or anyone to ask after them."

She nodded, and he saw realization in her eyes. She had no family, either. No one to ask questions if she should disappear. The doubt in her eyes was painful to see, yet he could not fault her for her fear. How many times had he warned her that she was not safe in his house? It amazed him that she was strong enough, brave enough, that she loved him enough, to stay when she had seen first hand what a vampire could do.

"You need not be present at the burial, if you'd rather not," he said.

"I want to go," she said. "I need to go."

Putting her on her feet, he gained his own. He went to the wardrobe and withdrew a modest gown of indigo blue and then proceeded to dress her as ably as any lady's maid. When she was properly attired, he brushed her hair, stopping now and then to run his hand over the long, silky length, or to bestow a kiss on the crown of her head.

He knelt at her feet and put on her stockings and her shoes, his hands caressing her calves. His touch

213

sent shivers of desire racing through her. It seemed wrong to feel desire when Sally lay awaiting burial.

"Will they become vampires now?" she asked.

"No."

She looked up at him. "Did you . . . ?" She couldn't say the words, couldn't ask if he had taken the precautions used by country folk to insure that those bitten by vampires did not rise again. She shuddered, remembering some of the images she had seen in one of Alesandro's books.

As always, he knew her thoughts. "There was no need," he assured her.

Rising, he took her hand and drew her to her feet. "Are you ready, 'Lisa?"

Her face paled a little, but she nodded. "Yes."

There was a small family cemetery a short distance behind the barn. The graveyard was perfectly square, enclosed by a wrought-iron fence. Unlike most graveyards, there were no crosses in evidence here, only three headstones. Analisa read the names. *Trevor Gallatin, Beloved Husband and Father. Dorothy Gallatin. Beloved Wife and Mother. Elizabeth Gallatin.* Elizabeth's inscription read, *"She lived and died alone."* Elizabeth's was the most recent date of death: March 27, 1746.

A pair of wooden caskets rested beside two freshly dug graves. She wondered who had built the coffins.

Analisa stood beside Alesandro, her hand in his, as Dewhurst and Farleigh lowered the caskets into the earth. Mrs. Thornfield and Cook stood across from her. The housekeeper's face was solemn, her eyes red-rimmed. Cook's face was pale. There was fear in the eyes of the servants. She noticed a small silver cross on a chain at Cook's throat.

When the bodies had been lowered into the earth, Dewhurst looked at Alesandro. Bowing his head, Dewhurst began to recite the Lord's Prayer.

Analisa closed her eyes, seeking comfort in the words of the prayer. If only she had spoken to Alesandro, begged him to let Sally and Robert marry.

Do not blame yourself, 'Lisa.

Alesandro's voice whispered in her mind. Looking up, she met his gaze.

She wondered, in the dim recesses of her mind, what effect, if any, the prayer had on him. Did he pray? He had told her he had no soul, but she refused to believe that.

When the prayer was over, Mrs. Thornfield and Cook dropped a handful of earth into each of the graves. Farleigh and Dewhurst did the same. Analisa looked at Alesandro, and then she scooped up a handful of earth. It was cold in her hand.

She knelt near Sally's graveside and then, murmuring, "I'm sorry, please forgive me," she dropped the dirt onto the casket. It made a soft, whispery sound she knew she would never forget.

Alesandro moved to her side and helped her to her feet "Come, 'Lisa, let us go back to the house."

She nodded, eager to be away from the cemetery. It could have been her they were burying, she thought. She often walked the gardens at night. She felt guilty for being alive, guilty for not talking to Alesandro before it was too late. He took her hand in his.

Walking away from the graves, she could hear Dewhurst and Farleigh shoveling dirt over the coffins.

She blinked back her tears, wishing she could dig a hole deep enough to bury her guilt.

Chapter Seventeen

The atmosphere in the manor house was subdued that evening. No one felt like eating dinner. Mrs. Thornfield retired to her room early, as did Farleigh and Dewhurst.

Aware of Analisa's distress, Alesandro took her into the library, settled her on the sofa, and covered her with a blanket. He asked Cook to bring her a pot of tea, then dismissed the man for the night.

Analisa refused the tea, but he insisted she drink it, hoping it would help to calm her.

He sat beside her on the high-backed sofa while she sipped her drink, his mind brushing against hers. Her emotions were tangled—love for him, tinged with a hint of fear, a deep loathing for Rodrigo, concern for her own safety, sorrow and guilt for Sally's death.

"You must not blame yourself, 'Lisa," he said quietly. Taking the empty cup from her hand, he placed it on the table, then slid his arm around her shoulders. "There is nothing you could have done."

"I'll miss her."

It occurred to him again that Analisa might be lonely. It was for that reason he had planned to take her to meet her neighbors that ill-fated night. Sally had been the only one on the staff close to Analisa's age, and now she was gone. It had been centuries since he'd had a close friend, years since he had socialized with others. Years since he had spent an idle evening dining and dancing or playing cards with his cronies. More years than he could recall since he had given thought to anything or anyone aside from his own survival.

He looked at Analisa thoughtfully. What right did he have to keep her hidden away from the rest of the world? She was young and beautiful, ignorant of the pleasures of city life. Did she secretly yearn to go out more? To spend time with people her own age? What kind of life was it for her, to spend her days in near solitude, waiting for him? Still, when he had offered to introduce her to society, she had refused to go.

" 'Lisa, are you happy here, with me?"

"Yes, of course. Why do you ask?"

"Are you ever lonely? Bored? Do you miss being around other people?"

She stared at him, a dozen emotions chasing themselves across her face.

"Tell me the truth, 'Lisa, not what you think I want to hear."

She considered her answer carefully. It had been nice, at first, playing lady of the manor, but she was used to working hard from dawn till dark. At home, there had been a cow to milk and pigs to feed, eggs to gather, a garden that was constantly in need of weeding. She had to admit she hadn't liked it much at the time, but it had kept her busy, given her a sense of accomplishment.

"Sometimes I get lonely during the day, when everyone else is busy," she admitted. "But I'm not bored. There are so many books to read, and Mrs. Thornfield has been teaching me proper etiquette, and Sally . . ." She bit down on her lower lip. "I'm going to miss her so!" Tears welled in her eyes, coursed down her cheeks. "Oh, Alesandro! She must have been so afraid!"

He drew her close, stroking her back while she cried out her grief. He murmured to her softly in his native tongue, his heart aching for her hurt, her loss. Hard-hearted creature that he was, the maid's death meant little to him personally. He was sorry she had died so horribly, angry that Rodrigo had dared to harm someone in his employ, but he'd had little interaction with the girl.

"I think I should take you away from here, my sweet one."

She looked up at him, blinking at him through her tears. "Away?"

"I have a small house in the city. I think the change of scene would do you good."

A fortnight later Analisa found herself walking through the fancy front door of a two-story house on the outskirts of London. Alesandro had said it was a small house, but it was small only when compared to Blackbriar Hall. The house had obviously been empty for some time. There were sheets over all the furniture; the air carried the faintly musty smell of disuse.

Mrs. Thornfield immediately began opening the windows. Cook went to look over his new domain. Farleigh stayed outside to see to the horses. Dewhurst moved in and out, carrying their luggage into the house.

Analisa stood in the middle of the parlor. It was a large room, decorated in dark wood. The ceiling was high; floral paper covered the walls; a carpet of deep blue and green covered the floor. There was a large fireplace with an overmantel on one wall, a bookcase and writing desk on another, an empty display cabinet on a third. A high-backed sofa and a pair of matching chairs were situated before the hearth. The walls were bare. She thought it odd that the cabinet was empty, that there were no paintings on the walls.

"Mrs. Thornfield, what shall I do?"

The housekeeper looked at her as if she had just offered to walk naked across Trafalgar Square. "Why, nothing, child. Why don't you go upstairs and have a look at the bedrooms and see which one you prefer?"

Analisa's shoulders slumped. Sometimes she felt so useless. Would it be so wrong if she did a few chores? She was young and healthy, after all. But whenever she offered, Mrs. Thornfield wouldn't hear of it.

"Go along now." The housekeeper made a shooing motion with her hands. "I'll look after things down here. Oh, Cook wants to know what you would like for dinner."

Analisa shrugged. "I don't care. Tell him to surprise me."

"Very well," Mrs. Thornfield said. Hands on hips, she glanced around the room, muttering something about needing to hire some help.

Analisa sighed. Hiring help seemed foolish when she had two good hands and a strong back, but there was no point in arguing.

After removing her hat and placing it on the rack, Analisa went exploring. The kitchen was downstairs, and off limits to all but Cook and his helper, should he hire one. The dining room was across from the drawing room. It was a large, rectangular room. The ceilings were high in here as well, the walls paneled. The table and chairs were of walnut, intricately carved, as were the sideboard and china cabinet, which was empty.

There was also a small breakfast room, similar to the one at Blackbriar. It seemed to be the only room not done in dark wood and fabric.

Going up the stairs, she found three small bedrooms, each with its own sitting room, and a large master bedroom. The next floor held the nursery and the schoolroom, and above that were the servants' quarters.

Going back down to the second floor, she went into the master bedroom. Removing her gloves, she tossed them on the chest of drawers and began plucking the sheets from the furniture. She immediately fell in love with the room. The walls were papered in a soft green and yellow stripe with white trim. The bed had a canopy. There were a dainty dressing table and chair, a matching washstand, a rocking chair beside the window. In the adjoining room were a large wardrobe and a full-length mirror.

A thick green carpet a few shades darker than the spread on the bed muted her footsteps as she dropped the sheets on the chair, then opened the window, which looked out over a small yard. It was a lovely view. There were a large leafy tree, flowers, and a small arbor.

She whirled around at the sound of footsteps, her heart pounding in anticipation even though she knew it was too early for Alesandro to be up and about. And indeed, it was only Dewhurst bringing her luggage.

"Where would you like these, miss?" he asked.

"Just put them there beside the bed."

"Yes, miss. Mrs. Thornfield said to tell you that Cook has prepared a light lunch. It's waiting for you when you're ready."

"Thank you, Dewhurst."

With a nod, he left the room.

The next few hours passed swiftly. She ate lunch,

unpacked her clothes, took a long, leisurely soak, washing away the dust of the journey. And all the while her thoughts were on Alesandro. Where was he now? She knew he was capable of moving rapidly from place to place. He never slept in his rooms at the Hall or the Manor; they were little more than places to keep his clothes.

She glanced around the chamber. Would he expect to occupy this room? It was, after all, the master bedroom, though she could not imagine him staying here. The room was too bright, too cheerful somehow. It made her wonder if he had ever stayed in this house at all. But if not, why did he have it?

Aware of the setting of the sun and the cooling water, she left the tub, dried briskly, and began to dress. First came the chemise which fell almost to her knees, then her stockings, then her drawers. Next came her corset, something she had never worn on the farm. She looked at it a moment, then dropped it on the bed, remembering that Sally was not there to lace it for her. With a sigh, she put on her robe. Sitting at the dressing table, she began to brush out her hair, studying her reflection as she did so. What did Alesandro see when he looked at her? She had never thought of herself as pretty. She had always been too plain, too thin. She leaned forward. She had paid little attention to her looks in the past, but now she studied her face carefully. She had filled out in the months she had been here. There were no hollows in her cheeks, no shadows under her eyes. Her skin was clear, her cheeks rosy. Her hair was thick and had a nice healthy sheen.

"I see a young and beautiful woman when I look at you," came a deep voice from behind her.

With a little cry of joy, she turned to face him. "Alesandro! You're here at last."

"Dare I hope that you missed me?"

"You know I did." Rising, she moved into his arms and rested her cheek against his chest.

"So, where would you like to go on your first night in the city?"

"Wherever you want, Alesandro. It doesn't matter to me, so long as we're together."

"Ah, 'Lisa, you make me weak."

"You, my lord?" she said with a smile. "That you could never be."

It was good to see her smile, good to see the sorrow momentarily gone from her eyes.

"I hope you don't mind that I've taken this room," she said.

"Of course not." He glanced around. The décor was far too feminine for his taste.

"It wasn't your room, then?"

"No. I have never lived in this house."

"Never?"

He shook his head. "I won it in a card game several years ago." He glanced around the room. "This is the first time I have been here."

"Is that why the display cabinet is empty? Why there are no paintings on the walls?"

"Yes. I won the house and the furnishings, but I

allowed Henry and his wife to take their personal effects."

"Are you sure you don't want this chamber? It's the largest one."

He shook his head. "You keep it. I shall take the room that adjoins it."

A faint blush warmed her cheeks at the thought of him having the room next to hers. It seemed so intimate, almost as if they were man and wife.

"So, my sweet," he said, "Lord and Lady Summerfield are hosting a gala tonight. Would you like to attend?"

She looked up at him, her gaze searching his. He wanted to take her out, and although it seemed wrong, with Sally so recently laid to rest, perhaps it would do her good to get out of the house, to think of something else besides Sally and Robert and the vampire who had killed them. She had thought of little else in the past two weeks, cried until she had no tears left.

"Do not think of it now," Alesandro said. "There was nothing you could have done, and I will not have you blaming yourself. If you must blame someone, lay that burden on me, where it belongs."

"It was not your fault, either."

"It pleases me that you do not think so."

"Have you known the Summerfields long?" she asked.

"Indeed," he said. "It was from Lord Summerfield that I won this house."

She looked up at him, laughing softly when she saw

the deviltry in his eyes. It was good to see him smiling, she thought, when he was far too often sober-faced and withdrawn. Perhaps it would do them both good to go out.

"What shall I wear?" she asked.

Going to her wardrobe, Alesandro withdrew a gown of ice-blue silk. It was a beautiful dress, but one she had never had occasion to wear.

She looked at him, waiting for him to leave the room so she could dress. But he only smiled at her.

"You have no maid, so I shall play the part," he said, and then cursed himself for his careless words.

He plucked her corset from the bed, laced up the back after she put it on. She stepped into her crinoline and tied it in place. Her petticoats came next, and then he slipped the silk gown over her head. The material felt sinfully delicious against her skin. The neckline was scandalously low, revealing a good deal of décolletage; the sleeves were slightly puffed at the shoulders, tapering down to her wrists, the skirt full over a modest bustle adorned with pink and white silk flowers. Kneeling, he placed her shoes on her feet.

"Will you do my hair, too?" she asked.

"Leave it down."

"As you wish, my lord."

"You look beautiful, 'Lisa."

"As do you, my lord Alesandro."

He lifted a brow at her. "Beautiful?"

"Yes, beautiful." And elegant, she thought. She had never seen a man to equal him. He wore a double-breasted tailcoat of fine black wool, a white shirt with a ruffled front, a black silk waistcoat embroidered with tiny black fleur-de-lis, a black bow tie, and black boots. Tall, dark, and dangerous.

He had never been a vain man but he smiled now, seeing himself through her eyes. She thought him elegant, did she? And dangerous. He couldn't deny that.

"Are you ready, my sweet?"

"Just let me get my gloves, and my bag." She plucked a pair of long white gloves from the dresser, along with a small silk purse that matched her gown. "Ready, my lord."

The home of Lord and Lady Summerfield was located in the fashionable heart of the city. Colorful lanterns lit the driveway; a liveried servant helped Analisa alight from the carriage. Taking Alesandro's arm, she walked with him up the winding drive to the house. Alesandro had planned it so they would arrive after dinner, so they were the last to enter. A servant took Analisa's wrap, and they went into the ballroom.

She paused inside the doorway. It was the first time she had ever been to such a soiree. An orchestra was playing a waltz and couples twirled around the floor, the men in sober black, the women like colorful butterflies. Servants moved among the guests who sat on the sidelines, offering drinks and dainty desserts.

"That is our host," Alesandro said, gesturing at a gray-haired man of medium height. "And that is his wife, Lady Summerfield." He pointed to a tall, angular woman who wore a dress that was a most hideous shade of yellow. "Come," he said, taking her by the hand. "Dance with me."

Alesandro waltzed her around the room, aware of the many masculine eyes that followed their progress. Analisa stood out like a rare diamond in a handful of fake gems. Her cheeks were flushed, her eyes glowed with excitement. He knew there wasn't a man present who didn't envy him; indeed, half a dozen unattached young men were lined up before the waltz ended, vying for the next dance.

Analisa looked up at him, confused. "Go," he said. "Enjoy yourself."

"But—"

"Go." He smiled as he placed her hand in that of the first young man.

"You won't leave me?"

"No."

Alesandro stood in the shadows, watching one man after another claim her for a dance. He heard the gossip around him as the matrons put their heads together, wondering who she was and why they hadn't seen her before. It was whispered that she was the daughter of a duchess, that she was a French courtesan, an actress from America, the bastard daughter of Lord Summerfield himself.

At the end of an hour, he cut in on her current partner and claimed her for himself.

Analisa smiled up at him, her cheeks flushed.

"You are the belle of the ball, my sweet," he said. "As I knew you would be."

"I don't know why they all want to dance with me. I don't even know most of the dances."

But he knew why. There was a freshness about her, an innocence that was sadly lacking in most of the other young ladies. There were worried looks on the faces of the matrons as they realized that there might be a new entry in the marriage market.

He kept her close for the next half hour before relinquishing her again. Fading into the shadows, he listened to gossip about himself while he watched 'Lisa move through the figures of a lengthy quadrille. For all that he was rarely seen in the city, his name was well known. People assumed he was the heir to the last Lord of Blackbriar Hall. Because he never aged, he was forced to leave Blackbriar every so often, returning as the son of the Hall's last occupant. It was a tiresome charade, but necessary.

He claimed her for the last waltz. Her cheeks were rosy, her eyes sparkling, as he whirled her around the floor, and he drew her closer, suddenly jealous of all the other men who had held her that night. He could smell them on her. He wrinkled his nose with distaste, wondering what madness had possessed him to bring her here in the first place.

A short time later, they bade farewell to their host. Alesandro was glad to have her alone in the carriage.

"Did you have a good time, 'Lisa?" he asked.

"Oh, yes! It was wonderful. Thank you, Alesandro."

He had been wanting to kiss her all night, and now, seeing her sitting there, her face flushed with happiness, her eyes glowing with excitement, he could resist the urge no longer. Sweeping her into his arms, he claimed her lips with his.

She yielded to him with a sigh, her eyelids fluttering down, her hand coming to rest against his chest, her fingers curling around his lapel as he deepened the kiss. She tasted of sweet tarts and champagne, the tastes alien on his tongue after so many years.

She moaned softly, her body moving against his, seeking to be closer—no easy task with the whalebone crinoline that seemed to take up half of the carriage.

Annoyed by that bit of feminine foolishness, Alesandro reached under her skirt, unfastened the ties at her waist, and yanked the thing off. The frame was collapsible, and he dropped it on the floor, then drew Analisa onto his lap.

"Thank you, my lord." She grinned at him, then wrapped her arms around his neck and kissed him.

Her tongue played over his lower lip, driving him to distraction as he lifted her skirts.

She laughed softly. "Alesandro, what are you doing?"

"Only what you want me to do."

"In here?" She glanced at the carriage's close quarters. "Is there room?"

"We will make room." His eyes flashed in the darkness. She felt his hands moving over her, rearranging her clothing, and then his own.

Miraculously, there was indeed room enough.

* * *

When they reached home, he carried her into the house and up the stairs to her room. She was asleep by then, a faint smile lingering on her lips. A smile he had put there. The thought pleased him greatly.

He laid her gently on the bed, undressed her, and settled her under the covers. He gazed down at her. In four hundred years, he had never seen anything more lovely, more desirable. It was beyond his comprehension that she loved him, that she willingly satisfied not only his hunger for blood, but for her sweet flesh as well. He had not known love in four hundred years. How had he survived without it? In a matter of a few months, she had become his sole reason for existence. How would he find the strength to go on if she left him? If she died?

He thrust the disquieting thought from his mind. She was young and healthy.

She ages every day while you do not.

He tried to drive that thought from his mind as well, but he could not shake it off. She might live to be forty or fifty, even sixty, but it would not be long enough. A few short mortal years, and he would be alone again. Unless . . .

His gaze slid over her neck, to the pulse beating slow and regular in the hollow of her throat. So easy to bring her across. So easy to make her his forever.

He imagined what it would be like, falling asleep with her in his arms as the sun chased the night from the sky, kissing her with his first breath at dusk. Having someone to share his existence. Someone to hunt with, someone who would understand the hunger that drove him, the guilt, the need.

Analisa.

It was a beautiful dream, but one that could never come true. He loved her far too much to condemn her to the dark half-life he led, to deprive her of the freedom to enjoy the sun, the opportunity to bear children, to live a normal life with a mortal man. How could he bring her across and subject her to the relentless hunger, the darkness of spirit, that had plagued him for centuries?

Bending, he brushed a kiss across her cheek.

"Sweet dreams, my 'Lisa," he whispered, and went to seek his lonely bed.

Chapter Eighteen

Rodrigo stormed through the night, his anger rising like the devil wind that sent his cloak billowing behind him. A string of foul oaths trailed in his wake. Gone! Alesandro was gone. He had not expected Alesandro to run. In four hundred years of conflict, despite the fact that Rodrigo possessed the greater strength, his enemy had stood his ground.

He streaked through the night unseen, his malevolence a force unto itself. Mortals who crossed his path were destroyed without a qualm, their throats torn out, their life's blood tasting like bitter bile on his tongue.

His hatred, his implacable need for vengeance, had been the driving force in his life for over four hundred years. It had given his existence meaning. He could have killed the other vampire years ago, but that would have been too quick, too easy. He had tormented Alesandro instead, knowing that the good doctor suffered greatly each time he arrived too late to save a life.

With the patience of a wild cat stalking its prey, Rodrigo had waited, knowing that, sooner or later, the perfect means by which to take his revenge would arrive. And now she was here. The woman, Analisa. She was what Rodrigo had been waiting for. For the first time in four centuries, Alesandro had found love. To take the woman from Alesandro, to destroy her as Alesandro had destroyed Serafina . . . Rodrigo took a deep breath. To inflict pain on the woman would hurt the vampire far more than merely taking his life.

He would find Alesandro again. No matter how long it took.

His hand closed around the throat of his third victim. Unlike the man fighting for his life, time was one thing Rodrigo had plenty of.

Chapter Nineteen

"A visitor?" Analisa looked up from her needlepoint in surprise. "Who would be coming to see me?"

"A young man," Mrs. Thornfield answered, handing her a small ivory-colored card.

"Mr. Geoffrey Starke," Analisa said, reading the name aloud. The name was vaguely familiar, but she couldn't recall where she had heard it before. "What does he want?"

"He's come calling," Mrs. Thornfield said. "He's waiting in the parlor."

Geoffrey Starke? Analisa frowned, and then it came to her. She had danced with him last night. Of all the young men who had partnered her, he had been the most persistent, claiming two waltzes and a quadrille. A fourth dance would have been a breach of etiquette.

"Miss?"

Analisa stared at the housekeeper, her thoughts befuddled. Never before had she entertained a gentleman caller, especially a member of Mr. Starke's class. "What should I do?"

"Why, you must make him feel welcome, of course," Mrs. Thornfield said. "I'll bring tea and some of the sweet cakes Cook baked this morning."

"What will I say to him?" Analisa asked, getting more flustered by the moment.

"If he's like most young men, you'll not need to say much," Mrs. Thornfield replied with a rare grin. "All you'll need do is nod from time to time."

Analisa slipped the card into her skirt pocket. "Couldn't I just send him away?"

"If you wish."

"What do you think I should do?"

"I think you should see him. He seems a pleasant fellow. It will do you good to make some friends in the city."

"Oh, very well. Do I look all right?"

Mrs. Thornfield looked her over carefully, then nodded. "You'll do. And don't worry, social etiquette dictates that his call will be brief."

Taking a deep breath, Analisa smoothed her hands over her skirt, patted her hair, then made her way toward the parlor. Outside the door, she took a deep, calming breath. Mr. Geoffrey Starke didn't know she was just a poor country girl with no home and no family of her own. And there was no need for him to know. Lifting her chin, she opened the door.

Geoffrey Starke stood as she entered the room. He was of medium height, with wavy brown hair, hazel eyes, and a fine straight nose. Clad in a crisp white shirt, buff-colored trousers and a matching coat, and carrying his hat and riding whip in one hand, he looked quite dapper. And quite handsome. Of all the young men she had danced with the night before, he had been the one she favored the most.

"Miss Matthews." He bowed over her hand. "I hope you don't mind my calling without an appointment."

"No." She withdrew her hand from his. "Sit down, please." She took a seat on the sofa, indicating he should take the chair.

"Thank you."

"I must admit, I was quite surprised when Mrs. Thornfield gave me your card."

"I hope the surprise was a favorable one," he said, smiling.

He had a ready smile. And a dimple in his left cheek.

They spoke of the weather, of the dance the previous night, of the masquerade ball Geoffrey was hosting the following week.

"The invitations have already gone out," he said, "which is why I came to call on you today." Reaching into his pocket, he withdrew an envelope and handed it to her. "I was hoping I could persuade you to attend. I know it's rather short notice, but . . ." He shrugged. "May I hope to see you there?"

"I'm not sure." She looked down at the envelope,

addressed to her in a bold hand, then placed it on the table beside the sofa. "I'll have to ask—"

"Of course. The gentleman who was with you at the ball, is he your guardian?"

Analisa was trying to decide how to answer that when Mrs. Thornfield entered the room. She served them tea and cakes, smiled reassuringly at Analisa, then left the room.

Mrs. Thornfield had spoken true. Analisa did not have to think of anything clever or witty to say. Mr. Starke dominated the conversation, telling her of his sister's upcoming wedding, the thoroughbred mare he had recently purchased from America.

Analisa had expected to feel ill at ease in his company, but, to her surprise, she was quite charmed by his quick smile and mild manner.

Half an hour later, Mr. Starke stood to take his leave. At the door, he took her hand in his. "I hope I may call on you again."

Flustered, she smiled politely and said that would be agreeable.

Returning to the parlor, Analisa sank down on the sofa. What would Alesandro say when he learned she'd had a gentleman caller? Would he be angry? Jealous? She didn't think he would be pleased.

She opened the envelope she had dropped on the table and withdrew the handwritten invitation. She read it once, then read it again:

Mr. Geoffrey Starke requests the pleasure
of Miss Analisa Matthew's company

Midnight Embrace

at an Evening Masquerade Ball
on Friday, April 8th.
An answer will oblige.
Dancing.

She felt a flutter of excitement. It was the first time in her life she had ever been invited anywhere. It had been such fun last night, being the center of attention, being flattered by handsome, well-dressed young men. She had not for a moment believed their flattering words, but they had been pleasant to hear nevertheless.

Leaving the invitation on the table beside the sofa, she went upstairs to dress for dinner.

A stranger had been in the house. Alesandro caught the man's lingering scent as soon as he entered the dwelling. He took a deep breath, his eyes narrowing. Geoffrey Starke. He did not have to wonder what the man had been doing there. He had seen the way Starke had looked at Analisa the night before, the way the man's eyes had followed her every move.

He fought down the jealousy that engulfed him. Whether he approved or not, Analisa had every right to have visitors. Once, he would have encouraged it. Once, he had thought to keep her with him only a short time, and then find her a husband. The idea no longer held any appeal. He could not abide the thought of her spending time with another man, smiling at someone else. Loving someone else. Once, he had told her they could not have a life together; now he could not imagine his existence without her.

She had said she was in love with him, but was she really? She had never known another man ... He closed his eyes, his hands clenching into tight fists at his sides. If she decided she wanted to marry a mortal man and raise a family, he would not stand in her way.

"Alesandro?"

He opened his eyes to find her regarding him curiously.

"Are you all right?" she asked, moving across the floor toward him.

He nodded. She was more beautiful each time he saw her, he mused, or perhaps it was only that he loved her more each day.

Rising on tiptoes, she kissed his cheek. It wasn't enough. Wrapping one arm around her waist, he drew her against him and claimed her lips with his. He kissed her hungrily, more forcefully than he intended, wanting to wipe the thought of any other man from her mind and heart.

She gasped when he released her, her gaze searching his. "What is it? What's wrong?"

"You had a visitor today."

She nodded, a guilty flush staining her cheeks. "Yes, Mr. Starke."

"Did you invite him here?"

She shook her head vigorously. "No, of course not."

"What did he want?"

"He invited me to a masquerade ball."

"And did you accept?"

"No. I said I would have to ask you."

He loosened his hold on her waist, suddenly ashamed. He was questioning her as if she belonged to him, as if he had every right to demand an accounting of her time, her actions.

"You need not ask my permission, 'Lisa. You are not a prisoner in this house. I am not your guardian."

"But . . ." She looked confused, and then hurt. "We . . . I thought . . ."

She looked away, but not before he saw the tears in her eyes. Feeling like a cad, he pulled her into his arms.

She buried her face against his chest. "You said you loved me," she said, her voice muffled.

"I do love you, 'Lisa. More than you can imagine." He ran his hand over her hair. "But you deserve to have a life of your own. Perhaps I should go away for a while and give you a chance to mingle with people your own age."

"No!" She looked up at him. "I don't want you to go. Please, Alesandro. I love you."

"Have you ever been courted, 'Lisa? Ever had a beau?"

"No."

"I would not deprive you of your youth." It was bad enough that he had stolen her innocence. "You should go to dances and parties, make friends, do all the things young women do before they settle down."

"You're trying to send me away again, aren't you? Like before. You're going to tell me this is for my own good, aren't you? Aren't you?"

"Analisa, listen to me. I just want you to be sure

that this"—he made a gesture that encompassed himself and the house—"is what you want. I do not want you to be sorry later, or feel that you have missed out on something that could have been yours. Think about it carefully, before it is too late. Think about what you will be giving up if you stay with me. Will you be happy with someone who can share but half of your life? Someone who cannot give you children. Someone who is no longer mortal. Perhaps not even human."

She stared up at him, her eyes wide, and he knew that, for the first time, she was seriously considering the consequences of being with him, loving him. It was no small decision.

"But I love you," she whispered.

"Have you ever been in love before?"

"No."

He swore under his breath, unable to believe what he was about to say. "Then I suggest you do as I said. Go out and meet people your own age. Find out if what you feel for me is truly love, or merely gratitude."

She looked up at him for a long moment, her eyes again reflecting her hurt and confusion, and then she nodded. "Very well, my lord, if that is what you wish."

Alesandro paced the floor of his study long after Analisa had retired for the night, wondering what perverse imp had taken over his tongue and mind that he should tell 'Lisa to go out and meet other men. He had never intended to fall in love with her. Never intended she should stay with him for more than a short time. He knew what he was, knew what atrocities he was capable of committing. He had never been one to lie to himself, to try to paint himself as anything but what he was: a hunter, a predator. A killer. He had done many things of which he was ashamed in order to survive. Despicable things. Cruel, evil things that weighed heavily on what was left of his conscience. He had never made excuses for himself, or for what he had done in the past. But wanting Analisa, wanting to keep her here, to share his wretched existence, was perhaps the worst sin of all. The least he could do was give her the chance to decide for herself, to make sure she wanted to stay here, with him. And she must be sure, for once she was truly his, nothing but death would take her from him.

Caught up in a maelstrom of emotions the likes of which he had not suffered in more years than he could recall, he willed himself out of the house and into the heart of the city. There were hours yet till dawn. Hours in which to torment himself.

He walked the quiet streets, gazing up at the darkened houses he passed, imagining the families inside, ordinary people living ordinary lives, worrying about finding enough food to eat, fuel to burn, raising children, always overshadowed by the specter of disease and certain death. How did they bear it? He had long ago forgotten what it was like to be weighed down by mortal worries, to be concerned about anything other than having a safe haven where he could spend the deadly hours of daylight, and the means to ease his insatiable craving.

He moved silently over the cobblestones, drifting like smoke through the darkness. Driven by his hunger, he left the residential area behind, his instincts taking him down a rabbit warren of dark streets until he came to a narrow alley where he found a tart plying her trade.

She looked at him over her trick's shoulder. "Be right with you, Your Lordship," she said with a wink.

Alesandro nodded. He could wait. If there was one thing he had in abundance, it was time.

Analisa sat at her bedroom window, staring out into the darkness. Alesandro had left the house. She had not seen him go, but she knew he was gone. His absence caused a sense of loss deep within her, as if a part of her soul had been cut out, leaving a great, gaping hole.

He wanted her to go out, to see other people. Other men. She knew he was offering her a way out, giving her a chance to make sure that what she felt for him was real and not girlish infatuation or gratitude. He was being noble, and it was making her angry, partly because he seemed so willing to let her go, and partly because, in spite of everything, she couldn't help having second thoughts from time to time.

He had been honest with her almost from the beginning. He was a vampire. He needed blood to survive. He was, in his own words, a predator, a killer. She thought perhaps she could learn to live with all that. But there were other aspects she had never dwelled upon. Like the fact that she would grow old and he would not. Her skin would wrinkle, her hair would turn gray, her body would grow old and weak, while he stayed forever young, strong and vibrant. If she stayed with him, could she bear it when she began to grow old and he did not? Would the love she felt for him turn to envy and then hatred when she peered into her looking glass and saw an old woman staring back at her? And what of Alesandro? How would he feel when she was no longer young? Would he grow to hate her? Pity her? Abandon her?

Alesandro, Alesandro, where are you? Where had he gone? To feed? It hurt that he had not come to her, as he usually did. Couldn't he see that what he was asking of her was going to cause a gulf between them? That it already had?

She slammed her fist down on the windowsill, her hurt turning to anger. If he wanted her to meet other men, then she would! She would show him! She would have men lining up outside the house, waiting to meet her. She would have so many men wanting to court her, she would have to turn them away in droves. She would marry the first rich man who asked her and have a dozen children and . . .

She dashed the tears from her eyes. She didn't want anyone else. She wanted Alesandro.

And she meant to have him.

Chapter Twenty

Analisa had Farleigh take her into the city the following day and spent the afternoon in a shopping spree the likes of which she had never imagined. She bought dozens of new dresses in every style and color available, as well as shoes, gloves, and hats to match. She bought ball gowns in deep blue silk and rich red velvet. She bought delicate undergarments and stockings. She bought a new nightgown that was no more than a whisper of lace and silk. She was fitted for a costume for Mr. Starke's masquerade. She bought anything and everything that caught her fancy, and charged it all to Alesandro.

It was near dusk when she returned to the house. Hurrying upstairs, she washed her hands and face, then dressed in a fine gray wool trimmed in ermine.

Sitting in front of her dressing table, she brushed her hair, thinking she would have to hire a new maid soon. She would have to speak to Mrs. Thornfield about it.

Though she had no appetite, she forced herself to eat a hearty supper, knowing that if she didn't eat, Mrs. Thornfield would tell Alesandro. He mustn't think she was unhappy about his decision.

She was sitting in the parlor, her feet curled beneath her, a book in her lap, when Alesandro entered the room.

He stood in the doorway a moment, his gaze moving over her. The light of the fire played over her face, casting her in a warm, golden glow. Her hair fell down her back and over her shoulders in waves of black silk, tempting his touch, but he stayed his hand, afraid that if he touched her he would drag her into his arms and ravish her there, on the floor, in front of the hearth.

He moved into the room, a wry smile touching his lips when he saw she was reading a book on vampire lore.

"Are you learning anything you did not already know?" he asked.

She looked up at him slowly, making him think she had been aware of his presence all along.

"Some of it sounds like nonsense to me." She looked down at the book. "Like this, where it says that if you surround a vampire with seeds, he'll have to stop and count them. What kind of foolishness is that?" She shook her head. "And this: 'One method of destroying a vampire is to steal his left sock, which must be filled with grave dirt and thrown out of the village in the direction of a river.' "

"Maybe it works," he said, fighting the uncommon urge to laugh out loud as he sat down on the other end of the sofa.

She made a face at him. "According to this book, a person might become a vampire if he is conceived on a holy day, or weaned too early, or if he eats a sheep that was killed by a wolf. Or you might become a vampire if a cat jumps over your corpse, or you're murdered and your death goes unavenged, or if your brother is a sleepwalker."

She shook her head again. "Are any of those things true?"

"No, Analisa. There is only one way to be made a vampire, and that is by another vampire."

"Does it hurt?"

He stared at her, flabbergasted by the question.

"The book says that to prevent someone rising from the dead you should cut off the head of the deceased and bury it in a separate grave."

"That would certainly do it," he muttered, still distracted by her earlier question. He told himself it had been based on curiosity, nothing more. There was no reason to think otherwise. Still, it troubled him.

"So," she said, putting the book aside. "Are you going to attend Mr. Starke's masquerade with me?"

"Of course. Unless you wish for Mrs. Thornfield to attend you. You are an unmarried woman. As such, you need a chaperone."

"Will you go in costume?"

"Perhaps. What are you wearing?"

"I thought I'd go as a biblical character," she said just to provoke him. "Delilah, perhaps, or maybe Salome."

Alesandro stared at her, his mind filling with images of Analisa clad in seven diaphanous veils, her thick black hair falling in wild disarray over her slender shoulders.

"Salome?" he asked, his voice suddenly thick.

Analisa nodded. "And you could go as King Herod. What do you think?"

He thought he would lock her in her room before he would let her out of the house in such provocative attire.

"I think you had best consider wearing something else."

"Oh?" she asked innocently. "Why?"

His eyes narrowed thoughtfully. Was she teasing him? What if he called her bluff? What if she was serious?

He was still trying to think of a suitable reply when she burst out laughing. "Oh, Alesandro, I wish you could see your face!"

He grunted softly. It was a common expression, spoken without thought, but it only served to emphasize, once again, the vast gulf between them.

Analisa's laughter stilled abruptly. "I'm sorry, Alesandro. I never should have said that."

He shrugged, as if it were of no consequence. He had not seen his reflection in four hundred years. It was the reason he'd had his portraits painted, so he could recall what he looked like. The artist had thought it odd when Alesandro had asked that the pool and the mirror reflect the head of a wolf instead of his own face.

Leaning forward, Analisa cupped his cheek. "It's such a strong, handsome face," she said quietly. "Such a fine straight nose," she went on, running the tip of her forefinger down its length. "A firm jaw," she said, stroking it lightly, "with just a touch of arrogance."

He lifted one brow, his whole body tingling at the touch of her hand.

"You know it's true."

He supposed she was right. He was arrogant. And stubborn. And selfish, or she would not be here.

His gaze caught and held hers. He heard the sudden increase in her heartbeat as the tension between them heightened, grew palpable. She was remembering the nights she had spent in his arms as clearly as he was. Remembering. And wanting.

" 'Lisa."

She moved toward him, drawn by his voice, the power in his eyes, her own desires.

His hands curled around her waist, lifting her effortlessly onto his lap. She stared up at him, her eyes cloudy with passion as he lowered his head, his lips claiming hers. Her arms twined around his neck, drawing him closer. As always, he was conscious of her warmth, her softness, the sweet scent of her blood, the flowery fragrance that clung to her hair and skin. She was perfection in the guise of woman, light to his darkness, goodness to the evil that lay dormant within him. An answer to the hunger that was never far from him.

He had sought nourishment elsewhere during the past few days, determined to put distance between them, to give her the chance to be sure that staying with him was what she wanted.

He rained kisses on her eyelids, her cheeks; his tongue stroked the sensitive skin behind her ear, his lips slowly drifting down her neck. She moaned softly. It was a sound filled with pleasure, a wordless entreaty for more of the same.

Desire and hunger stirred within him, urging him on, tempting him to ease her down on the sofa. She could satisfy all his hungers, leave him drowning in ecstasy even as she sated his hellish thirst.

Exerting his considerable self-control, he released her and drew back, his hands clenched at his sides.

She blinked at him, her lips parted and slightly swollen, her cheeks flushed. She was beautiful, so beautiful. What would he do if she decided to leave him, if she fell in love with some handsome young rake who could give her everything she deserved?

He feared that even his monumental self-control would not be strong enough to keep him from killing any man who dared lay hands on her. What misplaced sense of honor, what foolishness, had made him think he needed to give her a chance to meet other men? He was not noble or kind. He was a vampire, a creature who obeyed no laws of land or society but his own. And he wanted this woman as no other.

"Alesandro, is something wrong?"

He had stolen her virginity, yet she was still an innocent, as lovely as a night-blooming flower, without guile or deceit. Reining in his jealousy, he smiled at her.

"No, my sweet Analisa, all is well. We will attend Starke's masquerade, and any other entertainments you wish. And I will dress as Herod or Lucifer or a court jester, whatever pleases you."

She laughed softly. "A court jester, Alesandro?"

It was a costume well suited to him, he thought ruefully, for where Analisa was concerned, he was truly a fool.

The next five nights tested the limits of Alesandro's patience. Each day saw the arrival of a new suitor—sometimes two or three in one day. It seemed as though every young man she had danced with at the ball wanted to court her. Invitations arrived each day for parties later in the season.

Analisa spoke candidly of the men who came to call—this one was boring, that one was quite full of himself, another was rather crude, yet another too frivolous. But not all were dismissed out of hand. Mr. Huntington wrote her poetry. Mr. Wharton sent her a book of sonnets. Mr. Gray took her horseback riding. Mr. Starke took her for long walks in the garden, regaling her with tales of his recent voyage to India. It was obvious she quite preferred Mr. Geoffrey Starke over all the others. According to Analisa, he was the most handsome, polite, entertaining, witty, educated, and charming.

All the things he was not, Alesandro thought bleakly as he made his way into the parlor where Analisa was sitting in front of the fire, her head bent over a piece of embroidery. As always, he was captivated by her beauty, drawn by her warmth.

When she looked up at him and smiled, he felt his heart expand until he thought it might explode. Impossible as it seemed, he loved her more every day, or perhaps it was only the thought of losing her that made every moment, every smile, seem more precious.

"Alesandro," she said.

" 'Lisa." He moved toward her, feeling like a callow youth, his emotions in turmoil.

She put her needlework aside, her gaze settling on his face. "Where do you go now, to . . . to . . . you know."

Her question took him by surprise, but then, she had been doing that often of late.

"Alesandro?"

"Why do you ask?"

"Because—" her gaze slid away from his—"because I don't like thinking of you going to someone else."

He stared at her bowed head, unable to speak, unable to believe what he was hearing.

"Have you found someone else?"

" 'Lisa!"

She looked up at him. "Have you?"

"No, 'Lisa, there is no one else."

"Then I don't please you anymore?"

Dropping to one knee in front of her, he took her hands in his. Warm hands, soft, smooth. For a moment, he closed his eyes, remembering the touch of her hands moving over his skin. Thrusting the memory aside, he lifted one hand and kissed her palm.

"Everything about you pleases me, my sweet Analisa. The color of your hair, the sound of your laughter, the warmth of your smile, the touch of your body against mine, the taste of your skin . . ."

"Oh, Alesandro," she murmured. "That's so . . . so poetic."

"No woman I have ever known has pleased me as much as you do, in as many ways as you do."

"I still love you, Alesandro. Do you still love me?"

"You know I do."

"But you're still determined I should see other men?"

He fought down the jealousy that surged within him. He had wanted her to meet other people her age; he had not expected such an overwhelming response. Men swarmed around her like bees around a flower. Why hadn't he foreseen such a possibility? She was young and beautiful, with a sense of artlessness that set her apart from other women. She was innocent in the art of coquetry and guile.

"Alesandro?"

"Yes." The word was torn from his throat, and even as he uttered it, he wondered why he was trying to be noble when every instinct he possessed urged him to take her back to Blackbriar and hide her away from the rest of the world. And always, in the back of his mind, the thought of Rodrigo overshadowed everything else. Rodrigo, whose thirst for vengeance had endured for four hundred years. Rodrigo, whose hatred grew ever stronger. The other vampire would never stop looking for him, never rest until one of them had been destroyed. Rodrigo, who would like nothing better than to kill Analisa and, in so doing, bring his enemy to his knees once and for all.

As much as Alesandro yearned to keep Analisa for his own, he doubted his ability to protect her from the ruthless creature Rodrigo had become. Sally's image filled his mind, her throat ripped out, her dead eyes reflecting the sheer terror that had possessed her at the moment of death. The thought of Rodrigo finding Analisa, killing her as he had killed Sally, filled him with raw terror.

Analisa took a deep breath. "The masquerade is tomorrow night, my lord."

"I have not forgotten."

"Have you a costume?"

He nodded. Releasing her hands, he stood. "I bid you good night until tomorrow."

Chapter Twenty-one

The next afternoon, Mrs. Thornfield approached Analisa in the parlor. "I've found a girl who I think might suit as your maid," the housekeeper said. "Would you care to meet her?"

Analisa nodded, though a new maid was the furthest thing from her mind.

Moments later, Mrs. Thornfield ushered a short, plump young woman clad in a plain gray dress into the parlor. She had brown hair tucked under a lace-trimmed cap, light brown eyes, and a nose that was slightly crooked.

The girl made a graceful curtsey. "Good afternoon, miss."

"Good afternoon." Analisa looked at Mrs. Thornfield, wondering what was expected of her. She had never hired help before.

Mrs. Thornfield smiled encouragingly. "This is Frannie Smythe. She's ten and seven, and was recently employed as Lady Heywood's maid."

"How long were you employed by Lady Heywood?"

"Five months."

"Why did you leave her?" Analisa asked.

Frannie clasped her hands together. "I was let go. I could never please her."

Analisa nodded. She had met Lady Heywood at the ball she had attended with Alesandro and had had the misfortune to sit beside the lady for a few moments. The woman had complained of everything. The room was too hot. The music was too loud. The wine was too bitter.

"I think you'll do fine," Analisa decided. "How soon can you start?"

"As soon as you wish," Frannie replied with an eager smile. "Right now, if you like."

Analisa returned her smile. "That would be wonderful. I'm to attend a masquerade ball tonight. Please attend me at seven. Mrs. Thornfield will show you to your room."

"Thank you, miss." Frannie curtsied and then, beaming, followed the housekeeper from the room.

Analisa sat at her dressing table while Frannie brushed her hair. The girl had a nice, gentle touch.

She had helped Analisa into her costume, and seemed competent if a little nervous, but that was to be expected. Analisa thought they would get on well together once they got to know each other.

When Analisa's hair gleamed like spun silk, Frannie laid the brush aside. Rising, Analisa studied her reflection in the full-length mirror, wondering what Alesandro would think.

"Thank you, Frannie, that will be all."

"Shall I wait up for you, miss?"

"No, that won't be necessary."

"Very well, miss. Good night." Bobbing a curtsey, the maid left the room.

With a last glance at her reflection, Analisa went downstairs, wondering if Alesandro had arrived.

He paced the parlor floor, wondering how he would get though the night to come, wondering how he would abide watching Analisa dance with one man after another. This was the last time he would play the role of chaperone. In the future, Mrs. Thornfield could accompany 'Lisa.

He turned toward the stairs, scenting her presence, his body tightening as he waited.

She appeared at the head of the staircase, a faint smile curving her lips as she moved toward him. She seemed to float as she descended the steps. He grinned inwardly as his gaze moved over her costume. Apparently she had taken his words to heart. It was no siren coming down the stairs. Quite the opposite. She was clothed as an angel in a long white gown that floated around her like a cloud. A golden halo sat atop her thick black hair. Lacy wings fluttered with each movement she made.

She paused at the bottom of the stairs and struck a pose. "Do you approve, my lord?" she asked.

He felt a sharp pang in the region of his heart. Since his decision that she should make the acquaintance of other men, she rarely called him by name.

"It was to be a masquerade," he said. "And yet we have both chosen costumes that reflect what we really are."

Her gaze took in his costume. "Are you a devil, then, my lord?"

"Do you doubt it, my angel?"

She took her cloak from the hall tree where Frannie had left it for her. "It doesn't matter what I think," she answered as he took her cloak from her hand and placed it over her shoulders. "Is that how you see yourself?"

"A devil is the nicest thing I am," he replied. "Shall we go?"

The home of Mr. Geoffrey Starke was set amidst a vast green expanse of carefully manicured lawn. Gaily colored lanterns lined the broad, winding road to the house. Lights glowed in every window; the strains of a waltz floated on the night air.

Analisa felt a flutter of excitement as she tied her mask in place, then stepped out of the carriage. She had been a stranger at the last function she had attended; here, she would be welcomed as a friend of the host.

Alesandro offered her his arm and they entered the house. A maid took Analisa's cloak. The house was filled with music and laughter. Clowns mingled with kings and queens, a horse danced with a ballerina, Cleopatra danced with Cupid, Hercules stood in a corner, whispering in the ear of a plump lady in a medieval gown. A flame-haired Gypsy hung on the arm of a monk, a harem girl shared a glass of champagne with a Cossack.

The ballroom was ablaze with light. Benches covered in rich red velvet lined the dance floor. Musicians stood on a dais at the far end of the room. Servants in crisp black and white moved among the guests, offering champagne and sweetmeats.

Analisa looked up at Alesandro. "Will you dance, my lord?"

With a nod, he swept her into his arms and out onto the floor. Perhaps she really was an angel, he mused, because holding her was like holding a piece of heaven in his arms. Her hand rested in his, small and trusting. Candlelight shimmered in the wealth of her hair. He had fed earlier, but her nearness stirred his hunger even as it stirred his desire. Time and again, his gaze was drawn to the gentle curve of her throat, to the pulse beating there. Each beat of her heart called to him, reminding him of her sweetness. No other satisfied his hunger as she did. No other filled his heart with such aching tenderness, his soul with such peace. Analisa.

She looked up at him as though he had spoken her name aloud, a tentative smile curving her lips.

"I love dancing with you," she murmured.

"And I with you," he replied, and then scowled as he glanced over her shoulder.

"You look troubled, my lord. Is something amiss?"

"Young Geoffrey comes to claim you."

The ill-disguised jealousy in his voice pleased her beyond measure. He had been distant these past few days, making her wonder if he had stopped caring for her. But the look in his eye, the jealousy in his voice, proved otherwise. Perhaps she would tweak his possessiveness just a bit.

She smiled at Mr. Starke as he cut in.

With a curt bow, Alesandro surrendered her to the other man.

"I'm so glad you were able to make it," Geoffrey said as he took her in his arms.

"Thank you. Your home is lovely."

He nodded. "I can't take credit for it. My late mother took care of decorating it."

"She had excellent taste."

"Indeed." He smiled at her, his eyes filled with admiration. "Your costume suits you."

"But didn't fool you."

"No." He caught up a lock of her hair, let it run through his fingers. "I'm afraid this gave you away."

"I guess I should have worn a wig."

He shook his head. "It would be a sin indeed to cover such beauty."

"You are too kind, Mr. Starke."

"Geoffrey," he said. "I would be pleased if you would call me by my given name."

"Perhaps," she said, "when I know you better."

He laughed softly. "An occasion I shall look forward to."

The next hour passed swiftly, and not the way she had planned. She had hoped to make Alesandro jealous; instead, she found herself caught in her own trap, watching in silent fury as he danced with one woman after another, twirling them effortlessly around the floor, holding them far too close to please her. She was so intent on watching him, she paid little attention to her partners, hardly aware of who they were or what they said.

And then, to her dismay, she lost sight of him. She was about to go in search of him when a tall man clad in the costume of a white knight appeared before her. A silver helmet covered his head; there were leather gauntlets on his hands.

"May I have this dance?"

She started to refuse and then thought better of it. If Alesandro didn't want her, then she didn't want him, either.

She forced herself to smile at the knight, let herself be led onto the dance floor once again.

For a moment, they danced in silence, which suited Analisa quite well. She couldn't stop thinking about Alesandro, couldn't help wondering if he had gone in search of some private corner where he could be alone with his last partner.

"Your thoughts are far away."

The knight's words brought her back to the present. She looked into his eyes, pale gray eyes barely visible through the slit in his helmet—and felt a chill slide down her spine. She had never seen such empty eyes, almost as if there were no soul behind them.

She recoiled instinctively.

The knight's hold on her tightened. A knowing smile played across his face. "Not yet, my pretty one." His voice was a low rasp, filled with carefully controlled rage and subtle menace.

"Who are you?" she asked, refusing to meet his gaze. Looking into his eyes was like looking into the face of death. "What do you want with me?"

"Who am I?" He laughed. It was a cold, bitter sound, like dry leaves rattling over a grave. "Can't you guess?"

"Rodrigo!"

He inclined his head. "At your service, my lady."

She was shivering now, the foreboding within growing with each passing moment. "You killed Sally," she said, surprised to find that her anger was stronger than her fear. "Why? Why? She'd done nothing to you."

He dismissed the maid's death with a shrug. "I was hungry. She was there."

Analisa shook her head. "I don't believe you."

"I killed her to punish Alesandro." His laugh was harsh, filled with contempt. "He bruises so easily, my old friend."

She tried to pull away from him, but his hand tightened on hers, squeezing, squeezing, until she was afraid he meant to crush her very bones. Tears of pain welled in her eyes.

He smiled, enjoying her discomfort. "Many women have died in the last four centuries. But the debt is not yet paid," he murmured, his voice bitter. "The debt is not yet paid!"

Fear threaded through her, turning her insides numb, making her heart pound, her throat dry. She had known fear before—when she watched her parents die, when she lay in the hospital too weak and sick to care if she lived or died—but never like this. Never this gut-wrenching, paralyzing sense of terror. She could feel the evil that clung to him.

The music faded into the distance. The other dancers turned into a swirling mass of colors spinning in endless circles around her. The pain in her hand crept up her arm. She felt suddenly light-headed. Darkness seemed to enfold her and she felt herself slipping away, falling into the darkness. . . .

And then she heard Alesandro's voice, deep and filled with anger and authority. She concentrated on the sound of his voice, clinging to it like a lifeline.

"Rodrigo, let her go."

The other couples continued to waltz around the dance floor, laughing and talking, completely unaware of the tension that flowed between the two vampires. But Analisa could feel it. Power lifted the hair on her arms, beat against her skin, filled her with the urge to flee, but she couldn't move. Rodrigo's hand imprisoned hers like a vise.

"Let her go," Alesandro repeated, his voice blade sharp.

"And if I don't?" The challenge glittered in Rodrigo's soulless gray eyes.

"This is neither the time nor the place," Alesandro replied coldly.

The music came to a stop and the dancers began to leave the floor. Analisa stood there, waiting, wondering what would happen if Rodrigo refused to release her.

The tension between the two men was a palpable thing, overpowering her senses.

And then, abruptly, Rodrigo released her. Taking a step backward, he made a low bow in her direction, then turned and left the floor.

Analisa released the breath she had been holding. Feeling suddenly weak, she would have fallen if Alesandro hadn't slipped his arm around her waist.

"Are you all right, 'Lisa?" he asked. His gaze searched hers, his fingers gently explored her throat. "He didn't . . ."

"Bite me? No."

He led her off the dance floor, found her a quiet place to sit down, brought her a glass of champagne.

She took a sip and wrinkled her nose, not liking the taste.

"Drink it," he said. "It will do you good."

With a grimace, she did as he asked, then put the glass aside.

"How do you feel?"

She hiccuped. "Better."

He took her hand in his, his thumb lightly stroking the back. The pain eased at his touch. She moved her fingers tentatively, her eyes filled with wonder when she looked up at him. Was there nothing he couldn't do?

"Come," he said. "I'll take you home."

She didn't argue. He offered her his hand, and she took it, grateful for the strength of his touch.

He retrieved her cloak and settled it around her shoulders.

"Shouldn't we thank Mr. Starke for inviting us and tell him we're leaving?" she asked.

"Send him a note in the morning," Alesandro said. "I'm taking you home. Now."

She knew a moment of fear at the thought of going outside. What if Rodrigo was waiting for them? She had no desire to be caught in a fight between the two of them, but she need not have worried. Alesandro guided her into an empty room. Taking her into his arms, he held her close and willed them back home.

Alesandro swore under his breath as he placed Analisa on her feet. She looked pale, her face almost as white as her costume. She swayed unsteadily. Lifting her into his arms, he sat down on the chair in the corner and settled her on his lap.

"Analisa?"

She stared at him, her expression troubled.

"What is it?" he asked. "Your hand . . . ?"

A tremor ran through her. "No. Rodrigo. He . . ."

"What? What did he do?"

"He said . . . he said, 'The debt is not yet paid.' "

Alesandro's arms tightened around her. Fear. He had not felt fear like this for centuries, not since the night Tzianne had brought him across. But his fear now was not for himself, it was for Analisa.

"He means to kill me, doesn't he?" she asked. "The way he did Sally. To settle the debt he feels you owe him."

" 'Lisa—"

"It's true, isn't it?" Her voice rose. "Isn't it?"

He wanted to deny it, but he couldn't lie to her. "You will be safe here," he said.

"Sally wasn't safe."

"She would have been if she had stayed inside after dark. He cannot come in here, 'Lisa, unless he is invited."

"He was at the masquerade."

Alesandro nodded. "Someone must have invited him into the house. The butler, perhaps."

"What's to keep that from happening here?"

"Mrs. Thornfield knows better than to invite a stranger into the house. Or to look one in the eye."

She huddled against him, shivering uncontrollably.

He wrapped his arms around her and held her close. He had been content thus far to let Rodrigo live. In spite of all that had happened, he could not forget that Rodrigo had once been his closest friend, nor could he castigate Rodrigo for blaming him for what had befallen Serafina. The responsibility rested squarely on Alesandro's shoulders and no one else's. No matter that he had revealed himself to his sister

267

in hopes of saving her from a similar fate, no matter that she had died by her own hand; the fact remained that he was the one to blame. He could understand Rodrigo's pain and anger; knew he would suffer as deeply, and as long, if anything happened to Analisa. But, guilty or not, he would not allow Rodrigo's need for revenge to touch Analisa.

And so he held her close and rocked her until her trembling ceased.

"Stay with me tonight," she whispered. "I don't want to be alone."

"Tonight and every night, my sweet Analisa." His lips brushed her cheek. "By all that I hold sacred, I swear I will never leave you again."

He helped her out of her costume and into her nightgown, then carried her to bed. He tucked her in, then removed his clothing save for his trousers and slid into bed beside her. He put his arm around her and she snuggled against him, her head pillowed on his shoulder, one hand resting on his chest. He stroked her hair, his mind lightly touching hers, easing her fears so she could sleep.

He held her all through the night, his senses drinking in her nearness, reveling in the warmth of her hand on his chest, the silky feel of her hair against his shoulder, the scent of her perfume, the touch of her breath whispering over his skin. Holding her, being so close to her, was pleasure and torture rolled into one.

How had he survived so long without her? She had brought light and meaning into his existence. He had taken her to the opera and the ballet, had shown her London and Paris, and seen them anew through her eyes. He had smelled the warmth of the sun on her skin and in her hair, savored the near-forgotten taste of tea and chocolate on her lips.

It still amazed him that she knew him for what he was and loved him in spite of it, that she trusted him enough to sleep in his arms.

He stirred as he felt the night fading away. Slipping his arm out from under her shoulders, he left the bed. Drawing the covers up over her, he kissed her lightly.

"Rodrigo will not have you, my sweet Analisa," he vowed quietly. And then, with a last glance at her face, he left the room to seek his lair.

Chapter Twenty-two

Geoffrey Starke called on Analisa the following afternoon. She received him in the parlor, invited him to sit down, sent Mrs. Thornfield for tea and cakes.

She sat down, spreading her skirts around her. It was, she thought, getting easier to pretend she was a fine lady. Folding her hands in her lap, she waited for Mr. Starke to state the purpose of his call.

He removed his gloves, set his walking stick aside, ran his finger inside his collar, cleared his throat. "I seem to be making a habit of calling on you uninvited," he said, "but I couldn't help noticing you left rather abruptly last night."

"I'm sorry," she said, "it was rude of me."

"Did someone offend you?"

"No, of course not. I . . . I was suddenly feeling indisposed."

He cleared his throat again, his cheeks turning bright pink.

Fortunately, Mrs. Thornfield chose that moment to enter with the tea tray, relieving Mr. Starke of the necessity of a reply.

Analisa thanked the housekeeper, then turned her attention to pouring the tea. She handed Mr. Starke a cup, placed one of the tea cakes on a plate and handed that to him as well, together with a neatly folded linen napkin.

She sipped her tea, her thoughts not on Mr. Starke but on Alesandro. She glanced at the clock, counting the hours until she would see him again. Her Alesandro. Just thinking about him sent a shiver of excitement down her spine. He filled her waking thoughts. He filled her dreams.

Alesandro . . .

She blinked, aware that Mr. Starke was walking toward her. She stared at him, dumbfounded, as he dropped to one knee in front of her.

"Miss Matthews, I know this will shock you. I find it rather shocking myself, but, well . . ." He cleared his throat. "Would you do me the honor of being my wife?"

She stared at him. Shocked didn't begin to describe how she felt. Whatever had possessed him to propose to her? Didn't proper etiquette dictate a period of courting first?

He was watching her, waiting for her answer.

"Mr. Starke, this is so sudden. I don't know what to say."

"Say you will consider it."

"I . . . I hardly know you."

"I know this is sudden, and I apologize for that, but I haven't been able to think of anything or anyone else since we met." He smiled disarmingly. "And I'm afraid if I wait too long, you might marry someone else."

"I'm sorry, Mr. Starke, but I'm afraid I can't accept."

He nodded, sighed rather dramatically, and stood up. "I had to ask. I hope you'll forgive my impertinence."

Returning to the sofa, he picked up his gloves and walking stick. "May I call on you again?"

"If you wish."

"Good day to you, then, Miss Matthews." He bowed over her hand. "I look forward to seeing you again."

She smiled politely and started to rise.

"I can see myself out," he said, and left the room.

She sat there for several minutes, stunned by what had happened. Her first proposal! Even if she never married, at least she could say she had been asked. She should have told Mr. Starke she was in love with someone else, she thought, and she would, the next time he came to call. There was no point in letting him think there could ever be a relationship between them. She loved Alesandro, and even if he never asked

272

to marry her, she would never wed anyone else. Never. If she couldn't have Alesandro, she would never marry anyone.

The clock was chiming four o'clock when she left the parlor. Alesandro would be here soon.

Hurrying upstairs, she rang for Frannie.

Analisa was lingering over a glass of sherry when Alesandro entered the dining room. She looked up, her smile of welcome fading when she saw the look on his face.

"Starke was here again," he said flatly.

There was no point in denying it. "Yes."

Alesandro sat in the chair across from her, his dark eyes intense. "Did you invite him?"

"Of course not."

He swore under his breath. He had no excuse for his rudeness, save that he loved her beyond measure. "Forgive me, 'Lisa."

She put her glass aside and rose. "Shall we go into the library?"

With a nod, Alesandro stood and followed her. There was a chill in the room. He cast a glance at the hearth and a fire sprang to life.

"What did Mr. Starke want?" He hadn't meant to ask, but he could no more have stayed the question than he could have taken Deuce out for a ride in the sun.

"He . . . he asked me to marry him."

"Indeed? And what was your answer?"

Analisa blew out a sigh of exasperation. "I said yes, of course."

She had not expected him to take her seriously, nor was she prepared for the rage that blazed in his eyes. It slammed into her, as forceful as if he had struck her.

"Alesandro, I was only jesting. Of course I told him no."

She stared at him, waiting for the anger to leave him. She had seen him in pain, in need of blood, but never enraged like this. It was far more frightening than she could have imagined.

"I'm sorry," she said. "I shouldn't have . . . I . . ."

He closed his eyes, and a stillness settled over him. As she watched, the tension drained out of his stance, his face.

"Alesandro?"

He opened his eyes, savoring the sound of his name on her lips. "Once again I must beg your forgiveness." He moved to the sofa and sat down. "Come," he said. "Sit with me."

She did as he asked without hesitation. She smelled of lavender soap and sherry, of sunlight and the beefsteak and kidney pie she had eaten at dinner.

Need rose within him, the need to hold her, to taste her, to make her forever his. The thought went through him like a bolt of lightning. He had never made another vampire, had sworn he would never be responsible for passing the Dark Gift to anyone else. How could he even think of condemning the woman he loved to an existence of endless darkness, to the relentless hunger, the loneliness?

He looked at Analisa, imagining her as a vampire, her quiet beauty enhanced by the Dark Gift. Imagined her sleeping beside him during the long hours of daylight, waking in his arms. Imagined her lips stained with his blood . . .

"Alesandro, are you angry with me?"

"No, of course not."

"You look . . . I don't know . . . what were you thinking about?"

"You do not want to know."

"Why not?" She studied his face, her head tilted to one side, her expression thoughtful. "It was about me, wasn't it?"

He did not deny it.

"Tell me!"

He shook his head, certain it would frighten her to know that he had considered bringing her across, no matter how briefly.

She pouted prettily, making him smile in spite of himself. Sometimes he forgot how young she was.

"Please, Alesandro?"

"No, 'Lisa." He rose to his feet. "I must go out for a while."

"Don't go."

"I will be back soon."

She caught his hand. Holding it to her breast, she stared up at him through wide brown eyes. "You don't have to go."

He had not taken her blood since it was decided she should see other men.

"Please don't go!"

He gazed down at her a moment, then knelt at her feet. "Something is troubling you. What is it?"

"Rodrigo." Her hand tightened on his. "I'm afraid."

"He cannot come here."

She brushed a lock of hair from his brow with her free hand. "I'm afraid for you, Alesandro."

"There is no need for you to worry, 'Lisa."

"I can't help it. I love you so much." She pressed his hand to her cheek. "What would I do if something happened to you?"

"Nothing will happen to me."

"He hurt you before."

" 'Lisa." Her concern touched him in ways he barely remembered, made him recall emotions and feelings he had not felt since he was mortal. But he was mortal no longer. Gently, he captured her hand in both of his. "I cannot change what I am."

"Would you if you could?"

"Yes. But it is not possible. There is no going back."

"How do you know?"

He gestured at the bookshelves that surrounded them. "Do you think I have read all the books here and at Blackbriar simply to pass the time? For centuries I have sought a way to end this curse. Centuries, 'Lisa."

Her heart ached for the sadness she saw in his eyes,

the resignation in his voice. "It can't have all been bad. You've seen so much of the world."

"Yes. I have lived through wars and plagues. I have watched kings and queens rise and fall. I have seen advances in medicine and the arts." He looked down at her hand, caught in both of his. "And all of it alone."

She put her hand under his chin and lifted his head. "You're not alone now. I'm young, Alesandro. I'll stay with you as long as I live, if you want me to."

" 'Lisa." It was what he wanted, what he yearned for, yet how could he ask her to give up everything to be with him? How could he let her go? In that brief moment when he thought he had lost her to Geoffrey Starke, he had been filled with a torrent of rage and jealousy the likes of which he had not experienced in four centuries. He had known, in that instant, that he would kill Starke before he let the man claim Analisa for his own, had feared that he might kill her, too, rather than let another man have her.

Analisa bit down on her lower lip as she watched Alesandro's face. His expression was black, his eyes haunted. What was he thinking? What dark thoughts troubled him so?

Fearing she might be rebuffed, she cupped his cheek in her hand. "Alesandro?"

"What am I to do with you?" he asked quietly.

"Only love me, as I love you."

Did she truly love him? he wondered. Or was she enamored of his preternatural powers?

" 'Lisa, I am going away."

"What? When? Where?" Her gaze searched his face. "Why? What have I done?"

"You have done nothing. I am going away for a year, to give you time to yourself—"

"No! No! You made me come here. You made me see other people, other men—"

" 'Lisa I—"

"No!" She stood and faced him, her hands clenched at her sides. "I will not let you go away from me. I love you. I do not need to see other men to know that it's you I love. I will not stop loving you if you go away. I will not love you any less if you are not here."

He rose to his feet in one lithe movement to tower over her. But she refused to be intimidated. Holding her ground, she stared up at him. "If you do not want me, if you do not love me, then I'll go away and you need never see me again." She held up her hand when he started to speak. "I'm going to my room. Don't follow me. Think about it, Alesandro. I know what I want. I don't want to see you again until you know what you want. Good night."

With all the dignity and grace of a highborn lady, she turned on her heel and swept out of the room.

Alesandro stared after her, stunned by her outburst. She had grown up in the past few months, he mused, smiling faintly. She was a woman who knew her own mind and was not afraid to speak it.

She loved him. She had said it before, and he had believed her because he wanted to so desperately. But this time, for the first time, he knew she spoke the truth.

She loved him. And she had given him an ultimatum.

I know what I want. I don't want to see you again until you know what you want.

Bold words, brave words, for a mere slip of a girl. How beautiful she had looked glaring up at him, with her eyes flashing fire and her cheeks flushed with anger. How could he even think of letting her go? If he did, he knew he would regret it every night for the rest of his accursed life.

He was tempted to go to her, but another need clawed at him, a need that could not be denied.

Settling his cloak on his shoulders, he vanished into the night, searching for that someone who had what he needed. Who needed what he had.

Analisa's tears came hot and swift when she was in her room with the door locked behind her. She knew no lock would keep him out should he wish to enter, but she locked the door anyway. Why did he keep trying to send her away? Didn't he love her at all? But even as the thought crossed her mind, she knew she was being unfair. He loved her desperately, and it was because he loved her that he wanted what was best for her. She knew he felt guilty for loving her, and what was worse, he felt unworthy of her love.

With tears streaming down her cheeks, she paced the floor, wishing she knew how to convince him that she was old enough to know her own mind. Would she be wise to let him go? A year was not such a long time. It would not change her feelings for Alesandro, and if it would somehow put his mind at ease. . . . Moving to the window, she drew back the drapes and peered out into the darkness. A year. What would she do in that time? She could travel, but what fun would it be without him? She could go to parties and balls, plays and operas, meet a thousand men, but to what purpose? There was no room in her heart for anyone but Alesandro.

He wanted her to have a normal life, to play in the sunshine, to marry and have children. She placed her hands on her flat stomach and tried to imagine her womb swollen with new life. She had never given any thought to child-bearing before, had taken it for granted that she would someday marry and have children, though she'd had no idea who her future husband might be. She had caught the eye of one of the neighboring young men, but they had never done more than smile at each other and speak a few words, and now he was dead, killed by the same epidemic that had taken the lives of her family.

Was she willing to give up having children to be with Alesandro? The answer was an overwhelming yes. She was willing to give up everything and anything to be with him, to love him. She would spend the rest of her days trying to make him happy if only he would let her.

And that, of course, was the one question for which she had no answer. Would he let her?

Chapter Twenty-three

She woke early the following afternoon after a night spent tossing and turning. When she had finally slept, her dreams had been dark, fragmented, filled with blood-red eyes and dripping fangs, of a child's arms reaching out to her, of an empty crypt and a round stone cottage. She had awakened once, just before dawn, certain she heard a wolf howling out in the gardens. The sound, so lost, so lonely, had sent a shiver down her spine.

Now, in the light of day, she knew it had only been a dog barking. There were no wolves in the city.

She rang for Frannie, hoping she'd feel better after her cocoa and a hot bath.

The maid arrived a few minutes later bearing her chocolate. Dewhurst filled the tub, and while Analisa bathed, Frannie laid out her clothing for the day. Sensing Analisa's pensive mood, the maid said little as she helped Analisa dress, then brushed her hair.

"Will that be all, miss?" Frannie asked.

Analisa regarded herself in the mirror. Frannie had arranged her hair in a neat chignon at her nape. It made her look older, more mature. Would Alesandro think so? Would she even see him tonight? Would she ever see him again? Whatever had possessed her to talk to him the way she had last night?

Oh, but he made her so mad, always trying to be so noble, to do what he thought was best for her. And even if leaving him *was* best for her, she didn't care. Alesandro might have centuries, but she didn't. Life was too short to spend even a year without him.

Despite all that was on her mind, the day passed surprisingly fast. She spent an hour reading and another hour working on her penmanship. She went out and walked through the gardens, spent a quiet few minutes in the arbor watching a bird build a nest in a tree.

She went in for lunch, worked on her needlepoint, and then took a nap. She rang for Frannie when she woke, picked out the gown she would wear that evening, had the maid touch up her hair.

Sitting at the dinner table, she grew increasingly tense, waiting, wondering if Alesandro would appear, or if he would again avoid her, as he had in the past.

After dinner, she went into the parlor and sat in front of the hearth, trying to decide what she would do if Alesandro sent her away.

Her options were much more promising now than when she first arrived. She could read and write, she knew proper etiquette, her table manners were more refined. She might be able to find a position as a governess, or, at the least, a lady's maid.

Or she could accept Mr. Starke's marriage proposal. . . .

She stared into the flames. Mrs. Geoffrey Starke. She could do worse, she thought. He was a handsome man with pleasant manners and a lovely home. As his wife, she would want for nothing.

She looked up as Mrs. Thornfield entered the room.

"Can I get you anything, miss?" the housekeeper asked. "Cook made a lovely trifle. Perhaps you'd like some with a nice hot cup of tea?"

"Yes, thank you, Mrs. Thornfield, that would be wonderful."

With a smile, the housekeeper started toward the door, then paused and glanced over her shoulder. "Is everything all right, miss?"

"Yes, of course. Why do you ask?"

"You've fallen in love with him, haven't you?"

She didn't pretend to misunderstand. "Yes, I have. Does it show?"

The housekeeper nodded. "I recognize the signs."

Analisa studied the other woman for a moment, then murmured, "Oh, my," at the expression in the older woman's eyes. "You love him, too, don't you?"

Mrs. Thornfield nodded. "Yes."

"I'm sorry. I didn't know—"

"How could you?"

Analisa looked at the housekeeper as if seeing her for the first time. She must have been beautiful once, she thought, for she was still an attractive women in spite of her years and the gray in her hair.

"How long have you been with him?" she asked.

"Forty-seven years."

Analisa knew she was staring, but she couldn't help it. "How old were you when you met him?"

"I had just turned seventeen."

"But that would make you—"

"Sixty-four on my last birthday."

"But . . ." Analisa would have guessed the housekeeper to be in her early forties.

"But I look younger. Yes, I know." She lifted a hand to her neck in a gesture that Analisa knew she herself had made on more than one occasion. "When I was younger, there were times when I provided Lord Alesandro with what he needed. And once, when I was very ill, he saved my life, much as he saved yours."

"And that's why you—"

"Yes. Whatever it is in his blood that makes him what he is also has the power to slow the aging process in mortals."

"That's . . . I don't know . . . incredible."

"Yes, but true, nonetheless."

"And you've kept his secret all these years."

"Of course," the housekeeper replied softly. She lifted her head, looking past Analisa toward the door. "Good evening, my lord."

Now that she knew, now that she was looking for

it, Analisa wondered how she had ever missed the tenderness in the housekeeper's eyes when she looked at Alesandro.

"I'll bring your tea directly," Mrs. Thornfield told Analisa, and left the room.

Heart pounding, Analisa waited for Alesandro to join her on the sofa. As always, he moved soundlessly, appearing on the sofa beside her almost as if by magic. He wore a white shirt, open at the throat, buff-colored breeches, and calfskin boots.

He looked at her, one brow raised inquisitively. "What is it?"

"I wasn't sure I would see you tonight, my lord."

He grunted softly. "Something troubles you. What is it?"

"I . . . nothing."

"Tell me, 'Lisa."

"Mrs. Thornfield, she said . . . I didn't know that . . . I mean that you and she were . . ."

"Ah. She told you, did she?"

Analisa nodded. "She must love you very much."

"She did." He grunted softly. "I suppose she still does."

"Did you love her, too?"

"No. When I learned of her feelings, I intended to dismiss her from my service, but she begged to stay. She has been a loyal and trusted servant for many years."

"Forty-seven," Analisa murmured. She bit down on her lip, feeling suddenly self-conscious when the housekeeper returned with her tea and a bowl of trifle. Had Mrs. Thornfield overheard them discussing her?

"Would you care for a glass of wine, my lord?" the housekeeper asked, and there was nothing in her expression or her manner to betray her feelings.

"No, thank you, Mrs. Thornfield."

"Will you be wanting anything else this evening, miss?"

Analisa shook her head.

"Very well, I shall bid you both a good night, then."

"Good night," Analisa said. She stared after the housekeeper, thinking how awful it must be for her to have loved Alesandro for so long, to live in his house knowing he did not return her affection. And yet, how much worse to leave and never see him again.

Her hand was trembling when she picked up her teacup. She sipped slowly, her thoughts in turmoil.

Alesandro stretched his arm along the back of the sofa. "You gave me a rather stern ultimatum last night."

She nodded, not trusting herself to speak as she set the cup on the saucer.

"You want to stay here, with me?"

"Yes."

"You are sure this is what you want?"

"Yes, my lord."

"You say you are not afraid of me, of what I am."

His words, casually spoken, filled her with a sudden sense of unease. She met his gaze, waiting.

" 'Lisa?"

"I'm not afraid of you."

"We shall see."

Her heart slammed against her chest. "What do you mean?"

"We shall put it to the test, my sweet Analisa."

She looked up at him, her mouth suddenly dry, her palms damp. "And if I fail?"

"If you fail, you will no doubt be gone from my house by tomorrow."

Her heart was pounding so hard, so fast, she thought she might faint. She had seen him when he was wounded and in need of blood. Surely nothing could be more frightening than that.

"I thought I heard a wolf last night," she said, and wondered what had prompted her remark.

"Indeed?"

"It was you, wasn't it?" She waited, hoping he would deny it, knowing he would not.

He sat beside her, vampire still, his dark eyes watching her.

"The paintings in your bedroom at Blackbriar and at the Manor, they're you, too, aren't they? Both man and wolf."

Still he said nothing, only continued to watch her out of fathomless indigo eyes.

She swallowed, her hands worrying a fold in her skirt. "The night I came here, a wolf ran alongside the carriage. I thought I imagined it, but I didn't, did I? It was you."

He rose in a single fluid motion, moved several

paces away, and faced her. A dark aura seemed to surround him. His eyes darkened, his body shimmered, blurred, and a wolf stood before her. A large black wolf with indigo eyes.

She stared at him, a dozen thoughts tumbling through her mind. It was impossible. It was fantastic. How did he do it? Did it hurt? Would he understand her if she spoke to him? Were all vampires capable of shape shifting? What of Rodrigo?

She blinked, and Alesandro stood before her again.

"Lisa?"

"Yes, my lord?"

A faint smile lifted a corner of his mouth. "Are you going to faint?"

"I don't think so. Do all vampires have the power to change shape like that?"

"No." He sat down beside her once again, picked up her teacup, held it to her lips. "Drink this."

The tea had grown cold, but she did as he asked. Doing such a normal, everyday thing had a calming effect on her.

"Is that it?" she asked shakily. "Did I pass the test?"

"Nothing so simple as that, my sweet."

"What, then?" she said, her trepidation growing ever stronger. "Tell me."

"I want you to spend the night with me."

"That's all?"

He nodded, his expression solemn.

She stared at him, her mind racing. What could be so bad about spending the night with him?

"And the day," he said. "Until after sunrise."

And then she knew what he meant, knew what the test was.

He read the knowledge in her eyes.

"Not . . ." She bit down on her lower lip, knowing her words would be seen as a sign of weakness. "Not in the cottage?"

He shook his head. He would spare her that much, at least.

"When?"

"Tonight."

Spending the night with Alesandro. It seemed a simple thing, something she had yearned to do. To fall asleep in his arms after making love. And they would make love tonight. She knew it, felt it in every fiber of her being.

He blew out the lamps in the parlor, lifted her into his arms, and carried her swiftly up the stairs and down the long, dark corridor to his room. The door opened at his silent command and closed the same way. She heard the key turn in the lock; a moment later, a fire sprang to life in the hearth.

He was still holding her in his arms. Now he gazed down at her, his expression impassive. "If you wish to change your mind, you must say so now."

She shook her head.

Letting her body slide intimately down his own, he placed her on her feet, and then backed away from her. "I have instructed Mrs. Thornfield to unlock the door at half past eight tomorrow morning."

Analisa nodded.

"If you are gone when I rise in the evening, Mrs. Thornfield will contact you."

She started to ask how Mrs. Thornfield would know where to find her, then stayed her tongue. Alesandro had taken her blood. He would always be able to find her.

"You are certain you wish to do this, 'Lisa?"

"Yes."

"Then come to me, Analisa."

She had known, when they made love the first time, that her life would be irrevocably changed, but that paled in significance to this.

She moved slowly into his embrace, her heart pounding so loudly in her ears she was certain everyone within the walls of the house could hear it.

She gazed up into his eyes as he lowered his head toward hers, his lips claiming hers in a kiss that was at once achingly tender and violently possessive. His tongue plundered her mouth, his hands moved up and down her back, slid down to cup her buttocks and draw her close against him. He was fully aroused.

He carried her to the bed and lowered her onto the mattress, followed her down, his mouth never leaving hers. She clung to him, caught up in a maelstrom of yearning and desire, of overwhelming need to cradle him in her arms.

Their clothing disappeared as if by magic. Vampire magic. And then he was pressing her down onto the mattress.

His skin felt cool against the heat of her own, his

hands urgent as they caressed her, arousing her until she moved restlessly beneath him.

"I love you." She whispered the words as his body slid into hers. She arched upward, wanting more of him, all of him.

He groaned softly. " 'Lisa, 'Lisa. Four hundred years I have waited for you."

"I'm here." She cupped his face in her hands.

His gaze burned into hers, hotter than the flames crackling in the hearth.

"Tell me," she whispered. "Tell me you love me."

"I love you." He moved deep within her. "I will always love you."

"And I you."

She saw the doubt in his eyes, the fear that she would not be strong enough to endure what was to come.

Her hands moved restlessly over his back and shoulders, sliding up and down his arms, reveling in the strength that trembled there.

"Don't think of it now, Alesandro."

His tongue laved her neck, his breath hot against her skin. "Let me."

She closed her eyes and turned her head, felt his fangs at her throat. Pleasure and ecstasy mingled inside her. She felt what he felt as his body moved within hers, knew that for this small space of time, the beast within him lay quiet, sated by her blood and by the desire building, cresting, exploding in the deepest part of her.

A low growl rose in his throat as he thrust into her,

and for a moment, just a moment, an image of the painting hanging over his bed at Blackbriar Hall flashed through her mind, the images of man and beast melding into one as Alesandro followed her over the edge of desire.

Afterward, feeling blissfully content, she lay in the circle of his arms, her head pillowed on his shoulder, her fingers playing in the thick black silk of his hair.

"Did I hurt you?" he asked quietly.

"No, of course not." She smiled at him, her heart swelling with love and tenderness. Always, his first thought was for her. She looked at him, awed to be loved by such a man. A man who had lived over four hundred years, who could summon fire with a thought, who could crush her with a look. He had such strength, possessed powers she could not begin to imagine. Yet he held her gently in his arms and adored her with his eyes.

Lifting himself on one elbow, he gazed down at her, one brow arched. "What are you thinking about, 'Lisa?"

"Don't you know?"

He shook his head, his gaze intent upon her face.

"I thought you could read my mind."

"I do not make a habit of it."

She raked her fingernails lightly down his chest. "Afraid to know what I'm thinking?" she teased.

He nodded, his expression somber.

"Alesandro, I have nothing to hide from you, no secrets you cannot share. But something troubles you. I can see it in your eyes. You look so sad sometimes, so lost. Is there nothing I can do to help?"

He closed his eyes as if he were in pain, and then with a low groan he crushed her to him. He spoke to her in a language she did not understand, his voice low and ragged, filled with self-loathing.

As the words moved over her, her mind filled with images of Alesandro. He held nothing back. He showed her all the horror of his first days as a vampire. She felt the excruciating pain that engulfed him when he refused to satisfy his hunger, felt his agony when his sister went mad, his hurt and his rage when Rodrigo turned on him, his sadness when he left his home for the last time, never to return. She felt his isolation from the rest of the world, the loneliness that had been his companion over four centuries. And his need—she felt it in every part of her, the pain, the relentless need, and then the cessation of pain when at last he gave in to his thirst. It was a pleasure unlike anything she had ever experienced, as necessary to his survival as the air she breathed to live.

She felt the wetness of his tears on her cheek as he fell silent. She hugged him to her, one hand stroking his hair, until comfort became need and need became desire and they made love again, tenderly, so tenderly. The gentleness of his touch only made her love him more. Tears filled her eyes. Her heart swelled with love until she thought it might burst.

Held tightly in his arms, she closed her eyes and surrendered to the weariness that engulfed her.

Alesandro watched her all through the night, wondering if he would ever see her again, wondering what her reaction would be when she woke beside a body that was virtually lifeless.

He smelled the dawn, knew the sun was rising. His body grew heavy, his mind sluggish. He should have prepared her, he thought, warned her . . . too late now . . . too late. . . .

Chapter Twenty-four

Analisa woke slowly, aware that she was smiling. Unwilling to open her eyes, she rolled onto her side and pulled the covers over her head, hoping she could recapture the lovely dream she'd been having. Such a wonderful dream. She had been walking through a sunlit garden with Alesandro beside her. The pain and sadness were gone from his eyes; his skin was no longer pale but a rich golden brown. Hand in hand, they had walked and talked, then made love beneath a tree.

But the dream was only a memory now. With a sigh, she threw off the covers and opened her eyes. She started to smile when she saw Alesandro lying beside her, but the smile died unborn upon her lips. He did not move. He did not breathe. His face was beyond pale. Lifting a trembling hand, she touched his cheek and quickly jerked her hand away. His skin was as cold as the marble crypt at Blackbriar, his body hard and unyielding.

She stared at him in horror, then scrambled off the bed, every instinct she possessed shrieking at her to get away. She ran to the door and found it locked. The key! Where was the key?

She started to pound on the door, a scream rising in her throat. With an effort, she fought down her rising panic. There was nothing to fear. It was only Alesandro, and he would not hurt her. Could not hurt her, not now.

Slowly she turned around, her back pressed tight against the door. Crossing her arms over her breasts, she forced herself to look at him again.

There was nothing to fear.

"Nothing to fear." She whispered the words aloud over and over again as she moved toward the bed. "Nothing to fear." He wasn't dead, only asleep. *A sleep like death*. If she spoke to him, would he hear her? When she'd touched him, had he felt it?

Shivering, she pulled a blanket from the foot of the bed and draped it around her shoulders. It was then she saw the dagger on the table beside the bed. Curious, she lifted it, surprised at the way it fit so snugly into her hand. It was a heavy weapon, with a thick blade tapered to a sharp point. The blade was made of silver, the haft of wood inset with a blood-red ruby. Frowning, she turned the weapon over in her hands, and then, as clearly as if she heard Alesandro's voice, she knew he had left it there for her. He had given her the means to destroy him.

With a cry, she threw the knife into the fireplace, then sat down on the edge of the bed and waited for Mrs. Thornfield.

He woke as soon as the sun began to set. One minute he was held fast in the death-like sleep of his kind, the next he was awake and aware. And in that instant, he was conscious of everything around him: Analisa's scent clinging to himself and the bedding, the rain that had just begun to fall, the aroma of hot cocoa.

The fact that he was not alone.

"Good evening, my lord."

He sat up, unconcerned by his nudity. "Analisa." He could not disguise his astonishment at finding her there. "What are you doing here?"

"Waiting for you to wake up, of course. What else would I be doing?"

"You did not leave." He stared at her blankly, unable to believe his eyes.

"Only for a little while." She smiled at him. "I left long enough to bathe and have some breakfast, and then I came back here."

"Have you been sitting there watching me all day?"

She laughed softly. "Well, not quite." She pointed at the book on the bedside table. "I read for a while, and then I finished my needlepoint. And I took a nap after lunch."

"A nap?"

"Yes, in your bed," she said, answering his unspoken question. "I hope you don't mind."

He stared at her. "You slept here? Beside me?"

"Of course. That's what beds are for." Rising, she walked around the bed and sat down beside him. "I thought you would like to bathe when you woke up. Cook is heating the water. It should be ready soon."

" 'Lisa." He wrapped his arms around her waist, his face pressed in the valley between her breasts. " 'Lisa, 'Lisa." Only her name, filled with such love it brought tears to her eyes.

"So, my lord, have I passed the test?"

He drew back, his eyes narrowed. "You were not afraid of what you saw?"

"I was at first," she confessed. "It was frightening to see you lying there so still. I was afraid you were really and truly dead. But then I realized I had nothing to fear from you, Alesandro. Dead or alive, you would never hurt me."

He glanced at the bedside table, noting the absence of the dagger.

"I hope it wasn't an heirloom or anything," she said, following his gaze.

"What have you done with it?'

"I threw it in the fire."

"Ah, 'Lisa, you have the heart of a lioness."

"I could have had *your* heart," she retorted with a grin. "Did you really expect me to cut it out?"

"I would rather have you destroy me than leave me."

"I shall do neither, my lord." She drew the blankets

over him at the sound of a knock on the door. "That will be Dewhurst with your water." She dropped a kiss on the top of his head. "I shall leave you to your bath."

He caught her by the hand as she turned to go. "Will you not stay and wash my back?"

It amazed him that she could still blush after the night they had spent together. There was no part of her that he had not touched or tasted,.

"Yes, my lord, if that is your desire."

"Among others," he replied, a bold glint in his eye.

Laughing softly, Analisa unlocked the door.

Analisa laid her knife and fork aside, took a sip of wine, then sat back in her chair. Alesandro sat across the table from her, watching her eat. He had all but forgotten what it was like to partake of solid food, could no longer remember the texture of bread, the flavor of meat or fowl, the sweetness of honey or marmalade save what he sometimes tasted on Analisa's lips. Once, soon after he had been made vampire, he had eaten a slice of ham. It had made him violently ill. The only thing his stomach would accept was a bit of red wine now and then.

She looked at him over the rim of her glass. "Where do we go from here?"

He shook his head, not understanding her question.

"I passed your test. Does that mean you will stop trying to send me away?"

"Ah. It does begin to look as though I am stuck with you."

"Stuck with me!" She made a very unladylike face at him.

He laughed out loud. It was a rich, full-bodied sound, and she determined then and there to elicit it more often.

"Analisa, my sweet, you are such a joy to me."

"And you to me."

"You are sure you want to stay here with me, to spend the rest of your life with me? Think carefully on your answer, 'Lisa, for once you are truly mine, I will not let you go. The only thing that will part us is death. Yours, or mine."

"I've done nothing but think of it," she replied. "Don't you know that?"

" 'Lisa."

He spoke her name with such love, such emotion, that she couldn't stay her tears.

He was at her side in an instant, drawing her up into his embrace, his lips moving in her hair as he whispered that he loved her, would love her all the days of her life.

She clung to him, her arms tight around his waist, knowing, in the deepest part of her being, that she was where she belonged.

She offered no protest when he swung her into his arms and carried her swiftly up the stairs to his room.

He placed her on the bed, his eyes hot as they moved over her. She smiled with anticipation as he closed the door, shutting out the rest of the world.

* * *

"Will you now make an honest woman of me?" she asked.

She was lying on top of him, her arms folded across his broad chest, her chin resting on her arms.

"Is that what you want?"

"Yes, very much." She leaned forward and kissed him lightly. "Will you marry me, my lord doctor?"

"Whenever you wish."

"Truly?"

"Truly." He smiled as her face lit up like a child's at Christmas. "Where would you like to be wed?"

"I don't know." She hesitated a moment. "Could we be married in a church? With lots of flowers and candles?"

"If you wish."

"Oh, I do, very much."

"I shall arrange for the church. You will need a dress. Have Mrs. Thornfield take you into the city."

"She still loves you, doesn't she?" Analisa stroked his cheek. "Someday I'll be as old as she is," Analisa murmured, her expression troubled. "Will you still love me then?"

He cupped her face in his hands and kissed her. "I will always love you. Your outer beauty may fade, but you will always be beautiful on the inside. And I will always see you as you look now, your eyes filled with love and your skin glowing and your lips swollen from my kisses."

In a single fluid move, he rolled over and tucked her beneath him. "So, Analisa, my sweet, you need but name the day."

She frowned thoughtfully. "A week from Sunday? That should give me time enough to have a dress made, shouldn't it?"

He shrugged. "With enough money behind you, anything is possible. Spend whatever you wish." He smiled down at her. "Buy yourself a whole new wardrobe."

"Won't it be painful for Mrs. Thornfield to go shopping with me?" she asked. "I know if I were in her shoes, I should hate to watch another woman getting ready to marry the man I loved. Maybe I should take Frannie instead."

"No," he said adamantly. "She is too young. You will take Mrs. Thornfield. And have Farleigh accompany you as well. He can wait for you outside."

She looked up at him with a faint expression of alarm. "Why do I need Farleigh to stay with me? What are you afraid of?"

"Nothing. I am only being cautious—"

"Because of Rodrigo? But surely he can't hurt me during the day. Can he?"

"No, 'Lisa, but the city can be a dangerous place. I am not willing to take any chances, not now." He gazed down at her, his eyes dark with desire. "Will you stay the night with me?"

With a nod, she drew his head down and kissed him, all else forgotten but the need that burned so brightly between them.

When she woke in the morning, she was alone in his bed. Troubled, she wondered why he had left when he had asked her to stay. And then she saw the note. And the single red rose with the thorns cut away. Smiling, she unfolded the sheet of paper.

I love you, my sweet Analisa, and count the hours until I can hold you in my arms again.
Yours in life and death.
Alesandro

Laying the note aside, she picked up the rose. It was blood-red and perfect, the petals as soft as velvet against her cheek.

She rang for Frannie, knew as soon as the maid entered the room that Alesandro had informed the household of their upcoming nuptials.

"Cook is preparing your breakfast," Frannie said. She held out a robe for Analisa. "Your bath is ready. Farleigh will have the coach at the front door by the time you've finished breakfast."

"Thank you." Analisa belted the robe at her waist, picked up the rose and the note, and left Alesandro's chamber.

She found a dozen red roses in a crystal vase on her dressing table, as well as another note, which simply said, *I love you. A.*

Tossing her robe on the bed, she took a leisurely bath. She wished Alesandro were there to share it with her, wished she could feel his skin against hers, his hands moving over her. She blushed from head to heel as she imagined the two of them in the same tub, their bodies covered with soap suds.

Frannie came to help her dress and do her hair, and then Analisa went downstairs to a very late breakfast. There was a vase of red roses in the center of the dining room table, and a note that said, *I am dreaming of you, even now. A*

Lost in thoughts of Alesandro and the night she had spent in his arms, she paid little attention to what Frannie placed in front of her. Alesandro. Just the mere thought of him brought a smile to her face even as she wondered why he had left their bed. She had looked forward to waking beside him even though it was disconcerting to see him lying so still.

Too excited to finish her breakfast, she was about to leave the dining room when Mrs. Thornfield came in.

"The coach is ready whenever you are, miss."

Was it her imagination, Analisa wondered, or did the housekeeper seem more remote than usual? "Thank you, Mrs. Thornfield. Are you ready to go?"

With a nod, the housekeeper put on her cloak and bonnet and followed her out the door.

Definitely aloof, Analisa mused as she descended the front steps. Farleigh was waiting beside the coach. He opened the door and helped both women inside, then climbed up on the box. A moment later, the coach lurched into motion.

Analisa had known the housekeeper would be upset when she learned that Alesandro intended to marry. Analisa couldn't blame the woman for the way she felt. Still, she couldn't help being hurt by the housekeeper's reserve. Mrs. Thornfield had been the closest thing to a friend Analisa had had since leaving the hospital. The woman had made her feel at home, taught her to read and write, praised her efforts. Now she wouldn't even meet Analisa's eyes.

It was a long, silent ride. Analisa gazed out the window, watching the passing countryside, wishing she could think of something to say to ease the tension in the coach, but nothing came to mind. She felt that she owed the housekeeper an apology, but she wasn't sure why. It wasn't as though she had stolen Alesandro from her. According to Alesandro, there had never been any commitment between him and the housekeeper. It wasn't Analisa's fault that Alesandro hadn't loved the other woman. Analisa hadn't even been born at the time. Yet still she felt guilty.

With a sigh, she leaned her head back against the seat and closed her eyes. Alesandro's image immediately sprang to mind. She pictured him in the stone cottage, his body trapped in sleep. Did vampires dream? She would have to ask him tonight. She smiled, thinking of the hours she would spend in his arms. Alesandro. *Sleep and dream your girlish dreams, and I will make them come true.* She had heard him whisper those words once. At the time, she had thought she had dreamed them, but now . . . now she wasn't so sure. But, imagined or not, he had indeed made her dreams come true.

She woke at the cessation of movement. Peering out the window, she saw that Farleigh had stopped the coach in front of an exclusive dressmaker's shop.

Farleigh opened the door and handed Analisa out.

Then, instead of staying with the coach, he accompanied Analisa and Mrs. Thornfield to the door of the shop. Mrs. Thornfield followed Analisa inside.

As soon as they entered the building, a tall woman hurried forward to meet them. "Welcome to Womack's," she said, extending her hand. "I am Madame Devereaux. How may I help you."

"I'm getting married," Analisa said, taking the woman's hand. "I need a dress."

"She is also to have a whole new wardrobe," Mrs. Thornfield added. Mrs. Devereaux beamed at Analisa. "It will be a pleasure to serve you." Her gaze moved swiftly and professionally over Analisa's figure. "Have you any preference for a wedding gown?"

Analisa shook her head. "I don't know."

"Let me show you some sketches," the modiste suggested, and for the next hour, Analisa looked at sketches and fabrics, finally settling on a simple gown of white silk with long, fitted sleeves, a square neckline, and a full skirt with a modest train. She chose a full-length veil made of delicate lace.

Madame Devereaux took the necessary measurements and promised the gown would be ready in time for the wedding, then went on to show Analisa a number of other dresses, as well as undergarments. Lastly, Madame Devereaux showed her several lovely nightgowns, one so diaphanous it was like wearing little more than a whisper of black silk. It was quite the most provocative thing Analisa had ever seen. The thought of wearing it, of having Alesandro see her in something so immodest, brought a blush to her cheeks.

Madame Devereaux smiled knowingly as she added the nightgown to Analisa's purchases.

By the time Analisa signed the bill and arranged for everything to be sent to the house, her head was spinning.

Outside, she took a deep breath.

"Are you ready to go home, miss?" Farleigh asked.

"Not yet." She moved down the street, with Farleigh and Mrs. Thornfield trailing behind her. When she reached a café, she went inside and ordered a cup of tea and a hot buttered scone. Mrs. Thornfield refused to enter the establishment and waited outside with Farleigh.

Analisa sighed as she poured milk into her tea. Life was going to be quite unpleasant if Mrs. Thornfield continued to be so disapproving and aloof. Perhaps Alesandro would know what to do.

She was about to leave the café when Geoffrey Starke paused at her table.

"Miss Matthews," he exclaimed.

"Good afternoon, Mr. Starke."

He gestured at an empty chair. "May I?"

Slightly flustered, she nodded.

"You're looking quite well," Geoffrey remarked, taking the seat across from her.

"Thank you."

"Will you have another cup of tea?"

"No, thank you." She glanced out the window,

suddenly aware of the time. "I really should be going."

"Please," he said. "Stay a moment."

She didn't want to be rude, so she nodded and agreed to stay long enough for one more cup.

"I had hoped to call on you before this," Geoffrey remarked. "But, alas, my mother was taken quite ill and I've been afraid to leave her."

"I hope she's feeling better."

"Yes, thank you. Lady Fairfax is hosting a musicale next month. I should be most pleased if you would accompany me."

Analisa took a deep breath. She would never have a better opportunity than this. "I'm sorry, Mr. Starke, but I'm afraid I can't accept. You see, I'm going to be married."

Geoffrey stared at her. "Married? To whom?"

"To Lord Avallone."

"Avallone?" Geoffrey looked at her as if she had suddenly grown another head. "Dear Lord, you can't be serious!"

"Why not? He's a fine . . . a fine man."

"Don't tell me you've never heard the stories about him?"

"What stories?"

Geoffrey shook his head. "They say he's a ghoul, that he performs experiments on his patients, that he's looking for the secret of eternal life."

She laughed softly. "Surely you don't believe that."

He shrugged. "Perhaps not, but there are too many stories. There is likely some truth there, somewhere."

"I live in his house," Analisa said. "I've seen no evidence of such nonsense."

"His house?"

"Yes, didn't you know?"

Geoffrey shook his head. "I was told he rarely left Blackbriar."

"Then you've never met him?"

"No."

Analisa smiled faintly. "He was my escort at your masquerade."

"The tall man," Geoffrey murmured. "The one dressed as Satan?"

"Yes."

"And now you intend to marry him. Why?"

"Because I love him, of course."

"It happened rather suddenly, didn't it?"

"No. I've loved him for quite some time. He has only recently come to feel the same."

Geoffrey grunted softly. "Who can blame him?" He rose from the table, his tea grown cold and now forgotten. "I wish you all the best, Miss Matthews."

"Thank you, Mr. Starke."

He looked at her for several moments, dropped a few coins on the table, then turned and headed for the door.

Analisa stared after him, then quickly left the café. She had one more stop to make before she returned home. She glanced at the sky. She would have to hurry, she thought; the sun would be setting soon.

Chapter Twenty-five

Analisa felt a growing sense of apprehension as the carriage left the city behind. A thick fog covered the coach and spread out over the countryside like a dark shroud. Shivering, she drew the lap robe across her legs.

It would be full dark soon.

She glanced at Mrs. Thornfield. The other woman was staring out the window, her face pale, her brow furrowed.

Analisa heard the crack of the whip, felt the coach lurch forward as the horses increased their pace. Home, Analisa thought; soon they would be home. She smiled, thinking of the elegant dressing gown she had bought for Alesandro. It was blue, the same deep indigo blue as his eyes.

She was picturing how handsome Alesandro would look in it later that night when she heard a hoarse cry from the top of the carriage. Frowning, she peered out the window, screamed as Farleigh's body plunged over the side of the coach.

Analisa looked at Mrs. Thornfield. "What's happening?"

Mrs. Thornfield shook her head, her eyes wide. "Highwaymen, perhaps," she replied. "Just give them whatever they ask for."

Analisa clasped her hands in her lap. Farleigh was dead. She was sure of it. The thought filled her with pain, and fear for her own life and that of Mrs. Thornfield. It was not unusual for carriages to be robbed. She had never worried about it when she was with Alesandro, knowing that he would protect her. She wished suddenly that he was there now. He would know what to do.

She glanced out the window again, but there was nothing to see. Whatever lay beyond the coach had been swallowed up in the thick gray mist.

She looked back at Mrs. Thornfield. "Why aren't we slowing down? Who's driving the horses?"

The housekeeper shook her head.

Analisa felt a growing sense of terror as the carriage continued at breakneck speed. This was no ordinary robbery, she was certain of that. And, judging by the expression on Mrs. Thornfield's face, she knew it, too.

The carriage turned off the main road and onto a narrow, rutted lane. Tall trees lined both sides. Leaning out the window, Analisa saw they were approaching a house made of stone. A house that seemed to have no windows.

Moments later, the carriage came to a halt in front of the house. Analisa was reaching for the carriage door when it opened, revealing a bulky man clad in a heavy cloak.

"Get out," he said, his voice gruff. "The master is waiting for you."

Frannie clasped her hands together to keep them from shaking. She'd had little to do with the master of the house, and for that she was grateful beyond words. Seeing him now, his face dark with rage, his eyes blazing like the fires of hell, she hoped she would be as fortunate in the future.

"N-no, my lord, I . . . I haven't heard from Miss Analisa," she stammered. "She left this . . . this afternoon with . . . with Mrs. Thornfield. She . . . she said they would be home before dark."

Frannie watched him pace the floor, his long strides carrying him swiftly, silently, from one end of the parlor to the other. There was something passing strange about Lord Alesandro de Avallone, she mused, though she could not have said why she thought so. Something about the way he moved, as if his feet didn't quite touch the floor. The light of the fire cast eerie shadows over his face and hair; for a moment, it looked as though he were drenched in blood.

He stopped abruptly, turned, and stared at her. It

was a look that chilled her to the marrow of her bones.

She took a step backward, her hand going to her throat. "No—"

"Come to me, Frannie."

She tried to speak, tried to shake her head, tried to run from the room, but her feet refused to obey. She was horrified to find herself walking toward him. His gaze never strayed from her face. Try as she might, she could not draw her gaze from his.

And then she was standing before him. She cried out, her voice little more than a shrill squeak of terror as his arm slid around her waist. It was like being encased in iron. She thought she might melt from the intensity of his gaze.

"Do not be afraid," he said. "I will not hurt you."

She stared up at him, mesmerized by the slow seduction of his voice. She could hear the sound of her own heart beating wildly in her breast as he bent his head toward her. There was a sudden pain that was not quite pain just below her left ear. She felt herself being drawn into a swirling crimson vortex, and then she felt nothing at all.

Analisa stood beside Mrs. Thornfield, the older woman's hand clasped in her own as she glanced at her surroundings. They had been ushered into a large, well-furnished room that looked like any other room in any other well-kept house, except that it had no windows. A fire blazed merrily in the hearth. There were expensive paintings on the walls; a plush carpet covered the floor. A comfortable-looking sofa faced the hearth. A large mirror hung over the mantel.

She had tried the door as soon as they were left alone. It was locked, as she had known it would be, but she'd had to try.

"Where are we?" Analisa wondered aloud.

Mrs. Thornfield shook her head.

"Do you think we've been kidnapped?" Analisa asked. Since they hadn't been robbed, that seemed to be the most logical explanation. She knew Alesandro would pay whatever was asked to get them back.

Mrs. Thornfield squeezed her hand. "I hope so."

"But you don't think so?"

"I think—"

The words died in the housekeeper's throat as the door opened. A tall figure stood in the doorway.

"What do you think, Elisabeth?" he asked.

"How do you know my name?"

He shrugged, but made no reply.

Mrs. Thornfield squared her shoulders. "I think you had better let us go before it's too late."

His laughter filled the room. It was a dark, ugly sound, like dry bones rattling in a grave.

"Rodrigo." Analisa whispered his name.

He bowed from the waist. "You remember me. I am flattered. I, of course, remember you." He stepped into the room and closed the door behind him.

"What are you going to do with us?" Analisa demanded, and immediately wished she hadn't.

Rodrigo looked at her and through her, and she knew in that moment that she was as good as dead, and Mrs. Thornfield as well. They were simply pawns in an endless game of revenge.

"Alesandro—"

"He will not save you," Rodrigo said. "This is my home, and he cannot enter uninvited. Surely you know that?" His smile could only be described as fiendish. "He can prowl the outside, he can pound on the walls. He can listen while you scream. But he cannot come inside."

Rodrigo lifted his hand toward Analisa's cheek. She recoiled, only to find she could not move. Helpless, she could only stare at him in horror, a horror made worse by the fact that she could see her revulsion in the mirror, but no sign of the vampire. His hand caressed her cheek. She felt the coolness against her skin, and then he leaned forward, letting her feel his fangs against her throat.

"Do not worry," he said, his breath like hellfire against her skin, "I will not take you now. Not until he is here."

"Please, don't—"

"It is not personal, you understand?"

She grimaced with repugnance when his tongue slid over her neck.

"But I am fortunate," he went on, glancing at Mrs. Thornfield, "to have the company of the two women he cares for most." His eyes narrowed. "I think I shall dine on the elder first, and save the younger for dessert."

Releasing Analisa from his hold, he glided toward the other woman, his fangs gleaming in the light of the fire, his eyes as red as the coals in the hearth.

Mrs. Thornfield screamed and ran toward the door, her nails clawing at the wood, her cry rising in horror as Rodrigo's hand curled over her shoulder, his fingers sinking like talons into her flesh.

Analisa hurled herself at the vampire's back, her own safety forgotten. She cried out in fear and pain as the vampire reached behind him, took hold of her neck, and threw her across the room. Her head slammed into the wall, and everything went black.

Alesandro stalked the dark shadows of the night, his cloak billowing behind him like the shadow of death. Where was she?

His mind searched for her, called to her, but silence was his only answer. In desperation, he sought a link with Elisabeth. As soon as he established the link, her terror slammed into him.

Rodrigo! Alesandro swore under his breath. He should have known! By damn, he should have known!

Elisabeth's fear shone in his mind, bright as the sun at noonday. It was a simple thing to follow it, to follow the sound of her screams as Rodrigo savaged her throat. But he had no sense of Analisa. Was he already too late?

Analisa woke to the sound of a groan, only to realize it was coming from her own throat. Afraid of what she might see, she opened her eyes. Closed them. And opened them again.

She was in a dungeon, her arms chained over her head.

A wrought-iron wall sconce held a single candle. The walls and floor of her prison were cold gray stone. The air was musty. In the flickering flame, she could see that she wasn't alone. Mrs. Thornfield was chained on the opposite wall, held upright only by the manacles on her wrists. Her head lolled forward. Her hair had come loose; it fell forward, hiding her face. As far as Analisa could tell, the housekeeper wasn't breathing. There was dried blood on her neck, on the shoulder of her dress.

"Mrs. Thornfield? Mrs. Thornfield! Elisabeth!"

No answer.

Analisa bit down hard on her lower lip to keep from screaming. This couldn't be happening. It had to be a nightmare. Soon she would wake and find herself curled up on the sofa in front of a fire in Alesandro's study, or safe in her own bed, anywhere but here.

She shifted her weight from one leg to the other, only then realizing that her ankles were shackled as well. Her arms ached. Her shoulders ached. Her neck . . . oh, Lord, he hadn't bitten her, had he?

She stared at Mrs. Thornfield, felt panic rise up inside her. The woman was dead, she knew it; she was chained in a medieval dungeon with a dead woman. Did Rodrigo intend to leave her here to die?

Alesandro! Her mind shrieked his name as horrible morbid images filled her mind. Images of herself going slowly insane as Mrs. Thornfield's body began to decompose. Images of herself slowly starving to death while rats gnawed her feet . . .

The fear inside her was a living, breathing thing, feeding on itself.

She tugged against the chains that bound her wrists until her skin was raw and red, until blood trickled down her arms.

"Alesandro!" She cried his name aloud, tears running down her cheeks. "Come to me. Please come to me!"

Soft mocking laughter filled the air, and then Rodrigo materialized before her, his eyes a hellish red, his fangs gleaming in the light of the candle.

He laughed again, her terror exciting him, arousing his hunger, and his lust.

She pressed against the wall, but there was nowhere to go, no way to escape from the monster who stood before her, watching her as avidly as a cat at a mouse hole.

"Call him again," Rodrigo urged. "Let him hear your fear, the way your heart pounds in terror." He threw back his head and closed his eyes, his expression bordering on rapture. "Soon my vengeance will be complete," he murmured. "Soon my Serafina will be avenged, and I will . . . Listen! He is here."

Alesandro circled the house, his frustration growing with each passing moment. Analisa was inside, and he could not go to her. He tried to open the door, both physically and mentally, but entrance was denied him. He tried to speak to Analisa's mind, but she was blocking him. When had she learned to do such a thing? he wondered, and then realized it was not Analisa's doing, but Rodrigo's.

In his mind's eye he could see the other vampire bent over Analisa, his fangs lightly raking her throat. It was Rodrigo keeping him out. He could hear the other vampire's mocking laughter in his mind, hear his voice as clearly as if he spoke aloud.

I have won! At last my Serafina will be avenged. And you, my old friend, will know the pain I have suffered these four hundred years!

"No!" Alesandro prowled the perimeter of the house. Such an odd house, with no windows and only one door. He cursed savagely. Had there been a thousand doors, each one open, he could not have entered the house unless bidden.

He came to an abrupt halt, his mind seeking Elisabeth's. She was lethargic, on the very brink of death.

Elisabeth! Elisabeth, listen to me. You must invite me into the house. Now! Before it is too late.

Alesandro?

Yes. Hurry.

But it's not my house.

It doesn't matter. You are, in a manner of speaking, a guest in the house. Hurry!

Alesandro . . . you are . . . welcome here.

He was at the back of the house now. There was no door here, but that was no longer necessary. He moved through the wall with ease and found himself in the dining room. There were no lights burning in the house, but he needed none. He moved through the house as if he had been there before, following Analisa's scent.

A tall, narrow door led to a flight of circular stairs. He followed them down, paused at the bottom, somewhat surprised to find himself in a dungeon. There were empty cells on one side, ancient instruments of torture on the other. A rack, an Iron Maiden, a wooden table stained with the blood of eons past. In passing, he saw that it held an array of knives, a garrote, several pairs of shackles.

The flickering of a candle lit the far end of the room. He moved toward it on silent feet, surprised that Rodrigo had not detected his presence.

And then he saw the other vampire. He was bent over Elisabeth's throat, lost in the rapture of feeding. Analisa was watching him, her face as white as parchment, her eyes wide with horror. He felt a surge of anger when he saw that her hands were chained above her head. She had tried to free her arms. There was dried blood on her wrists where the rough metal had cut into her flesh.

Elisabeth! He spoke to her mind, but there was no response, only the barest flicker of life.

With a wild cry, he hurled himself at Rodrigo's back, his hands curling around the vampire's throat, his fangs driving toward his neck.

He heard Analisa's scream, but he shut it out of his mind. If he lived, she would live. But, for this moment, there was nothing in all the world but the vampire struggling in his grasp.

Analisa's hands clenched into tight fists as she

watched the near-silent battle. Of similar height and weight, the vampires seemed well matched as they lunged at each other, broke away, and lunged again, their hands formed into deadly claws, their lips drawn back to reveal bloodstained fangs.

She spared a quick glance at Mrs. Thornfield. The housekeeper's head lolled forward, and Analisa feared she was really dead this time.

Rodrigo screamed what was surely an oath at Alesandro, and her gaze darted back to the two vampires. They were horrible to see, but there was a kind of graceful beauty to their deadly ballet. Faces pale, eyes burning with the hatred of four hundred years, they circled each other. They seemed to float above the floor, cloaks billowing like dark wings behind them.

She gasped as Rodrigo's fangs sank into Alesandro's shoulder, tearing away cloth and flesh. Blood spouted from the wound, spraying over the other vampire's face.

With a wild cry, Alesandro wrenched free and hurled himself at Rodrigo. He drove him back, out of the cell, down the damp corridor.

Analisa leaned forward as far as the chains would allow, but she quickly lost sight of them. Heart pounding, she listened for some sound that would let her know how the battle was going, but for several minutes there was little to be heard other than an eerie silence punctuated by a curse or an occasional grunt of pain.

Sweat trickled down her spine, dripped from her

brow. Every muscle grew tense with worry and fear for what would happen if Alesandro lost the fight.

Alesandro, Alesandro, I love you.

She repeated the words over and over again, hoping that somehow he would feel her love and gain strength from it.

A shrill scream filled with rage and excruciating anguish rose in the air, reverberating off the high ceiling, the walls, the floor, ringing like a death knell in Analisa's ears.

And then there was only a silence as deep as eternity.

She stared at the entrance to the cell, waiting, wondering if it would be life or death that walked through the doorway.

Chapter Twenty-six

Ears straining, heart pounding, Analisa stared at the door. She heard nothing, but suddenly a tall form appeared in the doorway. His eyes were aglow with hatred and the heat of battle, his mouth stained with crimson. His white shirt was splattered with dark red blood.

She felt her breath catch in her throat, then escape in a long sigh of relief. It was Alesandro.

She whispered his name as he drew near.

At a word, the shackles on her hands and feet fell away. Moving toward Mrs. Thornfield, he released her as well. Catching her in his arms, he laid her gently on the cold stone floor, then turned toward Analisa once again.

" 'Lisa?" His fingertips moved over her neck, lingering where Rodrigo's fangs had penetrated the skin.

"I'm all right." Her gaze moved over him. He was pale. There were deep scratches on his face. Blood flowed from the wound in his shoulder, dripped from a dozen other gashes on his arms, his neck, his chest. "You are not."

He drew her into his arms. "Do not worry for me."

"Is Mrs. Thornfield dead?"

"Soon."

"You've got to save her, Alesandro. We can't just let her die."

"She has very little blood left for me to take, and I fear I do not have enough to give her."

"We have to do something! Can't you take my blood and then give it to her?"

"You would be willing to do that?"

Analisa glanced at Mrs. Thornfield, remembering the woman's kindness. "Yes, of course. Hurry!"

He considered it for a moment, then shook his head. "It is not safe for you."

"Why not?"

"Fighting with Rodrigo has left me weak. I need blood."

She could see that for herself. His skin was pale, his eyes burned with hellish need. He was afraid for her, she thought, afraid he would not be able to stop, afraid he would take too much.

Analisa glanced down at Mrs. Thornfield. She couldn't stand by and let her die. The housekeeper had been kind to her. She had taught her to read and write. And she loved Alesandro as much as Analisa did.

"Do it, Alesandro."

"You are sure?"

She nodded, hoping she would not regret her decision. Alesandro needed blood to heal, to replace what he had lost in the fight, what he was losing even now from the wounds Rodrigo had inflicted. She knew he usually healed rapidly, sometimes immediately. Why did the bite of a vampire take longer to heal?

She closed her eyes when she felt Alesandro's fangs at her throat. What if he couldn't stop in time?

Her apprehension quickly faded, replaced by the sensual pleasure of his touch. She could feel the change in her heartbeat as it slowed to beat in time with his. His breath was warm on her skin, his hands masterful yet gentle as they clasped her shoulders, holding her close. She felt the pain of his wounds. They burned like fire, as if someone had poured acid on his skin. But the pain was receding, growing less with each passing moment. The thought pleased her.

She moaned softly when he lifted his head.

"Analisa?"

Her eyelids fluttered open and she stared up at him, her gaze unfocused.

"Lie still," he said.

She nodded, surprised to find herself lying on the floor beside Mrs. Thornfield. She watched through half-closed eyes as he lifted the housekeeper into his arms. She saw his face, his gaze intent as he bent over the other woman. Mrs. Thornfield cried out, whether in fear or pain or protest Analisa could not say, as Alesandro's fangs pierced her skin.

For the first time, Analisa wondered if they were doing the right thing. Would Mrs. Thornfield be pleased by their decision, or appalled? Analisa blinked, trying to clear her mind. How would she feel if someone made such a decision for her? Would she choose to live as a vampire if the alternative was death? Could she drink blood to survive? The thought filled her with revulsion. As much as she loved Alesandro, she had no desire to become what he was.

Analisa lifted up on one elbow. "Alesandro, wait . . ."

But it was too late.

And then a new fear insinuated itself into her consciousness. Smoke! She smelled smoke.

Rolling onto her hands and knees, she crawled toward Alesandro and grabbed his arm.

He turned on her, his eyes blazing, his face the face of a stranger. Seeing her, he closed his eyes, and when he opened them again, it was Alesandro looking back at her. "What is it?"

She clutched his arm. "I think the house is on fire."

He lifted his head, nostrils sniffing the air, and then he swore a vile oath. "We've got to get out of here. Can you walk?"

She nodded, her heart pounding. Would this horrible nightmare never end?

Rising, he lifted Mrs. Thornfield and draped her

over his shoulder, then helped Analisa to her feet. "We must go. Now."

She followed him, none too steadily, out of the cell, down the dark corridor, and up the stairs. Smoke filled her nostrils and stung her eyes.

Alesandro put his hand on the latch, only to find the door locked from the other side.

Cursing Rodrigo, he slammed his fist against the wood, and the door shattered.

Analisa followed him through the opening. The smoke was thicker here. Coughing, she followed Alesandro, who made his way unerringly through the dark toward the front door.

She slammed into his back when he came to an abrupt halt. "What is it?"

"We cannot go out the door. The fire was started there."

Analisa wiped her eyes. "How will we get out?" she asked, fighting down the panic that threatened to overtake her. "There aren't any windows!"

"Follow me." Pivoting, he hurried down the hallway, looking into each room he passed until he came to the library.

She followed him into the room.

"Close the door," he said.

She did as he asked, fear spreading through her as she looked wildly around. There were no windows in this room, either. It was hopeless. Coming in here might prolong the inevitable, but there was no way out. They were going to die, all of them. Even preternatural flesh couldn't withstand fire.

"Alesandro?" She reached out for him. If she had to die, at least she could die in his arms.

He wrapped his free arm around her shoulders and hugged her tight. "Do not be afraid."

Not be afraid? Smoke was seeping under the door, burning her eyes, searing her throat.

"I am going to take Mrs. Thornfield out, and then I will come back for you."

"Out? How?" He might be able to carry her through the night with supernatural speed, but he couldn't carry her and Mrs. Thornfield through walls made of brick.

"The fireplace." He kissed her gently. "Do not be afraid."

Before she could argue, he was gone. She stared after him, ashamed of herself for wondering why he took the other woman first. She could hear the crackle of flames as the fire ate its way toward her.

"Alesandro, hurry!"

She moved toward the fireplace, stepped up on the hearth, and put her back to the door.

How long had he been gone? It seemed like hours, though it couldn't have been more than a minute or two.

And suddenly he was there, his arms wrapping around her, holding her close. Before she realized they were moving, they were outside. Mrs. Thornfield lay on the grass several yards away from the house, pale and unmoving.

Still holding Analisa, Alesandro bent down and

lifted the other woman over his shoulder, and then they were hurtling through the night.

The next thing Analisa knew, they were inside the stone cottage. The door closed quietly behind them, sealing them in darkness.

In his room below stairs, Alesandro set Analisa on her feet, then laid Mrs. Thornfield on his bed.

"Is she going to be all right?" Analisa asked.

He shrugged, his expression troubled. "That will be up to her."

"Maybe we acted hastily," Analisa remarked. "Maybe we should have asked her if it was what she wanted."

"There was no time," he replied. "Come, I will take you home."

"I want to stay here, with you."

"No, 'Lisa. You do not want to be here when she wakes."

"Can't you bring her to the house, then? So we can all be together?"

"No. It is not wise for her to be near mortals when the transformation takes place. It will be difficult for her. And if I have made a mistake in bringing her across . . ." His words trailed off, but she knew what he had left unsaid. If the housekeeper didn't want to be a vampire, he would destroy her.

He covered the housekeeper with a blanket, then gathered Analisa into his arms.

Moments later, they were in his bedchamber. "I want you to stay here tonight. Lock the door and let no one in. I will come to you as soon as I can."

She nodded.

"Will you be all right, 'Lisa?"

She nodded again, afraid to speak for fear she would throw her arms around his neck and beg him not to go.

"Do not be afraid."

He gazed down at her, his expression filled with love and tenderness, yet, for an instant, she saw him as she had seen him earlier, his eyes blazing, his fangs stained with blood as he fought with Rodrigo, saw him bending over Mrs. Thornfield's neck . . .

" 'Lisa?"

"I'll be all right," she said. "You'd better go."

He looked at her for several moments, then vanished from her sight.

She stood there a minute; then, feeling chilled, she climbed into his bed and pulled the covers up to her chin.

Sleep was a long time coming.

She dreamed of blood . . . a surging river of blood . . . and swimming in the river she saw Alesandro and Rodrigo and Mrs. Thornfield, all struggling to stay afloat. She saw Rodrigo go under, and then Mrs. Thornfield. Standing on the shore, she reached out to Alesandro, knowing that only she could save him. He caught her hand. And pulled her in. And under . . .

She woke gasping for air, the taste of blood lingering on her lips.

Flinging off the covers, she unlocked the door and ran out of the room. Needing to see the sun, to feel its warmth on her skin, she ran down the hallway and out of the house.

Outside, she lifted her face toward the rising sun, basking in its light.

A warmth, a light, that Mrs. Thornfield would never see again.

Sinking down on her knees, Analisa buried her face in her hands. What was she doing here? How could she be in love with a vampire? All these months she had known what he was, or thought she knew. But last night . . . last night it was as if someone had removed the blinders from her eyes and she had seen him for the first time, not as the man who had saved her life. Not as the man she loved. But as a vampire. He had told her he was capable of killing. Last night, she had seen death in his eyes. She had watched him fight with Rodrigo, had felt his anger, his power, and it had been a terrible, frightening thing to see. She had seen the blood lust in his eyes when he bent over Mrs. Thornfield.

But he could be kind. And gentle. She knew that as well. He had made love to her so tenderly, showered her with gifts, confessed his love and his need. Taken her into his home . . .

To have a ready source of blood.

But that had been in the beginning.

And now?

Rising, she began to walk through the gardens. What about now? She couldn't believe that his love-making had been a lie, that all his words had been nothing more than a way to keep her here. He had survived four hundred years without her.

She walked for an hour, lost in thought, wondering how she would explain Mrs. Thornfield's absence. Returning to the house, she found Frannie, Dewhurst, and Cook in the parlor. They all looked up when she entered the room.

"Oh, Miss Matthews," Frannie said, "we've been so worried!"

"Worried? Why?"

"The carriage came back last night empty," Dewhurst said. "We didn't know what had happened to you and the others."

"Are you all right, miss?" Frannie asked.

"Yes, yes, I'm fine."

"What happened last night?" Dewhurst asked. "Where are Mrs. Thornfield and Farleigh?"

"I . . . we had some trouble on the road," Analisa replied, thinking fast. "Robbers. Farleigh was killed—"

"Killed!" Dewhurst exclaimed.

Analisa nodded. "I'm sorry," she murmured. "I know the two of you were very close."

Dewhurst sank down on a chair, too shocked to be mindful of proper behavior.

"What of Mrs. Thornfield?" Frannie asked, her voice subdued.

"She was injured. The horses bolted, so I had to find another carriage to bring me home." She glanced from Dewhurst to her maid. "I'm sorry I didn't wake either of you when I returned, but it was very late."

"And where is Mrs. Thornfield now?" Dewhurst asked.

"Lord Alesandro showed up soon after the accident. He took her to the hospital."

"Will she be all right?" Frannie asked.

"I don't know," Analisa said, glad to be able to speak the truth at last.

"Will you be wanting breakfast?" inquired Cook.

"No, thank you." She couldn't eat, not after last night. "But I would like a cup of tea."

"Very well, miss. I'm glad you're home safe," he said, and left the room, obviously anxious to have something to do.

"Frannie, would you draw me a bath, please, and lay out my clothing for the day?" It felt good to be thinking of mundane things. It helped to hold the horror of the past night away.

"Yes, miss."

"I'm glad you weren't hurt, miss," the groom said, rising.

"Thank you, Dewhurst."

"Will you be wanting to visit Mrs. Thornfield later?" he asked.

"I . . . yes, of course. That is, the doctor said she wasn't to have any visitors just now."

"Very well, miss." Dewhurst looked at her oddly a moment, then left the room.

Analisa stared after them. They would think it strange if she didn't go and visit the housekeeper, and stranger still if Mrs. Thornfield never returned. And she couldn't return, Analisa realized. The master of the house might be allowed his eccentricities; the staff might whisper among themselves and think it strange that he kept such unusual hours, but they would not accept the same from a housekeeper.

Analisa sighed. Poor Mrs. Thornfield. She had been with Alesandro for so many years, but that was ended now. She recalled Alesandro saying that vampires could not share the same territory; certainly they could not share the same house without arousing suspicion.

It was a problem that was beyond her ability to solve, at least at the moment.

Feeling a headache coming on, she went upstairs, hoping a bath and a change of clothes would make her feel better.

The day seemed to stretch endlessly before her. The house felt empty and was far too quiet. She tried to keep busy, tried to read, to sew. She went outside and sat in the sun. But try as she might, she could not stop thinking of Mrs. Thornfield. How had she reacted when she discovered what Alesandro had done? Was she relieved to still be alive? Or horrified to learn she was now a vampire? Would Alesandro stay with her, teach her what she needed to know? Or drive her out of his territory? Somehow, try as she might, she could not picture Mrs. Thornfield prowling through the night, stalking some helpless mortal, drinking her victim's blood. The mere idea filled her with revulsion. How did Alesandro bear it?

And what of Rodrigo? She had thought, had

hoped, that he was dead, but he was the only one who could have set fire to the house. Where was he now?

That thought grew more and more worrisome as night spread its cloak over the land.

Chapter Twenty-seven

Thwarted again! It was beyond endurance. Damn Alesandro. And damn the woman! Damn them all!

Muttering an oath, Rodrigo stormed through the night, his rage growing, gathering like the dark clouds scudding across the sky. He had been so close, so certain he was about to have the revenge he craved. How had it all gone wrong?

He lifted a hand to his chest where Alesandro had stabbed him with a rusty knife. Had the other vampire's aim been better, he might be dead now. As it was, he had barely managed to escape. It galled him to know that, had Alesandro pursued him instead of going back to look after the women, he would most certainly be dead, his body moldering in the bowels of his house.

And where was the good doctor now?

Rodrigo paused. Lifted his head to sniff the air. The scent of cheap perfume was borne to him on the wind. A prostitute was plying her trade nearby. He smiled. Little did she know her next customer would be her last.

Chapter Twenty-eight

Alesandro stood beside his bed in his chamber at Blackbriar Hall. He had brought Elisabeth here as soon as the sun had set. No one save Analisa knew of his lair in the stone cottage. It was knowledge he would not share with anyone else, not even his trusted housekeeper.

Now he waited. Soon, Elisabeth would awake to find herself a changed creature. Would she hate him for what he had done? Embrace her new life? Or ask him to end her existence as a vampire before it had even begun?

She lay on his bed unmoving, still caught in the death-like sleep that held all vampires in its grasp from sunrise to sunset. She had died the night before; would she remember the horror of it, he wondered, or had the memory been mercifully blotted from her mind?

He had lit several candles in hopes the light would somehow make things easier for her. He wondered again if she would recall the night past. Rodrigo's memory of that fateful night so long ago had been hazy upon waking the next night. He recalled little save that he had followed a beautiful woman and awakened forever changed. Alesandro wished he had been so blessed. He recalled it all so clearly even now: his terror at Tzianne's vicious attack, his horror as he endured mortal death, alive yet not alive, not knowing he would rise the next night. His confusion when he realized what had happened to him, his refusal to believe it, the lethargy that had engulfed him, the pain of the sun scorching preternatural flesh while he hastened to find a place to hide . . .

Elisabeth woke abruptly. Bolting into an upright position, she glanced anxiously around the room.

"It is all right, Elisabeth. There is nothing to fear."

She swung her head around to face him. "Where are we?" She glanced around the room, frowning in recognition. "Blackbriar? How did I get here?"

He moved toward the bed and took her hand in his. "All in good time, Elisabeth. How do you feel?"

She blinked up at him, as if puzzled by his question. "I feel . . ." She frowned. "I feel very well. But I shouldn't, should I? Why are you looking at me like that?" She glanced around the room, as if she might find the answer to her question lurking in a corner. "Why does everything look so different? Your cloak . . . I can see every stitch, every thread. The sun just went down, didn't it? I can smell the night . . ."

She took hold of his arm, her eyes widening, the pulse in her throat beating rapidly. "Alesandro!"

"Elisabeth." He sat down on the edge of the bed and drew her into his arms. "What do you remember of yesterday and last night?"

She frowned again. "We went into the city. Analisa bought a gown for the wedding . . ." Her eyes widened. "Our coach was attacked. They killed Farleigh and took us to . . . Rodrigo! Rodrigo was there. What has he done to Analisa?"

"Analisa is at the townhouse. She is unhurt."

"Thank the Lord."

"Is that all you remember?"

"I think so . . . No!" Her hand flew to her throat. "Rodrigo! He bit me. Drank from me!" She shuddered, remembering the horror of it, the pain of it. "How did I get here? Where is that fiend now?"

"I found you and Analisa at his house," Alesandro replied. "You were very near death. I would have taken you to the hospital, but there was no time."

Her gaze met his, and in the depths of his eyes she found the answer she was looking for.

Slowly she shook her head, her eyes filled with horror. "No. No, tell me you did not?"

"I could not let you die when I had the power to save you."

"How could you?" Her fingers searched her throat. "You had no right to . . . to make me what you are." Pushing against his chest, she stood. "I can't be a vampire. I don't want to be a vampire!" She whirled around to face him. "Undo it, now!"

"I cannot, Elisabeth. You know that."

She doubled over, her arms wrapped around her stomach, a low, keening wail of pain issuing from her lips as the hunger made itself known.

"I remember now," she gasped. "I remember it all." She lifted her head, her gaze piercing his. "Help me!"

"You need to feed, Elisabeth."

"No!" She shook her head. "No, I couldn't. I can't."

But he could see the hunger in her eyes, the growing need. He recalled his own revulsion at the thought of needing blood to survive when he had been a new vampire, but it had merely been a holdover from his old life, a taboo that no longer had any meaning. He was a vampire. Taking blood was natural for him. It would be for her, too, once she got past her initial revulsion.

"Come," he said, taking her by the hand. "Let me show you the beauty of the night."

Analisa couldn't sit still. She tried to read, but, for once, books held no appeal. She picked up her embroidery, only to put it down after a few minutes. She nibbled on a bit of pudding, but had no appetite. She picked up her shawl, intending to go for a walk in the gardens, but thoughts of Rodrigo prowling the shadows quickly changed her mind. Dropping her shawl on the back of a chair, she wandered through the house, finally ending up in Alesandro's room. Sitting on the bed, she hugged his pillow to her chest. Where was he? Why didn't he come to her? Surely he knew how anxious she must be for news of how Mrs. Thornfield was adjusting to her new life.

Once again, Analisa tried to imagine Mrs. Thornfield as a vampire . . . tried to imagine herself as a vampire, forced to spend her days trapped in a deathlike sleep, forced to forever shun the daylight, to dine on blood. Given a choice between death and becoming a vampire, which would she choose? For the first time, it occurred to her that if she were a vampire, she could be young forever, live with Alesandro, forever.

She fell asleep with that intriguing thought.

Alesandro smiled at Elisabeth. "You see? It was not so bad, was it?"

Elisabeth looked up at him, her gray eyes shining. He had taught her to hunt, shown her how to feed, how to erase from the mind of her prey any memory of her feeding.

After she had fed, he had shown her the beauty of the night. With her vampire eyes and ears, she saw details and heard sounds mortals never saw, never heard. When she walked, it was as if her feet never touched the ground.

"Not so bad as I thought it would be, at least," she replied. She twirled around, her arms extended, her head back, the sound of her laughter floating on the wings of the night. "I feel so young! So strong. As if I could fly."

He laughed with her. For all that he lamented his lost mortality and despised the necessity of taking blood to survive, being a vampire had its rewards. Eternal youth. Eternal health. Supernatural powers. And time. The greatest gift of all.

Though he was not certain of Elisabeth's age, he knew she had to be in her sixties, though she looked much younger thanks to the small amounts of blood he had given her in the past. Now, infused with the full preternatural glamour of the Dark Gift, she looked younger still. Her hair glowed with vibrant health, as did her skin.

She put her hand on his arm to steady herself. "I haven't done that in more years than I can remember," she remarked, grinning.

He looked down at her, his smile fading as the expression on her face turned from exuberance to contemplation to desire.

"I have loved you most of my life," she said quietly. "I watched you stay young while I grew old, and still I loved you. I love you now."

"Elisabeth—"

"I knew there was no hope for us before, that you did not love me as I loved you, but now we're alike, Alesandro. I can share your life in ways that she never can."

"Elisabeth, I am in love with Analisa.

"But I loved you first!"

"I care for you. I always have, and that has not

343

Amanda Ashley

changed. But I am going to marry Analisa, if she will still have me. And you will not harm her in any way, do you understand?"

"And what am I to do?" she asked bitterly. "Where am I to go? Because of what you've done, I can't stay here, or go back to the Manor, or to Blackbriar."

"I have a large house in Milano. It is yours, and the income from the winery that goes with it."

"So far away?"

"We cannot hunt the same territory. It is not wise, or safe. In time you will learn that vampires are very territorial about their hunting grounds."

"What of Rodrigo?"

"He is a danger to all of us. You would be wise to stay out of his way." Alesandro glanced up at the sky. It would be dawn in a few hours. "You must find a secure place to spend the day."

"Where shall I go?"

He shook his head. "That is something you must decide. Never tell anyone where you sleep. Trust no one with that knowledge. Not me, not anyone. Do you understand?"

She nodded, her voice filled with sudden anxiety as she glanced around. "But I don't know where to go."

"Go to the Hall. The crypt in the garden is large. You can stay there until you find a resting place of your own."

She shuddered. "You want me to sleep in a tomb?"

"You will be safe there."

"How will I get in?"

"Lift the lid."

Her eyes widened. "It's too heavy."

He laughed softly. "Trust me, you will be able to lift it with ease." He saw the disbelief in her eyes. "Here," he said, pointing at a large boulder along the roadway. "Lift this."

"I can't."

"Try."

With a shake of her head, she took hold of the boulder with both hands. Amazement filled her eyes as she lifted it from the ground.

"How?" She lifted the rock over her head as if it weighed no more than a tea tray. "How can I do this?"

"Elisabeth, how have you lived with a vampire so long and not understood? You know what I can do. Those powers are now yours."

"Am I as strong as you, then?" She dropped the boulder on the ground. "As strong as Rodrigo?"

"No, but you will be, in time." He glanced at the sky again. "I am going home," he said. "Do not be afraid when you feel the Dark Sleep come upon you. Do not fight it. In time, it will seem natural."

"I don't want to be alone, not now. Stay with me, please."

He thought of Analisa, waiting for him.

"It's the least you can do," she said, her voice sharper than she intended.

"Go to the Hall. I will meet you at the crypt before dawn."

"You promise?"

He nodded. "And there is no need to lift the lid of

the crypt," he said with a faint grin. "All you need do is will yourself inside."

And then, before she could detain him further, he vanished from her sight.

Analisa awoke to the sound of Alesandro's voice whispering her name. Opening her eyes, she found him lying on the bed beside her.

"You're here," she murmured sleepily. Suddenly awake, she sat up. "Where is Mrs. Thornfield? Is she all right? Where have you been?"

Grunting softly, he rolled onto his back and drew her down on top of him. "Elisabeth will be fine. I just left her. She was upset at first, but I think she has accepted the change. In time, she might even be grateful."

"Grateful." Analisa shuddered at the mere idea. "What will I tell the household staff? How will I explain her absence?"

"I will take care of it." His gaze moved over her face, his expression thoughtful. " 'Lisa?"

She frowned at the solemn tone of his voice, the sudden intensity of his gaze. "What? Is something wrong?"

"So much has happened. Do you . . ." He turned away, an oath escaping his lips before he looked at her once again. "Have you changed your mind? About us?"

"No, Alesandro." Her gaze searched his face. "Have you?"

"No. I missed you."

"Did you?"

"You know I did. Will you stay here with me?"

"I cannot. I promised Elisabeth I would rest beside her."

Jealousy was not a green-eyed monster. It was a sharp stab of pain in her heart, an ache in her very soul.

" 'Lisa. It is only one day. She is afraid to be alone when the Dark Sleep claims her the first time." He ran his knuckles lightly over her cheek. "You understand?"

"I understand she loves you."

He didn't deny it.

"And now . . ." Analisa frowned. "And now she is what you are."

"It changes nothing between you and me."

"Doesn't it? The two of you share something now that you and I can never share."

He stared at her in disbelief. She was jealous. Jealous of Elisabeth.

"What will she do now?" Analisa asked. "She can't come back here. Does she have any family anywhere . . . oh, I guess she couldn't stay with them, either."

"I have a small estate in Milano. I told her to go there."

"So far away?"

He grinned inwardly, thinking her response was the same as Elisabeth's had been. "Would you rather she stayed here?"

"No," she replied quickly.

"There is no need for you to be jealous, *cara.*"

"Isn't there?

"No." In one fluid movement, he rolled over and tucked her slender body beneath his. "No reason at all." His kiss smothered the argument he read in her eyes.

She glared up at him, mutinous, but only for a moment. And then her eyelids fluttered down and she surrendered to the incredible need that his kisses aroused in her. She had never made love to anyone else, had nothing with which to compare the heat of his kisses, the way her whole body came alive at the merest touch of his hand, the sound of his voice.

Was it only her love for him that caused her to respond this way, or was it something more? Could any man's kiss drive her to such distraction?

"No, 'Lisa," he murmured, answering her unspoken question. "You were made for me. Can you not feel it?"

She had forgotten he could read her mind, sense her thoughts. And surely that was part of the wonder of their lovemaking, the joining not only of their bodies, but their minds as well. There were times when he knew what she wanted, what she needed, before she did.

His hand skimmed over her breast, teasingly delicious, making her ache for more. She put her hand over his, holding it in place, her hips writhing beneath him, seeking to be closer.

She heard the sudden intake of his breath as he was caught up in the tumult, heard him gasp her name as

348

she began to caress him, her touches growing more and more intimate.

He tore off his shirt and sent it flying across the room. His hand fisted in the bodice of her gown. One yank, and it was gone. Her undergarments as well. She tugged at his trousers as they rolled back and forth on the mattress. Clothing flew through the air. He sat up to remove her slippers and his boots, and then he lowered himself over her once again, the thought that the sun's rising was less than an hour away adding to the tension between them.

She gasped his name, her nails raking his back as she urged him on, everything else forgotten but her need for this man, this incredible man. . . .

Elisabeth circled the crypt. She had seen it countless times, had known what it was, why it was here, but she had never considered the possibility that one day she would occupy it. She didn't know where Alesandro passed the daylight hours, but she knew it wasn't here. Did Analisa know?

She glanced up at the sky, her preternatural flesh sensing the coming of a new day. Where was he? She couldn't enter the crypt alone. Even if it meant she'd burn up with the rising of the sun, she couldn't do it. She had always feared small, closed-in places, feared being buried alive. How could she endure this?

She ran her hand over the cold white marble, her thoughts chasing themselves like a puppy chasing its tail. So much had happened in such a short time. She still couldn't quite grasp all the changes she'd undergone. She'd had no time to prepare herself, no time to think about it, no say at all in the decision. Would she have agreed to accept the Dark Gift if she had been given a choice?

She stared at the crypt. She was sixty-four years old. How many more years would she have had if Alesandro hadn't changed her? Though she had been in good health for a woman her age, it wouldn't have lasted forever. All too soon, she would have been laid in a crypt such as this from which she would never return.

She shuddered at the thought. This was better. Much better. Though she had been thoroughly repulsed by what she had to do to survive, once she got past it, it wasn't so bad. Almost pleasurable, in fact.

A life against nature, Alesandro had said. But it was life. And she very much wanted to live.

Her skin felt suddenly tight, and she glanced up at the sky. It would soon be dawn. Where was Alesandro?

Analisa blinked back a tear as she watched Alesandro pull on his shirt. She wanted to beg him to stay. It wasn't fair that he should have to leave her, not now, when they had made love so tenderly. She wanted to rest in his arms, to fall asleep in his embrace.

As though sensing her thoughts, he sat down on the bed and drew her into his arms. "I do not want to leave you, 'Lisa, you know that."

"I know."

"I will come to you tonight as soon as I can."

"Promise?"

He nodded. "I love you, my sweet Analisa. Dream of me."

"I will." She lifted her face for his kiss, closed her eyes as he cupped her face in his hands and kissed her deeply.

When she opened her eyes again, he was gone.

Elisabeth whirled around at the sudden knowledge that she was no longer alone. She breathed an audible sigh of relief when she saw it was Alesandro.

"Were you expecting someone else?" he asked with a wry smile.

"I can't stop thinking about Rodrigo."

Alesandro grunted softly. Sooner or later, he was going to have to do something about Rodrigo. He had let his old friend terrorize his life for far too long, partly because of the love he had once had for the man, partly because of the guilt he still carried for Serafina's death. But he had Analisa to think of. And now he had Elisabeth to consider. Like it or not, he was responsible for her, too.

He looked up, askance, as she tugged on his arm. "Alesandro, the dawn . . ."

With a nod, he took her by the hand. "Just relax," he murmured, and dissolved into the crypt, drawing her with him.

"It's so dark!" Elisabeth exclaimed.

"There is nothing to fear." He settled down on the

feather mattress and drew her down beside him. "Do not try to fight it. Just close your eyes and let the darkness surround you."

"Will I dream?"

"No."

"Will I wake up?"

He laughed softly. "Of course."

He knew when the sun cleared the horizon, knew when the Dark Sleep took hold of her. Her hand tightened around his as it drew her toward oblivion, and then, abruptly, her grip loosened.

He could see her clearly in the dark. Enhanced by the glamour of the Dark Gift and her recent feeding, her skin was unblemished and had the bloom of youth. The lines around her eyes and mouth were less noticeable, her hair was thick and lustrous.

With a sigh, he closed his eyes and followed her into the dark maw of oblivion. His last conscious thought, as always, was of Analisa.

Chapter Twenty-nine

Rodrigo paused, his head bowed over his latest victim. Eyes widening in disbelief, he buried his fangs in the tender skin of the woman's throat. He had done it! After four hundred years, Alesandro had bequeathed the Dark Gift to another, something Rodrigo had never done. Rodrigo licked a drop of blood from beneath the woman's ear. What had it been like, to bring another across, to watch the hellish transformation, to know that you had robbed a woman of life and yet given her another life in exchange?

He glanced down at the woman in his arms. Her vivid green eyes stared back at him, empty of expression. Her skin was pale, almost translucent. His mind probed hers. She was twenty-five years old. Her husband had mistreated her and she had run away. She had no children. Both of her parents were dead. She had a younger brother who was in prison, and a sister who was a nun.

He laughed softly. A diverse family, to be sure.

And what did she have to live for? He probed her mind again. She lived in a small room above the bakery where she worked for room and board and a mere pittance. She had considered taking her own life on several occasions, but lacked the courage to do so.

He grinned as he stared down at her, curious to know how she would react if he bestowed the Dark Gift upon her, and even more curious to know what it would feel like to drain her dry and then fill her with new life.

He probed her mind one more time, searching for her name.

"Kathleen Fowler." He spoke it aloud, savoring it on his tongue as he bent his head to her throat once more.

She shuddered in his arms, her skin growing more pale, her lips turning blue as he drained her life's force, and then, when her heartbeat had grown so faint even he could scarcely hear it, he tore a gash in his wrist and pressed it to her mouth.

"Drink, Kathleen," he purred. "Drink your fill and then come and walk eternity with me."

He closed his eyes as her mouth fastened on his wrist, her throat working frantically.

Rodrigo smiled faintly. What would Alesandro think when he discovered that another vampire walked among them?

Chapter Thirty

Analisa woke slowly, stretched, and then sat up with a jerk. Rising, she went to the window, drew back the heavy draperies, and raised the sash. Sunlight poured into the room, over her skin. For a moment, she closed her eyes and let the warmth wash over her. How good it felt on her face and arms.

Opening her eyes, she gazed at the scene below: the greening grass, the multitude of flowers blooming, the way the late afternoon sunlight shimmered on the small pool in the center of the gardens. How beautiful it looked! Poor Mrs. Thornfield. She would never see the beauty of this place again. Poor Alesandro, to have dwelled in darkness for four hundred years.

Feeling hungry, she rang for Frannie and asked the maid to have Cook prepare her something to eat.

"Dewhurst wants to know if you'll be wantin' the carriage brought round."

"The carriage?"

"He thought you might be wantin' to go visit Mrs. Thornfield."

"Oh. I . . . that is, I think I'd better wait and talk to Lord Alesandro."

Frannie eyed her strangely. "Yes, miss, as you wish. Will that be all?"

"Yes, for now."

With a curtsey, Frannie left the room.

The staff would most likely think her a heartless creature for not going to the hospital, Analisa thought with a sigh. Would it be better to make the trip and pretend to visit the housekeeper?

Sitting at her dressing table, she picked up her brush and ran it through her hair. She hated lying, but she could hardly tell Frannie and the others the truth.

She stared at her reflection in the mirror, trying not to think of Alesandro spending the night with Mrs. Thornfield. She told herself she was being foolish, that there was nothing to worry about. But she couldn't help being jealous.

Frannie returned a few moments later and filled the ewer with hot water. Analisa washed quickly. Frannie helped her dress, and she went downstairs to breakfast. Everything seemed to remind her of Mrs. Thornfield and Alesandro. She looked at the food on her plate. Never again would Mrs. Thornfield be able to enjoy one of Cook's sumptuous meals; Alesandro had not eaten solid food in four hundred years.

With a shake of her head, she finished her breakfast and left the table. She sent Dewhurst into town to pick up the mail and then spent a leisurely hour reading the morning paper. She was about to put it aside when she noticed a small article on the last page.

Body of unidentified young woman found on the roadside. Police say possible cause of death may be an animal attack, due to wounds in the victim's neck and amount of blood lost.

Fear congealed in the pit of Analisa's stomach. The woman had been killed by a vampire. She knew it as surely as she knew the sun would rise in the east. But which vampire?

She laughed mirthlessly. Only a few months ago, she had not believed such creatures existed, and now she knew three of them, one of them intimately!

Frannie brought her a pot of tea a short time later. Feeling strangely numb, Analisa sipped it slowly. So much had happened since she'd met Alesandro. Her life had changed in ways she had never imagined. She had a closet filled with dresses and gowns, shoes and silk stockings and delicately made undergarments. She had learned to read and write, she knew how to do fancy needlework, how to behave at a large dinner party. She had fallen in love, experienced its joy, and its pain, basked in the pleasure of her lover's touch.

Her lover. Where was he now?

Putting the half-empty cup aside, she went outside to wander aimlessly through the gardens, trying not to imagine Alesandro and Mrs. Thornfield hunting for prey the night before, or lying side by side now, trapped in the Dark Sleep.

Finding herself standing outside the barn, she opened one of the big double doors and went inside. Alesandro's big black devil horse whinnied softly when she approached the stall.

"Hello, Deuce," she murmured.

The stallion's ears twitched at the sound of her voice.

"Do you miss him?" She took a step forward, warily reaching out with one hand to stroke the horse's neck. His coat was as smooth as silk. She stroked the stallion's neck for several minutes and then, growing braver, she took another step forward and rested her forehead on his shoulder. "I miss him, too," she murmured. "He asked me to marry him, you know, and I said I would, but now—"

"Now?"

She whirled around, her hand going to her heart. "Alesandro! You frightened me." She looked past him to the doorway, surprised to see that the sun was already setting. "I didn't know it was so late . . . where is Mrs. Thornfield?"

"She is up at the house, getting her things."

"Oh. What reason will she give for leaving your service?"

"She is going to tell them she has decided to retire." His gaze focused on her face, the blue of his eyes looking almost black.

"What's wrong?" she asked, disconcerted by the intensity of his look.

"Have you changed your mind, 'Lisa?"

She bit down on her lip. He must have heard her talking to his horse, she thought.

" 'Lisa?" He stood there, vampire still, waiting for her answer. He was wearing black again, and she wondered absently if there was some sort of vampire code that decreed they must always be attired in black.

"I haven't changed my mind." Seeing him, hearing his voice, chased all her doubts away.

"This is not the first time you have had second thoughts about us," he said quietly. "Not that I can fault you for that, considering all that has happened."

"I have no doubts when we are together," she said, "so perhaps you should never leave my side."

He closed the distance between them and drew her into her arms. "I never should have let it come to this," he remarked, shaking his head ruefully. "I did not intend for this to happen. In four hundred years, I have allowed no mortal to get close to me, to matter to me."

She tilted her head back so she could see his face. "Would you rather I were a vampire, as you are?"

He had thought of it many times, but it was the first time she had mentioned it. The idea filled him with excitement, and horror.

"It would make things easier in many ways," he admitted, "but I would not see you changed, Analisa. I love you as you are."

Amanda Ashley

"But I won't always be like this."

He brushed a lock of hair from her cheek, ran his thumb back and forth across the velvet smoothness of her skin. "You are the most beautiful creature I have ever seen," he said quietly, "but I am not in love with your appearance, 'Lisa. I love the gentleness of your heart, the bravery of your soul."

"So you would love me just the same if I were old and wrinkled?"

He nodded.

"And it would make no difference when we made love?"

"Perhaps I would blow out the candles."

She made a face at him, and then she laughed.

"It is good to hear you laugh." He brushed a kiss across the crown of her head, then drew her up hard against him. "What am I do to with you?"

"Marry me, my lord," she said, "as you promised." As soon as they were wed, she would order him some new coats, she thought. Of course, he looked elegant in black, but she thought he would look equally gorgeous in blue to match his eyes.

"You have but to name the day," he assured her, then rested his chin on the top of her head. "Rodrigo has bequeathed the Dark Gift to another."

"When? Why?"

"Last night. I do not know why." He frowned. "Who can say why that madman does what he does? Perhaps, like me, he grows weary of being alone."

"A good guess, Dr. Avallone."

Alesandro whirled around to face the intruder

360

standing just inside the barn door. "What are you doing here?" he demanded.

"I have come to settle what is between us once and for all," Rodrigo replied. His gaze moved slowly, insolently, over Analisa, and then he licked his lips. "And she will go to the victor."

Alesandro stepped in front of Analisa, shielding her with his body. She could feel the tension radiating from him like heat from a roaring fire.

"I would kill her before I saw her at your mercy," he said, his voice as cold as winter frost.

"Would you?" Rodrigo swaggered into the barn. "I wonder."

"Be gone from here," Alesandro said. "This is neither the time nor the place to settle what is between us."

"This is the perfect time," Rodrigo hissed. "The last time."

Analisa took a step backward, fear stealing the breath from her body.

Alesandro moved toward Rodrigo. The two vampires seemed to grow larger in her sight, blocking everything else from view.

They circled each other slowly, their mutual hatred crackling like lightning between them. Rodrigo bared his fangs.

Alesandro focused all his energy on his enemy. He had no thought for Analisa now. For this moment in time, she did not exist. If he were destroyed, she would die. And he could not let her die the death Rodrigo would surely give her.

He launched himself at Rodrigo, fangs bared, hands curled into claws. The suddenness of his attack took the other vampire by surprise, and he knew a moment of satisfaction at drawing first blood.

Rodrigo quickly met his attack with one of his own, his fangs ripping through Alesandro's shoulder. The scent of blood filled the air.

The horses thrashed in their stalls, disturbed by the battle, by the scent of blood. Alesandro's stallion kicked the stall door with such force, it flew open. With a toss of his head, the horse raced out of the barn.

Analisa pressed herself against the back wall, her fist pressed to her mouth to keep from screaming as she watched the vicious battle. She stared at Alesandro. There was blood everywhere—on his face, his arms, his shirt front.

How much longer could it go on? And where was Dewhurst? If he came in now . . .

But there was no time to worry about Dewhurst, not now. In a move too quick for her to see, Rodrigo had managed to drive Alesandro to the ground. He bent over him now, fangs bared, his hands locked around Alesandro's throat.

Unable to watch, she squeezed her eyes shut, only to open them again as an inhuman howl rang in her ears, sending shivers racing down her spine.

Rodrigo and Alesandro stood facing each other now. Both were panting heavily. Blood poured from a deep gash in Alesandro's throat, gushed from a wound in Rodrigo's chest.

So much blood. How much longer could they go on?

A movement at the door drew Analisa's attention, and she saw Mrs. Thornfield standing there. For a moment, Analisa stared at the housekeeper. She looked the same, yet not the same. Her hair was thicker, the gray gleaming like spun silver. She looked vibrant, almost youthful. How had she explained the sudden change in her appearance to Frannie and Dewhurst and Cook?

Alesandro and Rodrigo both noticed the other vampire at the same moment. Alesandro shook his head to warn her off, but he was too late.

With a cry, Rodrigo flew to the housekeeper's side and buried his fangs in her throat, drinking deeply. She struggled in his grasp, but she was a young vampire and no match for Rodrigo, even wounded and bleeding as he was.

A low growl rose in Alesandro's throat. Eyes blazing, he started toward Rodrigo.

Rodrigo thrust Mrs. Thornfield in front of him, his hands gripping her shoulders. He glared at Alesandro, dark red blood dripping from his fangs. "Stay there, or she dies!"

Alesandro came to an abrupt halt, his eyes narrowing as Rodrigo dipped his head and drank again.

Analisa stared, unable to believe her eyes. She could see Rodrigo growing stronger, his wounds closing, the color returning to his face.

"Alesandro!" She took a step forward as she called his name.

He looked at her, his need horrible to see. His face was drained of color, his cheeks sunken, his eyes ablaze with pain. His gaze narrowed, focused on the pulse throbbing in her throat.

He took a step toward her, and suddenly Rodrigo was there. Strengthened by the blood he had taken, he drove Alesandro back against the wall, his fangs buried in Alesandro's throat, his hands clawing at Alesandro's chest.

Analisa felt the bile rise in her throat. For a moment, she stood rooted to the spot, frozen in horror. She looked to Mrs. Thornfield for help, but the housekeeper was lying on the floor, gasping for breath.

Analisa glanced frantically around the barn. She had to do something. If she didn't, they would all die at Rodrigo's hand.

Almost before she realized it, she was moving, her hand reaching out, her mind refusing to accept what she was about to do.

"Lord forgive me," she murmured, and drawing back her arm, she drove the pitchfork into Rodrigo's back. The tines of the pitchfork pierced the vampire's back with remarkable ease.

Rodrigo whirled around, shrieking with pain and rage, the tines sticking out of his chest. Blood dripped from the points. He lunged at her, his hands reaching for her.

She screamed as his hand closed on her arm. And then, like the shadow of death, Alesandro rose up behind him. With a feral cry born of fear and rage and pain, he lunged at the other vampire, his body shimmering, changing. A savage growl rose in his throat.

Rodrigo spun around. Too late. Too late to flee, too late to do anything but cry out as the huge black wolf drove him down to the floor and ripped out his throat.

Analisa stared at the wolf growling over the body of the vampire, at Mrs. Thornfield, who was just now struggling to sit up, at the blood that stained the wolf's fangs and fur. It was too much, too much.

The floor rushed up toward her, and then everything went black.

Chapter Thirty-one

The sun shining in her eyes roused Analisa. Sitting up, she glanced around, surprised to find herself in her own bed, in her own room. How had she gotten here?

"Good mornin', miss. 'Tis a lovely day."

Analisa stared at Frannie. How could the maid be so cheerful after what had happened last night?

"I'll bring your chocolate directly," Frannie said. She opened the chest of drawers and withdrew a set of clean undergarments. "Will you be wantin' breakfast?" she asked, placing the garments on the foot of the bed.

"What? Oh, no." Analisa lifted a hand to her neck, felt the familiar warmth that always lingered when Alesandro had taken nourishment from her.

"It was so good to see Mrs. Thornfield lookin' so fit after her ordeal," the maid went on.

"Yes. Yes, it was."

"Imagine, retirin' to Milano! I've never been to Italy. I hear it's a lovely place. I'd have thought she'd stay until you found a suitable replacement, though."

Analisa nodded. "Yes, but she was anxious to go." How would she endure the hours until she could see Alesandro again?

"What will you be wearin' today?" Frannie stood at the armoire, waiting.

"It doesn't matter. The green wool will do."

Frannie pulled it from the hanger and laid it on the bed. "I'll be gettin' your chocolate, then," she said, and left the room.

Rising, Analisa went to the window and stared into the yard below. Had it all been a dream?

Shrugging into her robe, she left her room, hurried down the stairs and out into the yard.

Dewhurst looked up from the trough he'd been scrubbing. "Mornin', miss," he said, obviously startled to see her outside in her nightclothes.

"Good morning."

"Is there something I can do for you, miss?"

"No, I . . ." She shoved her hands in the pockets of her robe, wondering what excuse she could give for rushing outside in her night rail. "I was wondering if you could give me riding lessons." It was a weak excuse, but all she could think of.

"Of course, miss."

She nodded. "This afternoon, then? Say three o'clock?"

"Very good, miss."

She glanced at the barn. If she went inside, would she find blood on the floor? Would Deuce's stall be empty? It must have been a dream, she thought. All of it, else Dewhurst would not be out here as though nothing had happened.

"I was wonderin'," Dewhurst said, "will you be hiring a new coachman?"

"What? Oh, yes." She forced a smile. "I suppose I shall have to see about a new housekeeper, as well."

"One more thing, miss. Will we be returning to Blackbriar soon?"

"I don't know. Is there some reason you need to go back?"

A red flush swept into the groom's cheeks. He cleared his throat, then shook his head. "I was just wonderin'."

Most curious, Analisa thought, her anxiety over Alesandro momentarily forgotten. Whatever could have a man of Dewhurst's age blushing like a schoolgirl? The answer came with amazing clarity. A woman, of course. Dewhurst must have a woman in the village.

"I'll ask Lord Alesandro what his plans are when I see him."

"Thank you, miss."

Turning, she made her way back to the house.

* * *

She moved through the day, dressing, eating, speaking when spoken to, yet she felt as though she were watching everything from a great distance. She let Dewhurst give her a lesson in riding sidesaddle, yet when the hour was over, she remembered nothing of what she had learned.

She took tea at four, then spent an hour reading, yet she could recall nothing of what she'd read when she put the book aside.

Would night never come?

Where was Alesandro? Where was Mrs. Thornfield? Was Rodrigo truly dead?

After what seemed an eternity, the sun began its slow descent.

Analisa paced the floor of her room, her nerves drawn taut, as she waited for Alesandro.

And suddenly he was there, as tall and handsome as ever. No trace of the battle of the night before remained. There were no scars on his skin, no telltale signs of the life-and-death struggle of the night before.

She looked up at him, her gaze searching his face. His expression was impassive, betraying nothing of what he was thinking or feeling.

"My lord?"

" 'Lisa."

"Did it happen? Is he dead?"

"He is dead." There was a great sadness in his voice. "And with him, my last tie to my home, to my past."

Analisa stared at him, astonished that he grieved for one who had caused him so much pain. "I'm sorry," she murmured, but though she regretted that she had been partly responsible for Rodrigo's death, she could not be sorry he was dead. He had been a vile, evil creature, bent on their destruction. And yet she could not escape the horror of what she had done. She had tried to kill a man.

Something shifted in Alesandro's expression. "What will you do now, 'Lisa?"

"Do?" she asked, confused.

"I am leaving here."

She looked at him blankly. "Where are you going?"

He shook his head. "I know not. I care not."

"But . . . I . . . you said we were to be married."

He laughed, a short bitter sound. "I was a fool."

"Alesandro, what has happened? I thought you loved me."

"I am selling this place," he said. "I have made arrangements for you and the staff to return to Gallatin Manor on the morrow. I will speak to my solicitor and have the deed placed in your name. You will receive a monthly allowance. If it is not sufficient, you have only to let him know, and the amount will be increased."

She put her hand over her mouth, stifling the urge to beg him not to leave her. When she had her emotions in check, she took a deep breath. "That will not be necessary, my lord," she said, pleased that her voice did not betray the fact that her heart was breaking. "I thank you for all you have done for me, but I want nothing from you." She drew in a deep, shuddering breath. "Goodbye."

Knowing she had nowhere else to go, he was taken aback when she refused his offer. It would be useless to play upon her greed, he mused, when she had none. But he knew her weakness, and he took advantage of it shamelessly.

"I am closing Blackbriar. I had hoped to send Blackbriar's staff to Gallatin. If you refuse, not only will Frannie and Dewhurst and Cook have to seek other employment, but Annie and Elton, as well."

She glared at him. "Very well. Thank you for your generosity," she said curtly, and swept out of the room with all the dignity she could muster.

Please, she prayed, *please let him follow me. Please.*
But he did not.

Alesandro watched her go, his brave Analisa, her back straight, her head high. He knew he had hurt her deeply. It took every ounce of his considerable self-control to keep from going after her. She seemed to take the light with her, leaving him in darkness as black as his soul. He had been a fool to think they could have a life together. He had brushed aside the doubts she had expressed from time to time, determined to have her in spite of his own doubts. He had been alone so long, he had told himself he deserved her, but last night . . .

He muttered a pithy oath. His sweet Analisa had driven a pitchfork into Rodrigo's back. No matter that she had done it to save his life. The darkness of his life had touched hers, driving her to an act of violence. Only moments ago, he had sensed her horror at what she had done. It was better to leave her, to take himself out of her life, her world.

He would go abroad, or perhaps he would go to ground and sleep for the next hundred years. Lost in the Dark Sleep, he would not be tempted by the thought of silky black hair and warm brown eyes, by soft skin and softer lips. . . .

He grunted softly. He would make the necessary arrangements to insure that Analisa would be well provided for, and then he would bury himself deep in the earth, where he belonged. Perhaps, in a hundred years, he would forget her.

Chapter Thirty-two

Analisa stood at the parlor window gazing out into the night. Six months since she had last seen Alesandro. She had spent the first month weeping, the second raging, the third learning to accept his absence, the fourth in a flurry of redecorating the house. She had hired painters, bought new furniture, replaced the carpets and drapes, the silver and china, determined to rid the house of anything that would remind her of the time they had spent together. The only room she had left untouched was his bedchamber. She had not entered it since the night he left, save for the day her wedding gown arrived from Womack's. She had taken the gown into his room and closed the door. She had grieved for him that day, grieved for all they had lost. Sitting on his bed, her gown clutched to her breast, she had wept until she had no tears left, and then she had thrown the gown into the hearth and watched it burn. When she left his room three hours later, she had locked the door, wishing she could as easily lock him out of her heart.

Life was peaceful at Gallatin. She had hired a new housekeeper, Mrs. Dinsmore, who, if not as efficient as Mrs. Thornfield, made up for it with boundless energy and enthusiasm. Mrs. Dinsmore had a married daughter and five grandchildren who lived nearby, and she was grateful to have employment close to home. Analisa also hired a new coachman. Carlin McLeod was a handsome young man with dark red hair and roguish brown eyes. Frannie had taken one look at him and been smitten. Though Analisa did not begrudge Carlin and Frannie their happiness, it pained her to see the two of them together, to see the love in their eyes, the smiles they shared. With Analisa's permission, the pair planned to stay on at Gallatin after they married in the fall.

Analisa had run into Geoffrey Starke on one of her infrequent forays into the city. When he had learned that her marriage had been called off, he had invited her to a ball at the home of one of his companions. Since that night, he had been her escort on more than one occasion. She had danced with dozens of handsome young men, exchanged pleasantries with well-dressed, well-bred young women, even hosted a small party herself. She had received and refused two marriage proposals. But nothing touched her. She went through the motions, experiencing it all as if she were seeing it from a distance, watching it from outside herself. Her future seemed as dark and empty as the night outside.

With a sigh, she turned away from the window, gasped when she saw Alesandro standing just inside the door.

He inclined his head in her direction. "Good evening, Analisa."

"My lord." Her heartbeat quickened at the mere sight of him. He was clad in black, his cloak falling in graceful folds to the floor. As always, he was a sight to take her breath away.

His gaze moved around the room, noting the changes, before settling on her face again. A faint smile touched his lips. "I see you have made this house your own."

She nodded, a thousand questions chasing each other through her mind.

"How have you been?" he asked.

She shrugged, not trusting herself to speak.

He lifted one black brow. "Do you wish me to go?"

She lowered her head so he couldn't see the tears forming in her eyes. "No." The word was hardly more than a whisper.

" 'Lisa . . ." His hands curled into tight fists, his knuckles white with the strain as he fought the urge to go to her. " 'Lisa, look at me."

His voice surrounded her. Dark, sensual, filled with quiet power. And love. Slowly she lifted her head to meet his gaze.

"Where have you been?" she asked.

"I went to ground."

She frowned, not understanding.

"Sometimes, when vampires need to escape what they are, or the world around them, they bury themselves deep in the earth."

"You've been buried alive all this time?" she asked, horrified at the image his words conjured in her mind.

"I could not bear to be in this world and not be near you. I had intended to stay below ground until you were no longer a temptation." He took a step toward her, his eyes pleading for her understanding. "I could not stay away from you," he said. "I did not want you tainted with what I am."

"I've never felt that way."

" 'Lisa, you tried to kill Rodrigo to save me. I know how difficult that was for you, the pain it caused you, the way it defiled your soul."

"Alesandro—"

"I tried to stay away from you, 'Lisa. I thought that, by going to ground, I could forget you." He shook his head. "No matter how deep I went, I could not escape your memory. Vampires do not dream, and yet you were there. I felt your sadness, your anger, and I knew that the love we shared was even stronger than the blood bond between us." He took another step toward her. "I came here tonight to see if there was a chance that you still loved me. If there was any hope for us."

"I never stopped loving you, Alesandro. Even when I hated you for leaving me, I loved you."

" 'Lisa!"

She closed the distance between them and laid her cheek against his chest. The wall she had built around her heart cracked, unleashing a torrent of tears.

His arms went around her, crushing her close. She felt his lips move in her hair.

" 'Lisa, beloved, can you ever forgive me?"

"Only if you promise never to leave me again."

"I swear it on all I hold sacred."

"And will you still love me when I'm wrinkled and gray?"

"Young or old, I will always love you as I do now."

"Will you care for me when I'm old and feeble? Will you be at my side when I draw my last breath?"

"I will never leave you," he said fervently, though he knew it would be the worst kind of torture to watch her age, to see her take her last breath, to face life without her.

She leaned back so she could see his face. "And would you make me what you are, if I asked you to?"

" 'Lisa!" Once, he would have refused her, but no more. "Yes, my sweet Analisa, but only if you are sure it is what you want." He ran his knuckles lightly over her cheek, his dark eyes burning into hers. "Think carefully, my sweet, for once it is done, there is no going back."

"I have thought about it. A mortal lifetime with you is not long enough. I want forever."

"Ah, 'Lisa, will you be happy in my dark world?"

"It will not be dark if you are there to share it with me. I love you, Alesandro. Do you know how much I missed you?"

377

Amanda Ashley
=============

His arms tightened around her. "No more than I missed you."

She leaned into him, drawing him into herself, accepting all of him, the light and the darkness, and as she did so, she knew with unshakable certainty that she belonged here, in his arms, in his life. Breathless and unafraid, she whispered, "Show me."

" 'Lisa!" Cupping the back of her head in his hand, he bent down and claimed her lips with his.

One dark kiss, filled with aching tenderness and an unspoken vow of love, a kiss that held the promise and the power of forever.

Dear Reader:

I hope you enjoyed *Midnight Embrace*. I loved Alesandro and I enjoyed writing his story.

When my editor, Alicia Condon, read it, she said, "Your readers are going to love this. It's just what they've been waiting for. The perfect vampire story." I hope you agree.

I love to hear from my readers. You can write me at P.O. Box 1703, Whittier, CA 90609-1703, or e-mail me at DarkWritr@aol.com.

Madeline Baker
a.k.a. Amanda Ashley

MADELINE BAKER WRITING AS

A Darker Dream. In all of his four hundred years, Rayven has never met a woman like Rhianna McLeod. She is a vision of light, warmth, and everything he can never be. And Rhianna, although she senses danger behind his soft-spoken manner, and although Rayven himself warns her away, finds herself drawn to this creature of the night—and loves him as she can no other.
____52208-X $5.99 US/$6.99 CAN

Deeper than the Night. The townsfolk of Moulton Bay say there is something otherworldly about Alexander Claybourne. But never scared off by superstitious lore, Kara Crawford laughs at the local talk of creatures lurking in the dark. No matter what shadowy secrets Alexander hides, Kara feels compelled to join him beneath the silver light of the moon, where they will share a love deeper than the night.
____52113-X $5.99 US/$6.99 CAN

After Twilight

Amanda Ashley
Christine Feehan
Ronda Thompson

A man hunts for a woman. Yet what if he is no ordinary male, but a predator in search of prey? A dark soul looking for the light? A vampire, a werewolf, a mythic being who strikes fear into the hearts of mortals? Three of romance's hottest bestselling authors invite you to explore the dark side, to taste the forbidden, to dive into danger with heroes who fire the blood and lay claim to the soul in these striking tales of sensual passion. When day fades into night, when fear becomes fascination, when the swirling seduction of everlasting love overcomes the senses, it must be . . . after twilight.

___52450-3 $5.99 US/$6.99 CAN

Sacrament
SUSAN SQUIRES

AVAILABLE MARCH 2002!

FROM
LOVE ✦ SPELL

Sacrament
SUSAN SQUIRES

It begins with an illicit kiss stolen under a hot Mediterranean sun. It makes the blood sing in her veins, burn in her body in ways she has never felt before. It is a pulsing need to be something else . . . something she doesn't yet understand. It is embodied by Davinoff. The dark lord is the epitome of beauty, of strength. He is feared by the ton, and even by fleeing to Bath, Sarah cannot escape him. His eyes hold a sadness she can hardly fathom. They pierce her so deeply that she feels penetrated to her very core. What they offer is frightening . . . and tantalizing. All Sarah knows is that the sacrament of his love will either be the death of her body or the salvation of her soul. And she can no more deny it than she can herself.